The Watercress Girls

By Kay Seeley

ISBN-978-1-9164282-4-9

To Mick

Author's Note on Watercress

In the nineteenth century watercress provided the working class with a good portion of nutrition for the day. Street sellers, mainly children aged between six and fourteen, would buy it and form it into bunches which were eaten in the hand like an ice cream cone. Hackney watercress beds were fed by the fast flowing waters of Hackney Brook. In 1861 Henry Mayhew wrote in *London Labour and the London Poor*:

"The first coster cry heard of a morning in the London streets is of 'Fresh wo-orter-creases'. Those that sell them have to be on their rounds in time for the mechanic's breakfast, or the day's gains are lost."

No piece about watercress sellers would be complete without mentioning Eliza James, who as a child of five sold wild watercress around factories in Birmingham. She later earned the nickname 'The Watercress Queen'. She was reputed to be the biggest owner of watercress farms in the world. Despite her wealth she still turned up every morning to work on her stall at Covent Garden Market which she had been running for over fifty years, arriving every day on a watercress cart. She trademarked the name *'Vitacress'* which was then sold on. Reporting her death in 1927 the *Daily Mirror* described her life as *'one of the most wonderful romances of business London has ever known.'*

http://watercress.co.uk/about/historical-facts/

Chapter One

"His mother's deserted him, it's the foundling hospital or the workhouse for him now," Dorcas said with a grimace. "Poor little mite."

"I can't believe you're saying that, Ma," Hettie said, sudden fear gripping her. "You can't turn him out, he's only a bairn. It's not his fault." She stared at her mother.

"Aye a bairn wi' no one to fend for 'im." Dorcas folded her heavy arms across her chest. "His ma's run off and left us in the lurch. Who's gonna pay for 'is keep that's what I'd like to know. We can't keep him, that's for sure, I can't afford to feed and clothe a growing lad. He'll be out of that cot in no time. Who's gonna pay for 'im then?"

Hettie drew in a sharp breath. She couldn't believe Dorcas would turn the child out – not Annie's child. "Annie paid well enough for us to look after him before and she'll make up what she owes – I'm sure of it."

"Sure of it are you? Well, why hasn't she been in touch? She's left him and left you wi' a baby on your hands and nowt to pay for 'im. She's moved on and she'll not be back. I always knew she was good for nowt. Flighty miss. She took you in good and proper didn't she? No, workhouse'll take 'im in."

Hettie bridled. "I'll not see him put in that place as long as I've breath in my body."

"So, you're gonna take 'im on are you? Wash him, feed him, buy 'is clothes...You can't afford that any more than I can. If I can't pay the rent we'll lose the house – then it's us as'll be out on street."

Hettie sighed. That was true enough. Their tenancy teetered on a knife edge. She'd relied on Annie's money to pay towards the rent and now, with only one lodger and Dorcas's laundry money coming in, things were tighter than ever. Still, she couldn't see the little mite put out. She'd promised Annie.

She turned to gaze at the child sleeping in the makeshift cot. She touched his cheek and he stirred in his sleep. "He sleeps in my room I'll see he's no bother. I'll take care of him."

"Take care of him will you? One thing when you was getting paid to do it. Different matter now though. I expect you to do your share around here. I can't afford to pay Sarah extra with nowt coming in."

"I'll do my share and look after Billy," Hettie said, her face reddening as her defiance mounted. "I'll pull my weight, just as I've always done."

Dorcas's jaw clenched. She shook her head but relented. "On your head be it," she said and stalked off to the kitchen.

Hettie stared at the sleeping baby, his wispy infant curls and long eyelashes dark against his velvet skin. That cute little boy with his sunny smile and big blue eyes had captured her heart the first moment she saw him. But her mother was right. He'd need a lot of minding as well as food and clothes and she hadn't heard from Annie for weeks now. She hadn't sent money for his keep either.

It wasn't like Annie not to keep in touch. Since she'd moved out she visited Billy as often as she could and Hettie had expected her to come home for Christmas but still they'd heard nothing. "Don't worry, she'll get in touch soon and everything will be all right," she said to the sleeping child. He couldn't hear her, but it made her feel better to say it out loud.

Hettie sighed. Was Dorcas right about Annie? Had she moved on and left him behind?

If they didn't hear soon Hettie may be forced to go back to her job at the bakery and then they'd have to find a place for him, no matter how great the betrayal or how fiercely Hettie fought it. Dorcas had taken Annie and her brother in when their mother died. Money was tighter now and

Dorcas older and perhaps more bitter. Was taking them in something she'd come to regret? Hettie wondered what had hardened her heart. Her mind spiralled back to that day so many years ago...

A sorry number of people stood shivering around the open grave.

Hettie wiped tears from her eyes, tears resulting more from the bitterness of the March wind than from any feelings she had for the deceased. Mary Flanagan was laid to rest with little ceremony. Corry, her twelve-year-old son threw in a handful of gravel, her daughter Annie, who was nine and, according to her mother a mistake, stepped forward and tossed in a daffodil. "I hope you're happy now, Ma," she said.

Hettie, who was a year older than Annie, squeezed her friend's hand. She barely knew Annie's mother. She'd only met her once, last summer when she took a bundle of her cast-off clothing along to the house for Annie. When she opened the door, Mrs Flanagan was wearing nothing but a gaudy silk gown wrapped around her slight body. The house smelled of stale beer, the unpleasant fug of tobacco and the sweat of the two dock workers who occupied the upstairs rooms. Hettie handed the bundle over in exchange for a thruppeny bit. Mrs Flanagan had told her to thank her mammy. Hettie ran all the way home.

The pastor nodded to the gravedigger leaning on his spade nearby and the task of shovelling earth over the coffin began. Dorcas laid a posy of violets by the grave, Hettie some primroses. There were no other flowers.

Back at the house, Dorcas Bundy had sandwiches and cake laid out ready. She prided herself on the cleanliness of her house and her ability to whip up a good spread from next to nothing. The children tucked into the sandwiches as though they'd not eaten for a week, which was quite likely. Dorcas handed the pastor a mug of hot tea.

"It's very good of you to take the children in, Mrs Bundy," he said picking up a cake.

Dorcas huffed, hoisting up her ample bosoms. "Better than leaving it to the parish to feed and house them," she said.

Hettie heard the pastor say something about a reward but he also mentioned heaven so she guessed it wasn't to be immediately forthcoming. Anyway, Dorcas hadn't been that keen to have them.

"They can share my room, they'll be no trouble," Hettie had said as soon as the pastor suggested it, but it was only Annie's persuasive nature, Corry's promise to pay and the pastor's assurance that they could pay their way that had opened Dorcas's heart.

Annie put her small hand into Dorcas's rough, work-hardened one and said, "Please Mrs Bundy, please."

"We'll pay," Corry said, his mud brown eyes glinting, his hands clenched. "We don't want no charity."

"And the parish will help if you need anything," the pastor said.

It was well known that Dorcas took in lodgers so, to please the pastor, she agreed.

Mary Flanagan's meagre belongings were sold to pay for the burial, the remainder being given to Dorcas towards the children's keep. Corry insisted their mother's own mementos, bits of jewellery, letters, photos and personal items, be put into a box as a keepsake for Annie. When Hettie saw it she thought it a poor legacy for a lifetime.

Chapter Two

Hettie stirred in her sleep, half aware that Annie no longer lay in the bed beside her. Darkness filled the room. It must be past midnight, she thought, but not far enough past for any light to edge in and lessen the gloom. She shivered as she rolled over and lit the candle on the table beside the bed. Annie was up, pulling on a too small jumper over her cotton dress. Her feet were bare on the wooden floor.

"What are you doing? It's the middle of the night. Where do you think you're going?" She kept her voice to a whisper so as not to wake Dorcas in the next room.

Annie glanced at her. "I'm going for the cress. Do you want to come wi' me?"

"Where?"

"Hackney. There's no frost. If it stays dry and it's not too bitter out we could do all right today, if you've nowt better to do."

Hettie saw that Annie had drawn back the thin curtain and the windowpane was black and frost free but there was a sharp chill in the air. She'd never been out so early in her life. Still, she thought it might be an adventure, and going out with Annie would be more enjoyable than staying in helping her mother with the bundles of washing she took in. She'd seen Annie in lessons at the pastor's school. She always seemed to be having more fun and greater freedom than Hettie. If Annie was going anywhere, she was eager to go with her.

"I'll have to ask Ma," she said her excitement mounting.

Annie shrugged. "Tell her you'll be out earning, that usually works."

Annie was right. Ma approved of hard work and had no time for idle hands. Her reputation for being careful with money was well known in the street. Hettie smiled and jumped out of bed.

She rummaged through the chest of drawers where her clothes were kept and pulled out a pair of thick woollen stockings, a flannel vest and a petticoat. It was cold in the bedroom, but it would be a lot colder outside.

"Course you'll have to have something to start, but I'll help you," Annie said.

In the flickering light of the candle Hettie noticed the bed Corry had slept in was empty too. The thin blanket he'd slept under was haphazardly heaped half on the bed and half on the floor. It was obvious both the Flanagans were early risers.

"Where's Corry gone?" she asked as she pulled on her vest.

"He'll be out early for the tide an' he'll want to get a good spot."

"Mudlarking?" Hettie knew of the gangs of boys who hung around the shoreline of the Thames delving in the deep mud to recover anything they could sell that had been dropped by barges navigating their way to and from the Pool of London, but didn't know Corry was one of them.

"How else d'you think we're gonna pay rent? Two shillings a week your ma said. It's a lot for Corry to find on his own. We'd best be getting out an' all or we'll miss the freshest pickings." She paused and smiled at Hettie. "With two us we should make twice as much. Your ma'll be happy with that."

Hettie grinned and quickly finished dressing. Being with Annie would be like having the sister she'd always dreamed of. In time she hoped they'd be able to do all sorts of things together. Her heart had warmed with joy when Dorcas had agreed to take them in rather than sending them to the workhouse. Now, with Corry as well, it would seem like a whole new family.

They tiptoed downstairs, but any hope Hettie had of not waking Dorcas was in vain. In the darkness she heard the sound of movement and a door closing. Annie was just helping them to some bread from the larder when Dorcas appeared in the kitchen doorway.

"What's going on 'ere then?" she said, folding her arms across her chest.

"We're going out for the cress, Ma," Hettie said. She stuck her chin out in a rare act of defiance. She was determined not to be kept home. "Annie's going to help me and we're going to earn the rent."

"Oh, you are are you?" Dorcas stared at Annie. Bare-legged and wearing threadbare slippers, there were holes in the two-sizes-too-small jumper she wore over her tattered mud-stained cotton dress. Hettie recognised the dress as one of the old cast-offs she taken round in the summer. Annie's long unruly curls hung like rusty bed-springs past her shoulders.

"You'll need sommat warmer than that if you're going out in this weather," Dorcas said.

Annie stared down at her dress. "It's all I've got."

"Did your mother never teach you to darn?" Dorcas eyed the holes in Annie's pullover.

Annie's lips quivered. "Ma never taught us 'owt," she said.

Dorcas huffed. She grabbed a petticoat, dress, jumper and a pair of Hettie's woollen stockings from the clothes horse where they were drying by the fire. "Put these on and let me have yours," she said. "I'll wash and darn 'em for you this time, then I'll teach you to do it yourself."

Annie snatched the offered clothes. Standing in the warmth of the stove she stripped naked and put them on. They were too big. She tied some string around her waist and the tops of her legs to keep the jumper from flapping about and to keep the stockings up.

Dorcas shook her head. "Your education's been sadly lacking," she said. "I can't think what your ma was about."

Hettie grimaced. She had a good idea where Mary Flanagan's talents lay, but she also thought that the scrubbing, polishing, laundering, baking, darning and mending Ma had taught her had brought her little joy. She envied Annie her ignorance. Perhaps if she'd been as ignorant she could spend her time like the other children in the street playing their raucous games outside.

Dorcas made them both a drink and gave them bread and butter before they set out. She gave Hettie money for the cress and a penny each to buy a hot drink.

"Don't let anyone say as how I don't pay for me own," she said. She found an old woollen shawl for Annie as she had no coat. Hettie wore a cloth coat and wrapped a shawl around her head and shoulders. It was still early enough in the year for a bitter wind and a light frost.

"Make sure you get to your lessons with the pastor," Dorcas said before they left.

"Yes Ma," Hettie said with a grimace. Selling watercress around the streets sounded a lot more exciting than lessons.

Hettie and Annie both attended the ragged school run by the pastor for four hours a day.

Annie was often absent from lessons, but those she did miss she quickly caught up. Annie was what the pastor called a 'quick study'. There was no doubt about that.

Walking down the deserted streets it wasn't long before the cold from the frosted cobbles seeped into Hettie's toes. She pulled her shawl closer around her. The air was fresh and she heard birds chirping from somewhere far away. She watched fascinated as a sliver of dawn crept over the roof tops, warming the street and burning off the mist drifting in from the river.

They walked in silence at first, their breath vaporising in the cold air.

"Doesn't Corry go to lessons?" Hettie asked Annie after a while.

"Corse 'e does," she said. "'E goes to Pastor Brown in the evening, but only if he's sold all his pickings."

Hettie followed Annie who had obviously walked this route many times before. If they did see anyone Annie would give a cheery 'good morning' and always got a smile and a wave in response. There seemed to be some sort of bond between the early morning people. It felt like a whole new world.

Annie pushed her hands under her shawl. "When we get there I'll show you the best place to buy. You should get a good handful, as much as you can carry for a penny but with thruppence you'll get a lap full, enough to make a good few bunches. We can sell 'em for a ha'penny a bunch but in the shops they try to knock you down to a farthing. I usually settles for giving 'em three for a penny."

Hettie skipped along trying to take it all in.

"Don't worry. I'll show you when we get there," Annie said.

They walked for about an hour before they reached the watercress beds. Hackney Brook flowed through lush greenery, a stark contrast to the greyness surrounding them. Hettie was surprised to see how busy it was. Men knee-deep in water bent over cutting the cress into baskets which were carried to the bank and quickly surrounded by a cluster of young girls. Hettie shuddered. Most of them were bare-legged and wearing only a thin shawl over their cotton dresses.

Annie pushed her way to the fullest basket. Holding out her skirt she showed Hettie how to pick out the best stalks until she had a lap full. Hettie did the same, although Annie's stalks looked fresher and greener than hers. They sat on a nearby doorstep and tied them into bunches with raffia.

"You have to make the posies look big or they won't buy 'em," Annie said. "If you've got some that looks a bit droopy you can freshen 'em up under the pump."

Hettie did her best but her fingers froze. Annie's experienced fingers tied three bunches to Hettie's one and Hettie's fell apart when she held them under the pump. Annie didn't seem to feel any discomfort as she twisted the cress into bunches and held them in the cold water.

Annie laughed. "Don't worry – you soon get used to it," she said. "I don't feel the cold no more."

Hettie looked at Annie's thin carpet slipper shoes and then at her own slightly sturdier ones and guessed Annie didn't feel it in her feet neither, although Hettie's feet were numbing like her fingers.

They tied all the cresses into bunches. By that time pale sunlight had chased away the dampness of the dawn and gradually the sky lightened. Annie loaded the cress onto her tray and they set off calling out: "Water creeeeeesses, fresh water creeeeesses."

Annie's voice was loud and strong but Hettie could only manage a thin, high-pitched call. She was sure no-one would hear her. She tried harder but her voice seemed to be lost in the rumble of cart wheels and clatter of horses' hooves now moving along the street. A couple of men on their way to work stopped and bought bunches from Annie to eat as they walked along.

Despite the early hour by the time they got to Liverpool Street the road teemed with carts, cabs and costers wheeling their barrows to the market. Street sellers of fish, fruit, hardware and household items called out their wares and Hettie watched and listened as gradually the city came to vibrant life.

Annie took some bunches to sell to the butcher, fishmonger, baker and grocer while Hettie stood on the corner with the tray of cress. She shivered in the cold, the wind burnt her face. She stamped her feet and flung her arms around her body to keep warm. When a man stopped in front of her her heart raced.

"You look frozen," he said with a chuckle. "Here, give us one." He took a bunch from the tray, dug his hand into his pocket and gave her a ha'penny. Suddenly Hettie stopped feeling the cold. The next customer gave her a penny for two bunches. As soon as she was able to sell one or two bunches, handing them out in exchange for ha'pennies, she felt better. Annie was right, you soon forgot about the cold. She even got used to calling out watercreeeses, fresh watercreeses.

Hettie soon saw how successful Annie was at street selling.

"Morning Missus," or "Cold one today," she'd say to the people passing. She beguiled them with her charm and it seemed that few could resist when she offered them the watercress bunches.

When they got to the Strand they stopped at a crowded coffee stall to buy a hot drink. The cress on the tray was dwindling.

"I'm glad I came with you today," Hettie said. "It's better'n helping with washing and hanging it out." And she realised she really meant it.

As they walked along to Covent Garden, Hettie realised how different Annie and Corry's lives would be from now on. "I'm sorry about your ma," she said.

"Aye, me an' all," Annie said. "She weren't the best ma in the world but she cared for us, me an' Corry. Never lifted a hand to us she didn't, never beat or braided us for wrong-doing." She sighed. "She was always telling us tales of big houses and great adventures." Her face lit up at the memory. She turned to Hettie. "She wasn't all bad you know – not like people think. She was good to us..."

Hettie thought she saw a tear in Annie's eye but Annie walked on so fast Hettie had trouble keeping up.

At Covent Garden Hettie stared wide-eyed at theatre goers and late night revellers mixing with early market people setting up their stalls. Annie walked Hettie around the baskets of watercress where they filled their skirts again. Eliza, the stallholder, was nice and she knew a lot about growing cress. "My cress is the best in the world," she said. "One day I'm going to have my own farms and supply all of London." Hettie never doubted it for a moment.

Hettie found tying the stalks into bunches much easier as her fingers weren't so numb and, watching Annie, she'd got the hang of it. Soon they were out again selling their cress to carriage boys on their way to work and people on their way home from dancing establishments and oyster houses. One man, wearing a heavy coat and top hat, obviously well oiled from his night out on the town, gave Annie a thruppenny bit 'just for the brightness of your smile,' he said.

As they made their way back through the city with their fresh supply of cress, Annie picked out the wealthiest looking, stepping in front of them with her basket and giving her brightest smile. "Fresh watercreeeeeses, all fresh this morning, ha'penny a bunch," she sing out, walking backwards in front of them.

A few pushed past her, hurrying on to their place of work, but many smiled and bought the offered bunches. Sure enough, by lesson time all the cresses had gone.

After lessons at the pastor's school, which varied between two and six hours depending on who he could entice in to teach, they made their way home.

Dorcas made them drinks and bread and butter with a slice of ham for their tea.

"Wash your hands before you eat," Dorcas said so they duly washed their hands in the cold water in the kitchen sink.

"How was your lessons?" Dorcas said. "Did you get there on time?" She eyed them suspiciously in case they missed lessons, as Annie often did.

"Yes," Hettie said. "And we sold all our cress." She puffed out her chest.

"We can out again for the evening trade," Annie said. "If that's all right with you Mrs Bundy." She touched Hettie hand. "I'll look out for Hettie an' all."

Hettie pulled her hand away. "I can look out for meself," she said.

Then Corry arrived home.

"You'd best wash your hands and feet," Dorcas said when he walked into the kitchen.

Corry scowled. "I washed 'em under the pump afore I came back," he said but Hettie noticed he went to the sink and washed his hands again before plonking himself on a chair at the table. She also noticed he'd said 'afore he came 'back' not 'home'.

Gathered around the table they each spoke about their day. Hettie chatted happily, Annie put in a few words and Hettie's heart lifted when she saw Corry smile. For the first time it felt like a real family.

After tea they set out again for the evening trade. The nights were drawing out and it was still light enough before the street lamps were lit. A soft breeze blew and Hettie was glad of her coat. As they neared the market she gasped at the lights along the Strand. Music could be heard from the various pubs they passed. Even at night the West End was bright as day.

At the market they bought more cress from Eliza and looked out for anything else they could find to sell on. Annie picked up flowers dropped by the flower sellers to make into bunches she could sell in the evening to the theatre goers as well as selling her cress.

Before they went home Annie counted out the money. She put sixpence aside for buying cress the next morning and bought them each a hot pie and a drink. Hettie's heart swelled. She threw some crumbs from her pie to the birds gathering around.

"Aw. What did you want to go and do that for?" Annie said. "Now they'll bother us all the way home."

Hettie shrugged. She thought the birds looked hungry.

Annie grimaced and shooed the birds away. She gave Hettie sixpence which Hettie thought most generous, seeing that Annie had done most of the selling.

When she got home Hettie gave her money to Dorcas.

"I used to give all my takings to Ma an' all," Annie said sadly.

Chapter Three

Over the next weeks Hettie made sure she was up and getting ready before Annie, anxious not to hold her back from getting out for the best pickings. Some days she even woke before Corry left. Then she'd lie in bed watching him through half-closed eyes. His trousers were ragged, his shirt too small, his jacket threadbare and in need of patching. He jammed a flat cap on his head over his dark curls. Tall and skinny, dressed in tattered clothes he might not have looked much, but to

Hettie he was steadfast, reliable and kind. True, he was as stubborn and hot-headed as his sister, but there was no one in the world she'd rather have as a big brother.

Dorcas had mended Annie's dress and sorted out a warmer jumper as well as finding her a petticoat and some woollen stockings. Every day they went out selling cress. As the weather brightened and Easter drew nearer they found more customers. Hettie enjoyed the early mornings best, watching the pale glimmerings of dawn as it rose over the city, gradually lightening the streets. It was quiet and it felt special being out so early. She soon came to recognise the people she met on the way to the market; the lamplighters, the knocker-upper, the newspaper boys setting up their pitches. She greeted each one with a smile and a cheery 'good morning'.

When they'd collected their share of cress and tied it into bunches they set out on their rounds. As spring turned to summer Hettie felt a surge of pity for the girls working in the factories along by the river. They worked long hours winter and summer and had no freedom to get out, breathe the fresh air and feel the sun on their faces.

Annie tutted when Hettie gave a sickly, poorly clad crossing-sweeper a bunch of watercress for nothing.

Hettie shrugged. "He looked so sad and sorry for himself," she said. "His need seemed greater than ours." She looked side-ways at Annie. "There's lots worse off than us, Annie. Anyway, the pastor says..."

Annie clasped her hands to her ears. "Spare me from another of the pastor's sermons," she said laughing. "I gets enough of his wisdom in church on Sundays."

Hettie chuckled. It was true; Annie never missed a Sunday service. Hettie suspected she only went to lessons so as not to lose her place in the Sunday choir. It wasn't the Lord she was praising either, Annie just loved to sing.

The other thing Hettie discovered about Annie over the months they went out together was that she loved clothes. Now she was able to keep some of the cress money for herself, after paying her share of the rent, she'd scour the markets for new clothes and shoes. Dorcas taught her to sew and mend so she could alter what she bought to fit her petite frame. It became her new passion. She also started to wash more frequently and brushed her auburn hair until it shone. Yes, Annie was becoming a real lady.

Over the summer months the cress became more plentiful and the selling easier. The streets buzzed with life. Everyone seemed more cheerful than in the long cold winters. On a good day they'd buy ice creams instead of the hot pies they enjoyed in winter and Hettie thought there was nothing better in life than that.

One day, as they were walking towards Liverpool Street, Annie carrying her tray with their cress and chatting about the amount of cress they hoped to sell, a burly lad, about fifteen, jumped out in front of them. Dressed in frayed trousers, heavy boots and a coarse jacket over a worn striped shirt, he glared at Annie, a look as hard as his steel-toed boots.

"Well, if it isn't little Annie Flanagan," he said with a wide grin showing his uneven, brown teeth. A livid white scar stretched across his cheek from his mouth to his left ear.

A vague fear rose inside Hettie. She swallowed it back.

Annie flinched. "Get out of my way, moron," she said. "I've got nowt to give you an' I wouldn't if I could."

The boy chuckled.

Hettie's fear mounted.

"It ain't a question of giving," he said. "If I wants owt from you I'd take it, no question." He gave a menacing sneer. "You're lucky I ain't interested. I got bigger fish to fry. Tell Corry I'll be looking out for 'im after lessons tonight. He'd better be there or it'll be the worse for all of you." With that he gave a raucous, throaty laugh, lunged forward and upended Annie's tray sending the bunches of cress cascading to the floor.

Hettie let out a shout but Annie stood frozen to the spot, eyes blazing, fists clenched and a look of pure hatred on her face. Within seconds the boy had vanished, melting into the hotchpotch of people crowding the street, hurrying past. The last Hettie saw of him was his squashed pork-pie hat disappearing up a nearby alley.

For the first time in her life Hettie felt scared. The lad's manner shocked her. She'd never felt so threatened. She feared not for herself, but for her friend and, more especially for Corry.

She stooped to collect up the scattered cress, tears stung her eyes. "Oh, Annie," she said. "Who on earth was that? What did he want? What was that about Corry?" She could hardly breathe. "Should we go home and tell Ma?"

Annie stared at her and then at the cress crushed in Hettie's hands. She took a deep breath and seemed to relax a bit although her eyes narrowed. "Nowt your ma can do," she said. "He's all wind and trousers anyway. He wouldn't do owt. It's all bluff and bluster, but I'd better warn Corry to look out for 'im."

Hettie put the cress back on the tray. "So you know him? Who is he? What does he want with Corry?"

Annie picked up a bunch of cress and inspected it. She laid it back on the tray and glanced around before replying. "He's called Gander, he's the leader of the mudlarks and he runs one of the street gangs. It's mostly petty thieving and the like, but he's not above making trouble for them as cross 'im. I keep telling Corry to keep away from him but it's difficult when they're all working along by the river." She took a breath, sniffed and started walking. "We can freshen the cress up under the Market Street pump. It'll be good as new," she said.

Hettie followed Annie to the pump but the encounter had affected her far more than she cared to admit. Suddenly the day seemed darker and selling cress less fun than it had previously been. She carried the fear with her for the rest of the morning, wary of seeing him again.

She shuddered and her heart shrivelled whenever a young, burly lad approached her and it only swelled again when he smiled, bought some cress and wished her a good day.

When they'd finished that morning's cress Hettie left Annie to go round the market and took a walk along the riverbank. She thought if she saw

Corry she might be able to warn him about the encounter with the boy called Gander. The fear still played in her mind. At least if she told Corry she might feel better about it. He'd know what to do to reassure her.

She enjoyed walking by the river, watching the boats. In the city streets the air was grimy and hot. By the river the air was cooler and there was the illusion of space – something missing from the crowded streets in town. She walked to Wapping Steps where she knew she'd see the young boys knee-deep in the narrow strip of mud.

The river was running fast as the tide rose bringing in the flotsam from the boats. Soon the water would cover the mud and the boys would have to move further up river. At first she couldn't see Corry, then she spotted him sitting on the steps dabbing at his foot with a damp rag.

She ran up to him "What on earth...?" she said.

Corry glared at her. "Cut me foot didn't I?" he said.

Hettie stared at his foot where a long gash trickled blood onto the rag. He'd obviously tried to wash it clean but with little effect. Brown mud still clung all around the wound. She glanced into his bucket where he kept his 'finds' and noticed a bloodstained piece of rusty iron. Sickness coiled inside her. All thoughts of the morning's fear vanished.

"What are you going to do now?" she asked.

"I'm going back in," he said attempting to wrap the rag around his foot to stop the bleeding.

"You can't do that," Hettie cried, trying to grab the rag from him. "That needs proper dressing and probably a stitch. Let me see."

Corry pushed her away. "Stop fussing. It'll be all right." He bound the rag tightly around his foot and stood up. "See – good as new."

"It's not," Hettie argued. "It'll get infected and that'll be the end of you. Let me help."

"And lose the best part of the day? I can't afford to do that. I'm going back in."

"But isn't it painful?"

"Can't help that. Anyways, water's cold enough to numb it."

Hettie glanced over to where a group of young boys were wading in to the rising tide to find anything hidden in the mud or floating in the dirty water.

"But you can't, not with that foot."

Corry smiled. "Can't go without it neither," he said and limped off back into the mud.

Hettie worried all the way home.

When Corry got home that evening his foot was large with blood-soaked bandages, turned brown.

Dorcas pulled them off and bathed his foot with carbolic acid.

"Ow, Ow, that hurt," he said but Dorcas carried on. When she was satisfied that the wound was clean she smothered it with honey and wrapped a clean strip of material, torn from an old petticoat, around Corry's foot.

"No need for all that fuss," he said.

But Hettie wasn't surprised when he went down with fever the next day and was too weak even to rise from his bed.

"What am I going to do wi' him now?" Dorcas said, worry creasing her brow. "I've enough to do without a sick child to care for."

"I'll stay and look out for him," Hettie said when she saw the state he was in.

Corry would have complained had he strength enough but Annie settled the matter. "I'll get two lots of cress and I'll split the money," she said. "You won't lose out, Mrs Bundy."

Dorcas shook her head but there wasn't much she could do about it. Corry was in no fit state to work and he'd need someone looking after him. Hettie sat with him bathing his forehead and offering sips of laudanum. Soon the fever passed. He complained bitterly when Hettie changed the bandages on his foot but Hettie wasn't deterred.

After a couple of days he was well enough to get up and a day later he went back to the river.

"Hmm," Dorcas said. "You'll be lucky if you don't get lockjaw."

"Lockjaw? What's lockjaw," Corry said.

"It's what you die of if you go wading in the Thames' mud with a gashed foot," Dorcas said.

It was several days before Hettie could step out confidentially with the cress, putting the memory of Gander behind her. She was determined to do her best and be as good as Annie. Soon she had her own tray of cress and found the best places to sell around Clerkenwell, Bethnal Green and Mile End in the morning. Then she'd meet up with Annie at Eliza's stall in Covent Garden and they'd chat and compare notes.

"West End's best for the evening trade, people going to the theatre and that," Annie said. "When I grow up I want to be on the stage, wear fine dresses and have men gaggling after me. Won't that be the best thing ever?"

Hettie smiled, but she wasn't so sure Annie's dreams were the 'best thing ever'.

One late summer's day they were sitting tying cress into bunches when Hettie asked Annie about Corry. "He goes out early and comes home so late," she said. "I'm not sure he's even eating anything he's got so thin and pale. Is he all right?"

"He misses Ma that's all," she said.

Hettie knew that wasn't all. She'd heard Corry sobbing at times during the night. She wouldn't say anything but her heart went out to him. "It must be dreadful for him," she said.

"They were close and he's more sensitive than you might think. Mudlarking's hard and he's worried he might not make enough to pay the rent. Sometimes I worry about him too but there's nowt I can do."

There was nothing Hettie could say or do either. Corry was Corry, too stubborn and independent to ask for help, even if he could admit to himself that he needed it, which was unlikely.

Annie shrugged. "Come on, let's get on. I don't want to miss the city crowds."

Every day Hettie and Annie went out selling their cress in the mornings before lessons and again after lessons in the evening. Hettie continued to give her cress money to Dorcas and Annie gave Corry a shilling a week toward the two shillings Dorcas charged for their keep. The rest she saved to buy herself a new shawl, thicker boots and a warm petticoat, ready for the coming winter when the wind would be sharp and the frosty air cold. In winter the cress would be less plentiful and the buyers fewer so money would be tight again.

Chapter Four

he last of the summer sun lingered until late September. October brought in a chill wind and cooler weather. The days were shorter and the nights longer. They'd been getting up in the dark for months but now, with the colder air the temptation to stay longer under the covers grew. Annie never seemed to mind. She'd be up before Hettie and hurrying her on and out of the door.

One morning towards the end of the month damp drizzle filled the air and Hettie was doubtful they'd find many customers on such a dull day. "It's Corry's birthday next week," Annie said. "I've seen just the thing to get for his present."

Hettie's heart skipped. Corry's birthday? Why hadn't she known that? Did Dorcas know? She hadn't mentioned it. And, just as important, when was Annie's birthday and did Dorcas know about that too? She suddenly realised how little she knew about her new brother and sister. A swell of sadness washed over her. Perhaps they weren't a real family after all.

"There's a harmonica on a stall in the market," Annie said. "If we each put something towards it we can get it for him, then he can play a tune and we can dance. What do you think?"

Hettie smiled. Annie was including her, so perhaps she'd got it wrong. They were a real family. "I think it's a grand idea," she said. "I'll ask Ma to bake him a cake as well. We'll make it the best birthday ever." She could imagine Annie dancing, she'd be light as a feather on her feet but I'll be cavorting like a carthorse, she thought.

The following week Annie and Hettie got home early to help Dorcas prepare a feast for Corry's party. He'd been let off lessons that evening and, to Hettie's surprise, the pastor called with some books and a pair of boots for Corry.

"Fancy the pastor remembering Corry's birthday," Hettie said to Annie as they were laying out the table.

Annie grimaced. "He always remembers Corry's birthday. Never misses giving him a present neither." She pouted. "Forgets mine though." Hettie caught the flash of resentment in her voice.

"He's never bought me a present either," she said. "If that makes you feel any better."

Annie laughed. That was one thing Hettie loved about Annie. She could never stay mad for long. If anything upset her she get over it in a heartbeat. She never dwelt on disappointment.

After tea, with ham and cress sandwiches followed by a fruit filled cake, Corry opened his present from the girls. His eyes lit up. "Where did you get it?" he asked. He blew into it. "It's amazing, jus' what I wanted. You're so clever."

Hettie's heart burned with pleasure.

It didn't take Corry long to get the hang of it. In no time at all he managed to play a decent tune. Hettie and Annie danced around the room as Dorcas and the pastor clapped and hummed along to the music. Hettie even saw the pastor's feet tapping.

Annie sang some of the songs her mother used to sing and Hettie saw a tear in Corry's eye. He quickly wiped it away. The pastor put his arm around Corry's shoulders. "Your sister's a rare talent," he said. "Her singing would bring a tear to a glass eye."

After the singing and dancing they sat around the fire playing parlour games and telling stories until Dorcas said they'd best be off to their beds. "You've an early start in the morning," she reminded them. Then, to everyone's surprise and Corry's great delight, she said, "I've made up the box room for you Corry. At thirteen you need to have a room of your own."

The smile on Corry's face stretched wider than the Thames.

Hettie and Annie helped him move his stuff into his new room. Hettie would be denied the pleasure of watching him dress in the mornings now, but she was glad. It was what Corry had always wanted.

That Christmas would be the first Annie and Corry would spend without their mother so Dorcas and Hettie vowed to at least make the day special for them.

Dorcas got Corry to light the front room fire first thing in the morning. Usually it wasn't lit until the evening to spare the coal. Over a special breakfast of bread and jam they each opened their presents.

"Oh, it's beautiful," Annie said when she saw the embroidered muff Hettie had made for her. "How did you do it without me seeing? I'll wear it every day to keep my hands warm."

Next, Corry opened his gift from Hettie, a needlecord waistcoat with a smart striped lining. He smiled broadly and slipped his arms through the armholes. Then he marched up and down in his new finery. "It's great, Hettie, thank you," he said. "I know where to come now if I want any new togs." Hettie glowed with pleasure.

"Open yours next," Annie said to Dorcas, handing her a loosely wrapped parcel. "It's from me and Corry. I hope you like it."

Dorcas undid the wrapping and held up the crisp white apron they had given her. "It's just what I need." She wrapped it around her ample middle. "My old one's well past mending." She smiled at the children. "Thank you kindly," she said.

Annie was delighted with the hairbrush, mirror and profusion of coloured ribbons Dorcas gave her and couldn't wait to try them out, but Dorcas tutted when she started to brush her riot of unruly curls at the breakfast table.

Corry bought her a book of paper dolls to cut out with dresses she could fit on them. "This is the best present ever," she said to Corry and gave him a kiss. Corry blushed redder than the jam on his bread.

Next, Hettie unwrapped her present from Annie and Corry. She hadn't expected anything but tears filled her eyes when she saw the book of poems she'd admired in a shop window sitting there in her hands. "However did you manage it?" she said glancing at each of them in turn. "It's lovely." She hugged Annie and ventured a kiss on Corry's cheek, which he wiped off with a grin.

Dorcas bought Corry a pack of playing cards and a book of tricks he could learn to keep them amused. Annie gave him a penknife with a strong blade.

After breakfast they put their gifts away, banked up the fire and put their coats and boots on to go to church for the Christmas Day service.

Dorcas had invited Pastor Brown to join them for Christmas lunch after the service. When he arrived he gave Dorcas a small bottle of sherry and the children some prayer cards. "This is most kind and unexpected," Dorcas said, her eyes shining. Her face gradually turned pink. Grinning broadly she shuffled them all into the parlour where Hettie had set the table for lunch.

They enjoyed a substantial Christmas dinner. Pastor Brown provided a goose, a gift from one of his parishioners, and Dorcas supplied the roast potatoes, sprouts, carrots, swede, parsnips, chestnut stuffing and thick gravy.

"I can't remember when I've ever eaten so much," the pastor said, patting his stomach. "A feast to praise the Lord," he said with a broad smile.

Dorcas blushed and hurried out with the plates.

After Christmas pudding, brandy butter and mince pies, Hettie read to them from the pastor's copy of *A Christmas Carol* by Charles Dickens.

Corry said he'd have preferred *The Pickwick Papers* but they all booed him down. In the evening, Corry played some music on his harmonica and Hettie and Annie sang. It was the happiest Christmas Hettie could ever remember.

The months after Christmas were heavy with frost, snow and no cress, so Annie went out scrubbing doorsteps for a penny a time, sweeping pavements or running errands and doing whatever cleaning jobs she could pick up. Hettie was back indoors with Dorcas helping with the laundry. She was taking a bundle of clean washing back to a house in the better part of Stepney Green when she saw Gander. She recognised him immediately from his demeanour and his squashed pork-pie hat. He was dodging in and out of the gardens in front of the houses, peering in through windows and knocking on doors.

Hettie crossed the street. The last thing she wanted was a confrontation with him. He's up to no good, she thought, but couldn't work out what he was gaining from his peculiar actions. Perhaps he was selling something, although he had nothing with him. Maybe he was offering some service like bringing in the coal or chopping logs. She couldn't imagine it. She shook her head and moved on.

Keeping out of his way was her first priority. Other than that she really didn't care.

Corry still went to the river looking for scraps of wood, metal, coal or even old bones he could pick up which would make a fire. Again, pickings were small as there were so many boys out. Most of what he brought home ended up on their fire so at least they had some warmth.

When it was too damp, wet or cold to go out in the evenings, there were no jobs to be had and there was no cress to sell anyway, Hettie and Annie sat indoors by the fire. Hettie helped Annie with her sewing or they played together with Hettie's dolls. Corry still went out to see what he could find, but pickings were poor and he often came home empty-handed, although he always managed to find money for their rent.

Dorcas became more and more concerned about Corry. "He's falling into bad company," she'd complain to Hettie when he stayed out late at night and seemed to have more cash than could be accounted for with pickings from the river being so poor.

"No good'll come of it," she said.

Hettie worried too. The evening lessons finished at nine and Hettie remembered that dreadful boy Gander saying he'd be waiting for Corry after lessons. That was some time ago but still, if he ran one of the gangs of boys who went out thieving after lessons... Hettie worried that Corry had been led into thieving. She mentioned her fears to Annie.

"He wouldn't do that," Annie said. "He's too much sense to follow those lads. He's probably working somewhere as a surprise for us when he's saved enough. Corry'd never do anything bad."

One evening when Hettie was at home with Dorcas sewing material into a shirt for Corry, there came a loud banging on the door.

"Who could that be at this time of night?" Dorcas said, putting her sewing aside and heaving her substantial frame out of the chair. "Someone up to no good for sure."

Hettie followed her to the door and saw a young boy, not more than six, barefoot and in dirty clothes standing on the doorstep. "It's Corry, Missus," he said, fear filling his eyes. "He's been taken in for thieving."

"I knew it," Dorcas said, snatching off her apron and grabbing her shawl from a hook in the hall. "I knew he was up to no good."

Hettie's heart sank. What would become of him and Annie now?

Chapter Five

"You stay here and tell Annie what's happened," Dorcas said. "I'll go see the pastor. See if he can sort it out." She gave the young lad a ha'penny for his trouble and bustled out into the rain. Hettie waited for Annie to come home. As soon as she heard the front door open she rushed out into the hall.

Annie started in shock seeing Hettie in such a state.

"Hettie, what on earth...?"

"It's Corry," Hettie said. "He's been taken in."

"Taken in? Whatever for?"

"Thieving," Hettie blurted out. "He's been taken in for thieving."

Annie paled. "Where? How? Who?"

"A young lad came to the door. Ma's gone round to see the pastor to see if he'll speak for him. He's fond of Corry you know, I'm sure he'll do his best."

She ushered Annie into the parlour and made her sit down. Annie shook her head, bewildered. "I'll never forgive 'im if he's put away," she said. Tears brimmed her eyes. "He didn't need to go thieving. I'd have worked longer and helped more if I'd known how bad things were."

She jumped up and paced the room screwing her handkerchief in her hands. "I'd do owt to help him, he knows that. Why did he have to go thieving?"

"I don't know. I thought things were going all right," Hettie said.

"It's that Gander," Annie said. "I bet a pound to a penny he's got something to do with it."

Hettie sighed. "You don't know that."

Annie stared at her. "A pound to a penny," she said.

Hettie thought she was probably right but there was nothing they could do about it. "All we can do is hope the pastor can help."

Hettie made Annie tea and sat with her, a heavy stone of dread filling her insides. Poor Corry, he didn't deserve to be put away, whatever could have driven him to thieving?

It was after midnight when Dorcas returned with Corry and the pastor. Annie and Hettie both jumped up as soon as they heard the door open. A few seconds later Dorcas, Corry and Pastor Brown walked into the room. Annie rushed up to Corry and hugged him.

Dorcas hung up her shawl and, smiling broadly, said, "Pastor Brown spoke up for 'im, he did. They let 'im go provided there's no more thieving. That's right in't it, Corry." She glared at a woebegone

Corry, who, once Annie let him go, shuffled his feet and looked as though he wished he could disappear through the wall.

"Why did you do it, Corry? Why?" Annie said her face stained with tears. Then she glared at him. "It's that Gander isn't it? He's at the back of it."

Corry's lips tightened.

"What did he do?" Hettie asked, unable to believe that Corry would go out on purpose to steal.

Corry hung his head and gazed at the floor. "I wasn't making enough in the mudlarking. Everyone does it, only I got caught."

"Everyone?" Dorcas said. "Who?"

Corry swallowed under Dorcas's unwavering gaze. "The lads at the school. They's all in it." He glanced at the pastor and then at Annie. "You know what Gander's like. He checks out what's good to prig and after lessons sends everyone out thieving. You can't say no to him. I'm not the only one."

"No, but you're the only one lives under my roof," Dorcas said, eyes blazing. "So, you ain't going to do it no more – right?" She glared at him. "What'd happen to Annie if you got took in for good? Have you thought of that?"

Corry obviously hadn't.

"I can look out for meself," Annie piped up. "Corry was only trying to help." She moved to beside Corry. "That Gander's a wrong 'un. Always has been." She turned to Corry. "I told you to keep clear of him."

Pastor Brown took a deep breath. "I'm afraid she's right, Mrs Bundy," he said. "I know a lot of the lads at the school go out thieving. We seem to have several gangs operating on the streets. I do what I can to discourage them but..." He shrugged his shoulders.

"It's that Gander should be taken in," Annie said.

"He don't go out thieving himself," Corry said. "He sends us lads to do it. No way he's gonna get taken in."

"That's true," Pastor Brown said. "Corry's not a bad lad, Mrs Bundy. I'll see what I can do for him to get him away from Gander and the rest of the gangs that rule the streets after dark." He turned to Corry. "Come and see me tomorrow."

He turned to Dorcas. "Don't be too hard on him, Mrs Bundy. There's much temptation for the lad. It's a brave man who can resist when pride and belonging's involved."

Not to mention avoiding a beating, Hettie thought.

Dorcas huffed her disapproval. "Whatever you say, Pastor," she said. "But I've never seen no good reason for thieving."

The next morning Annie and Hettie were up early again to go for the cress as usual, expecting to leave Corry to Dorcas's tender mercies. But Dorcas wasn't having of that. She had no time for idle hands. "There's ways of earning a penny or two that don't involve thieving," she said to Corry. "See what you can earn in the market helping out the costers or opening carriage doors for gents afore you go to see the pastor. That'll keep you out of mischief." She pushed him out of the door with the girls.

Hettie felt sorry for him, he looked so dishevelled. She offered him a penny for a hot drink but he refused.

"I can fend for meself," he said, anger burning in his eyes. "I don't need no help from any girl." Then he ran off in the direction of the market.

Annie sighed. "He feels responsible," she said, "him being a boy, but I can fend for meself an' all. I wish he'd let us help."

That morning the cress sold slowly, the dampness of the day keeping the buyers inside. Hettie and Annie ended up knocking on doors to sell their bunches. Hettie got used to having the door slammed in her face but Annie did better. She had a way about her and usually managed to charm a penny or two from most households. Still, she'd had to give four bunches for a penny, which left them short. Overall it was a dismal day.

When they got home Dorcas was alone, struggling with a pile of washing she'd taken in.

"Where's Corry?" Annie asked, fearful of his having been taken in again.

Dorcas smiled. "He's up at brewery yard. Pastor's got him a job there helping with the horses. Landed on his feet this time he has. Better than he deserves."

Annie pouted at Dorcas's words, but Hettie's heart soared. With a proper job Corry would no longer have to go mudlarking in the river and he'd be able to hold his head high again. With that and the cress things didn't look too bad at all.

That evening when Corry came home from the yard his boots were covered in stable mud, bits of straw clung to his jacket and the smell of manure reached Hettie and Dorcas well before he did.

"Take your boots off afore coming into my house," Dorcas said. "Take 'em out back and under the pump. I don't want you stinking the place out."

"It's honest work and honest stink," Corry said. "I've shovelled enough muck to fill the Pool of London today." He grinned. "Still, it's better 'an scrabbling around in the mud."

Over dinner he talked about the horses and the work at the stable yard. "There's one called Hercules," he said, "and another called Gideon. He's my favourite. Gentle as a lamb he is, not like some who won't come out and you have to get a couple of lads to help pull 'em out."

"What's the governor like?" Annie asked. "Good bloke is he? I mean, will you get on?"

Corry chewed a mouthful of bread before answering. "Joe's nice enough, but you have to move when 'e says move or you're for it."

He stopped going to the pastor's lessons in case he ran into Gander again, but on the evenings when Hettie was home she sat with him and helped with his reading and writing.

Gradually winter turned to spring and Hettie had never been so glad to see the early morning mist clearing and the sky brightening. At last the cress was becoming more plentiful and they hadn't to work so hard to sell it. By summer they found they could sell more than a lapful each so they bought a basket full to share. Annie, being the smallest, piled her share onto her tray while Hettie balanced the basket on her hip as she walked the streets.

One morning on their way to collect their day's cress, Hettie and Annie ran into Gander again. It was as much as Hettie could do to stop Annie going for him.

"I heard about Corry's new job," he said. "Tell 'im if he dobs me in it it'll be the worse for 'im."

"We ain't afraid of you," Annie said, sparks flying from her eyes. "You comes near us or Corry again I'll have the rozzers on you sure as eggs."

Gander laughed. "Eggs is easily broken," he said and stalked off, disappearing into the stream of early morning workers flooding the street.

Over the next few years Hettie and Annie sold their cress while Corry worked at the brewery yard. With the coming of the railway Hettie and Annie found more customers for their cress among the railway workers and builders working on the new housing. There were new streets and houses springing up and Hettie and Annie weren't slow to take advantage of the growing number of workers coming into the city via the railway.

With the opening of a station at Hackney things were changing fast. Even the cress was coming in by rail from the farms as distant as Essex and Kent on the east and Oxford in the west. The Hackney cress farm disappeared when the land was sold and a row of terraced houses built on it. Hettie and Annie bought their cress from Eliza in Covent Garden.

"Why don't you girls try the hotels and boarding houses as well as the shops?" she said one day when they were filling their baskets from her stall. "The streets full of sellers but none have tried the hotels as far as I know."

Hettie grinned. "I'll give them a try," she said.

As Hettie grew older she filled out. She paid more attention to her clothes swirled her long chestnut hair into a twist pinned up on top of her head and held it down with a felt hat befitting a street seller of good quality cress. She acquired quite a few admirers too. The paper boy at the corner tipped his hat and whistled as she passed and even the carriage boys called out 'good morning'.

That summer Hettie noticed the girls flocking to the baskets around the cress market appeared to be getting younger. Then she recalled that Annie had started selling cress when she was seven. Many of the girls she saw now were as young as five, barefoot and ragged lining up for their handful, or those who could stretch to it, lapful of cress.

She sighed at the memory. She'd been selling cress for years now. Was it time to move on and find a more lucrative line of work? She put the thought behind her.

Chapter Six

Hettie wasn't the only one who'd filled out and blossomed over the years. By the time Annie was fifteen she was a real beauty. Petite next to Hettie she had a doll-like delicacy. Her wild, unruly curls shone like burnished copper and no matter how hard she tried to tame them they escaped from under her perky beribboned hat to curl like corkscrews framing her pale as marble face. She'd started to dress in outrageously bright, colourful outfits, extravagantly decorated with sashes and bows which Hettie thought more suited to appearing on stage than walking the streets selling watercress. She felt dowdy in comparison.

When Dorcas mentioned her lavish wardrobe Annie's eyes flashed. "Nowt wrong with a bit of colour," she said. "We don't all want to look as though we've dug up and stole the clothes off corpses." Then she stormed out.

"Silk stockings?" Dorcas said to Hettie another time when she was sorting out the washing. "Why can't she wear woollen ones like the rest of us?"

"She hankers after a life of glamour and excitement, Ma," Hettie said. "She dreams of going on the stage." She pouted at Dorcas. "Can't deny her her dreams can we?"

Dorcas huffed. "That's as maybe, but a right little madam she's turning into." She turned away. "Like mother like daughter I dare say," she muttered.

Every day, when they'd finished the cress, Annie made her way to Covent Garden to pick up what flowers she could from the flower sellers and make up bunches to sell to the evening theatre goers in Drury Lane and Haymarket. Then she'd disappear for hours. Hettie would grow impatient waiting for her, but when she asked where she'd been, Annie would only say, "Oh, so you're the governor now are you?" Then she'd laugh and run off.

When Hettie went to look for her, tired of waiting, she'd invariably find her hanging around the entrance to some theatre or other, goggling at the posters or trying to catch sight of one of the performers arriving or leaving the building.

"It's no use hanging around here all night, getting your hopes up. It's a different world," Hettie said. "This is no place for the likes of us."

"The likes of us!" Annie nearly exploded. "And what would you recommend for the 'likes of us'? A lifetime of street selling, or taking in washing perhaps?" She scowled. "I've got my sights set a lot higher than that and I'll make it one day, you see if I don't."

It was when she was out late at night Hettie worried the most. "What would Corry say if he knew you was going down Haymarket and round the theatres at night?" she said. "You know what goes around there don't you?"

But again Annie laughed. "Don't be so soft. It's not as bad as you think and there's many a toff out there who'll buy a few flowers for his lady friend and they give me a generous tip as well. If you don't believe me come and see for yourself."

So Hettie followed Annie along Haymarket one night and saw for herself. The pavement was crowded with people, despite the late hour. As well as a number of well dressed toffs in silk top hats, canes and evening wear she saw respectable ladies walking along with their eyes averted.

She nudged Annie when she saw women with painted faces, wearing gaudy, extravagantly decorated clothes, their dresses hiked up so she could see their pink silk stockings. Some wore summer hats and some wore no hats at all. Annie nodded to one or two of them but Hettie pulled her away hurrying on. "You know what they are don't you?" She sighed. "Asking for trouble you are, Annie Flanagan."

"Don't worry about me I can take care of meself."

Hettie shuddered at the thought of what went on there but it was no use saying anything to Annie, she was stubborn as the mules that pulled the costers' barrows. All she could do was keep her mouth shut and hope everything was all right.

Summer was fading, the leaves on the trees turning gold and red. Soon the summer flowers would be replaced by the rich tapestry of autumn. Hettie decided to make her way early towards Covent Garden where she hoped to meet up with Annie for a hot drink and a bite to eat.

It was almost lunch-time when a hackney carriage drew up alongside her. The driver jumped down and lashed the horses' reins to the carriage brake handle. "Annie? Annie Flanagan?" he said standing in front of her.

Hettie stared at him.

"Annie? My name's Jack. I'm a friend of Corry's. There's been an accident. I'm to take you home then to the hospital."

Hettie's brain froze. For a moment she couldn't understand what the man was saying. Something about Corry. It took her a few seconds to gather her thoughts and find her voice. "Corry? Accident? Hospital? What's happened," she said, her heart pounding. "Is he all right?" Fear gripped her stomach, squeezing it like a fist. Something had happened to Corry.

"He got crushed when barrels fell off wagon," Jack said.

Hettie's heart flipped. "Crushed!"

He shrugged. "Well, knocked down." His brow furrowed. "I dunno how bad it is. I'd just run into the stables to give the horses a drink when it happened." He patted the horse nearest to him. "I took Corry to the voluntary hospital in Whitechapel, quick as I could, then I drove round to 'is lodgings. The lady there says to find Annie who'd be out with the cress and bring her home so that's why I'm here." He moved to help Hettie into the carriage. "Come on, we'll be there in no time."

Hettie's mind raced. She had no idea where Annie was. Her first instinct was to go with this man to see Corry. She knew she should tell him the truth and send him on his way to find Annie, but she could be anywhere and she wasn't selling cress neither. In fact she hadn't been selling cress for several days...

With only the slightest hesitation Hettie jumped into the hackney. She'd sort things out with Annie once she'd found out how bad Corry was. If worse came to worst she'd be the best one to break the news to Annie – she was her best friend after all.

When they arrived back at the house Dorcas climbed into the hackney with Hettie. "Where's Annie?" she said. "I sent Jack for Annie. If owt's happened to Corry she should be first to know."

Hettie could contain herself no longer. She burst into tears and held her head in her hands sobbing. Between sobs she managed to get out the fact that she had no idea where Annie was or what she was doing.

Dorcas's face reddened, her jaws clenched. "You wait 'til I catch up with that young lady," she said, eyes flaming. "She's a piece of my mind coming and no mistake." She shook her head. "Like mother like daughter," she said.

Her face softened as she looked at Hettie. "It's not your fault. She always was a wrong 'un that one."

When they arrived at the hospital the manager of the brewery yard was there, wringing his cap in his hands as he paced up and down the waiting room.

"Well?" Dorcas said.

"He was helping load barrels when the rope slipped," he said. "We got 'im here fast as we could. Doctor's with 'im now." With that he went and sat down. Dorcas and Hettie followed.

Jack said how sorry he was and if there was anything he could do they'd find him at Hackney End.

Dorcas thanked him and offered him two shillings but he wouldn't take it. "Least I could do for Corry," he said. "He's a good lad and helps with the horses when I bring 'em into the yard. Anything I can do just let me know." Then he was gone.

Dorcas and Hettie sat for what seemed like hours waiting to hear from the doctors. The manager of the brewery yard apologised and left, saying as how he had to get the wagons out afore dark. All the while Hettie's stomach churned. The worst possible scenarios ran through her head. What was she going to say to Annie? Shouldn't she be out looking for her rather than sitting here doing nothing? She wanted to go but fear held her back – fear of what the doctors might say and the greatest fear of all – fear of losing Corry and because of it losing Annie as well.

"He's a bit battered and bruised," the doctor said when he finally came out to see them. It was after midnight and Annie had arrived all in a dither, having been told of the accident by Dorcas's neighbour.

"But he'll be all right won't he?" she gasped, out of breath from rushing. "Corry's strong as a horse. He'll pull through."

The doctor smiled. "In time," he said. "We've patched him up as best we can. His shoulder and hip took most of the fall, they're badly crushed. His arm and leg are broken as well. The bones will mend in time. Nothing much else we can do."

"Thank you, thank you, doctor," Annie cried, rushing into his surprised arms. "We're all most grateful."

The doctor disengaged himself, pushing Annie to arms length, his face turning pink. "He'll need rest and it'll be a while before he'll be able to walk again – if ever," he added with a grimace. "We'll keep him here for a few days in case there are any nasty developments."

"What nasty developments?" Dorcas said, eyeing the doctor as though she knew he was holding something back.

The doctor sighed. "In cases like this we can't be sure how bad the damage is. All we can do is treat the cuts and bruises, splint his arm and leg and hope for the best."

"And what would that be?" Dorcas persisted.

The doctor took a breath. "The best we can hope for is that he manages to walk, but if he does it's most likely to be with a limp and there'll be a shortage of strength in his arm. If he's ever able to work again it'll be light duties only, nothing strenuous or tiring." He frowned. "That's if he recovers. Some never do."

"Can I see him?" Annie pleaded. "I'm his sister. We've only got each other."

"Just a few minutes then. He's very weak and needs to rest."

"Wait for me, Hettie," Annie called as she sprinted off to the wards. So Hettie sat and waited again.

Chapter Seven

Annie visited the hospital every day taking in whatever fresh fruit she could pick up from the market. Most of it sat untouched.

Hettie went once or twice, but couldn't bear to see Corry held captive by his injuries. She sat by his bedside, not knowing what to say. He looked so pale, fragile and heartbreakingly vulnerable. It was an effort to keep cheerful when all she could think about was his not being able to walk again. She took careful note of the drugs being used to dull his pain.

Even the pastor visited. He didn't say anything, just stood at the end of Corry's bed, a crushed look of great sadness on his face. Hettie knew he'd spoken to the doctors, but not what they'd told him.

Rain dampened the streets, bouncing up from the road, raindrops clinging to the bare branches of the trees and dark clouds filling the sky. The grimy streets seemed shrouded in Hettie's misery. Walking home from the hospital her shoes were soaked and her skirt sodden. All she could think about was what lay in store for Corry for the rest of his life.

It was a week before he was allowed home. Jack helped Dorcas move Corry's bed downstairs where it would be easier to nurse him. Then he went with Dorcas to collect him. Hettie and Annie waited at home, each lost in their own thoughts about the future.

Jack carried him in and lay him on the bed. "If there's owt else I can do..." he said.

"We'll manage no doubt," Dorcas said. "But thanks for the offer."

Hettie and Annie added their thanks and Jack tipped his hat and left.

Dorcas slumped down in a chair, anxiety etched in the deep lines in her face. Hettie guessed it was the loss of his wages that worried her most of all.

"We'll help out," Hettie said. "I'll work extra and so'll Annie, won't you, Annie?"

"An' who'll be looking after Corry?" Dorcas asked. "He'll need nursing."

Hettie's heart sank.

The next day Hettie and Annie were too distressed to leave him, which meant another day's takings were lost.

Dorcas busied herself with the bundles of washing she'd taken in but it was clear that even she worried about him. The atmosphere in the house was tense and miserable, as damp and depressing as the weather outside.

"How are we going to pay the rent now?" Annie said to Hettie when Dorcas went out to return the bundle of washing. "If I had owt to sell I'd sell it but even if I sold everything we have it wouldn't amount to anything. What are we going to do now?"

Hettie grimaced. "Don't worry. Ma won't throw you out if I've owt to do with it. We'll work something out. Leave Ma to me. She won't want to look bad in front of the pastor. I'll see what I can do."

Annie smiled for the first time in days. "You're right," she said. "Everyone has a weakness. If you can find it you can have anything in the world."

That evening Hettie went to see the pastor. She found him in the room at the rectory he used as an office. It had been some time since she'd had the opportunity to study him so closely. She saw an upright, agile man, fit for his years, sitting behind his desk intensely studying the papers in his hand. Dressed in clerical black, his white collar accentuated the light tan on his kindly face. His wiry hair, almost touching his shoulders, was grey but there was a lightness in his eyes.

He glanced up as she entered and rose to usher her to a chair, his face creased with worry. "How is he? What do the doctors say? Is there hope for his recovery?"

"The doctor says he needs to rest and won't be fit for some time," Hettie said. "We are all praying for him, but it's early days yet and no one can be sure."

Pastor Brown nodded and sat at his desk again. "Of course," he said at last.

Hettie sniffed and took out a handkerchief to wipe her eyes. "We'll feel the loss of his wages," she said pouting. "And he'll need nursing. I can do that but it means the loss of cress money as well."

"It must be difficult," the pastor said. "Even without the accident."

"It's a concern," she said. "Annie and I do what we can but with the bad weather we hardly make anything these days. Annie does some bits of cleaning but without Corry..." She shrugged and looked pleadingly at the pastor.

"I wish there was something I could do," he said, glancing around the room. He sighed and sat back deep in thought. Then he glanced up at Hettie again as though considering something. "Well," he said at last. "You're bright enough and a good reader, you could help with the boys in the school in the evenings. I can't pay much but it will help and I'll ask around to see if there's anything else you can do."

Hettie smiled. She could fit in a few hours in the evening at the school and still nurse Corry at home during the day and Dorcas couldn't object to her helping the pastor. A wave of gratitude washed over her. "Thank you," she said. "You won't regret it. I'll be the best teacher they've ever had."

The pastor grinned. "Come on then let's go see your mother and see what she says. I was wanting to see Corry anyway."

When they got back to the house Dorcas was laying out the tea. She invited the pastor to join them.

As Hettie predicted, Dorcas was happy to let Hettie stay at home to nurse Corry and help out at the school in the evenings as long as Annie could bring in enough to cover the rent. "She can give me a hand with the washing an' all," she said, brightening considerably. "It's a lot for me to do at my age."

The next morning Annie set off early to see what she could find to sell that would bring in a few extra pence. She'd found that if she spent her money on fish she could make a greater profit than selling cress.

Hettie watched Corry as he slept. At nineteen he was almost a man. He'd filled out from the skinny lad who'd first come to live with them. She noticed the dark shadow of bristles on his chin and how his tousled hair, black and shiny as a raven's wing, curled on his neck. His skin was smooth; his good arm muscled and tanned from working in the yard while his other shoulder was bound in heavy bandages. His arm and his leg were both held by wooden splints. She sat spellbound for what felt like ages, listening to the rise and fall of his breathing and watching the way his head turned as he mumbled in his sleep. A deep well of tenderness opened inside her. He looked so pale and so very defenceless.

Gloom descended like a rain cloud. Supposing the doctor was right, he'd never walk again. He'd be an invalid in need of care for the rest of his life. Unbearable sickness swirled inside her. Whatever happened she'd never leave him, never, no matter what. The sickness inside her hardened to form a rock of determination.

When he woke she bathed his face and held his head up. She held a glass to his lips dispensing the drugs that softened his pain. He slept most of the day, so while he slept she scrubbed the floors, did piles of washing, and cooked the potatoes and little bits of meat that Dorcas brought home to make the broth to go with the bread and butter they had for dinner.

Every evening she fed him a little broth and sat with him. How wonderful it must be to be able to nurse the sick back to health, she thought. She'd read about Florence Nightingale nursing in the Crimea and wished with all her heart that she could so something like that. Wouldn't it be lovely, she thought. Of course, in her position she knew it was an impossible dream, but it didn't stop her thinking about it.

She watched, her heart squeezed with worry, as days passed with Corry heavily sedated, drifting in and out of consciousness. Once in his delirium he called out in the night.

"Ma, Ma," he called. Hettie, lying awake unable to sleep for worry, jumped out of bed and ran down to sooth him, bathe his face and reassure him.

"I'm here," she said. She held his hand, heart pumping, until he calmed and drifted into sleep again. A swell of pleasure washed over her and she glowed inside.

Another time he called out for Annie but still it was Hettie who rushed to his side.

In his more lucid moments he'd talk about Annie, their childhood and the different lives they'd lived. Hettie wondered what sort of life they'd had when their mother was younger, more glamorous and obviously popular. What had happened to bring them from what appeared to be a reasonably well off living to this rundown street in Wapping?

Gradually the pain lessened and he'd lie awake for several hours before dropping off to sleep again. Hettie was heartened as each day his recovery became more marked. After a couple of weeks he was well enough to enjoy her reading to him from books she'd borrowed from the pastor's library. She'd feel his gaze upon her and heat would flush her face.

The pastor visited. He brought a chess set for Corry.

"I can't play," Corry said frustrated at the gift.

"I'll teach you," the pastor said. And so he did.

Jack was a regular visitor too. He'd sit and play cards with Corry in the evenings when Hettie was teaching at the pastor's school.

Sometimes, in the late evening when everyone was in bed, Hettie would hear Corry playing sad songs on his harmonica. She'd lay and listen, until the music lulled her to sleep.

Corry was an impatient patient. Hettie saw his frustrations at his incapacity. Some days he'd be in a foul temper at his enforced confinement, then Hettie knew to keep quiet and get on with her work. Other days he'd lay back and let her fuss around him assuring him that, in time he'd be fit again. She prayed with all her heart this was true.

Pastor Brown brought him a pair of crutches he'd been given by a parishioner.

"It's early days yet," he said. "But you'll soon be up on your feet again and these'll come in useful."

Corry couldn't wait to try them out. With Dorcas and the pastor's help he got out of bed and managed to stand on his good leg. With one crutch under each arm he hopped across the room to sit in a chair in front of the fire. Hettie wrapped a blanket around his legs and Dorcas put a shawl over his shoulders. Corry grinned.

"Be galloping down the road in no time," he said.

By Christmas he was recovered enough to hop on his crutches into the kitchen where Hettie was delighted to see him eat a hearty breakfast. After breakfast they exchanged gifts. Annie bought Hettie a tambourine so she could join in the music making and Hettie gave Annie a songbook filled with the latest songs from the music halls.

She bought Corry a book about ships and Dorcas gave him a notebook and pen.

Corry had no money as he wasn't working and couldn't get out but he surprised everyone by producing gifts for them all. First he gave Annie an intricately carved wooden box lined with felt for her jewellery.

Thrilled, Annie said, "How on earth did you manage this?" She glanced at him, his arm and leg still in plaster. "You've only one arm."

Corry grinned. "Jack helped. He smuggled the wood and some tools in from the yard under his coat. I worked on it in the evenings while you were out." The look of pride on his face made Hettie beam.

He gave Hettie a small box, also delicately carved, for hairpins, and Dorcas a colourful mat of woven raffia to stand her pots on. "You have been busy," Hettie said her eyes shining. "It must have taken ages."

"Hours," Corry said. Then blushing added, "Well, I'd nothing else to do."

Pastor Brown joined them for lunch and the rest of the day was spent around the fire. Annie sang, Corry played the harmonica, Hettie joined in as best she could with her tambourine and Dorcas and Pastor Brown clapped along. Hettie relaxed at last, seeing Corry enjoy himself despite his injuries.

After New Year Hettie went back to selling cress with Annie. Corry was well enough to manage with only a little help to get up and dressed in the morning and Hettie left him in Dorcas's tender care.

It didn't take her long to notice a change in Annie. She was just as friendly to the people in the market in the mornings, but Hettie noticed she'd disappear for long periods of time during the day and refused to say where she'd been. As the evenings lengthened Annie stayed out later and later.

"You've missed supper," Hettie said one evening. "I've saved some for you."

"It's all right, I've eaten," Annie said and swished her skirts as she strode past Hettie and up to bed.

Another time she came in obviously the worse for drink. "Annie Flanagan, you're drunk," Hettie said.

Annie laughed. "And you're boring," she said pushing Hettie to one side.

"Don't let Corry see you like that," Hettie said.

Annie stopped in her tracks and stared at Hettie. Her eyes narrowed. "He's no angel," she said. "Don't go getting ideas about Corry. He's a man. He'll let you down, they all do."

Dorcas's disapproval permeated the air in the house and it was only Corry's being laid up and the pastor's frequent visits to check his progress that kept Dorcas quiet and her opinions unexpressed.

Then, one evening Annie came in bubbling with excitement.

"I expect you've all been wondering what I've been up to," she said, eyes bright with glee.

Hettie raised her eyebrows. Dorcas glared. "Up to no good if I knows you," she said.

Corry's face clouded over. Hettie jumped up. "Ma," she said. "Give Annie a chance, can't you see how excited she is. Go on, Annie, tell us your good news."

Annie bounced up and down, almost dancing around the room. "I'm going to be on the stage," she said. "In the theatre. It's what I've always dreamed about. Imagine, Hettie, me on the stage."

Corry shook his head. "On the stage?" he said. "Where?" His face darkened. "Not one of those penny gaffs, Annie? I won't allow it."

"No," Dorcas chimed in. "Corry's right. Whorehouses and temples of obscenity they are. If that's the best you can do you'd better stick to selling cress."

"Well, it's not one of those if you must know. It's a proper theatre in the Strand patronised by the well-to-do." She huffed and stood with hands balled on her hips. "I've been working with street theatre entertaining the queues and that," she said. "Then this lady comes up to me and says I ought to audition for the proper theatre, so I do. And guess what? I got the job." If the moon had landed in her lap she couldn't have look more pleased with herself. "The lady what took me on said I had potential. Thought very highly of me she did."

"A lady took you on?" Corry said. "Not a man then?"

Hettie saw his point. Annie drew men's lust like a magnet, but not many women fell under her spell.

"No, a lady. Dance teacher I think she said."

Despite Dorcas and Corry's disapproval there was nothing they could do to stop Annie doing exactly as she pleased. "I'm sixteen," she said. "I can make up me own mind." It was clear that her mind had been made up.

"First sign of trouble and she's out," Dorcas said but Hettie knew that Dorcas's heart was softer than she'd let people know. As long as Annie paid the rent she could stay as long as she liked, but Corry's disapproval, that was a different matter.

Later that evening Hettie sat with Annie and Corry while Dorcas was out. "Tell us about this theatre then," Corry said. "Are you sure it's all above board, not a front for something else? A lot of these places are no more than knocking shops."

Annie bridled. "And you think I'd be interested in working in one of them? Give me some credit, Corry," she said. "It's a proper theatre with ballet dancers, plays, musicals and even a dancer from Paris." Annie's eyes shone with excitement. "Oh, you should see it, Hettie, there are magnificent chandeliers, a huge pit for the orchestra, refreshment rooms and private dining rooms. It's amazing – so many people there, dancers, singers and performers. It's light and bright with mirrors and velvet curtains. It's a whole different world. I've never seen anything like it in me life."

Hettie watched Corry battling contrasting emotions. Fear, worry and confusion flitted across his face but in the end he could say nothing. Clearly he wasn't convinced.

"I'm going to be on the stage – just like I've always wanted." Annie grinned. "Please say you're happy for me, Hettie – Corry."

Hettie's heart crunched. "Of course I'm happy for you," she said. "But are you sure?"

"Yes, look at the programme, it says 'absolutely free from objectionable material'. It can't be clearer than that can it?"

Hettie sighed. Corry's eyes narrowed. Hettie saw anger simmering in them at his helplessness and frustration.

Chapter Eight

Gradually, Corry's limbs mended. Two months after the accident Jack took him to the hospital to have his plasters removed. He still needed his crutches but Hettie was relieved to see him trying to walk again.

He grinned at her. "I'll be back on my feet in no time," he said. "I might not be up to dancing but I could chase you around the room."

Hettie laughed. She hoped his good humour would remain once he did get back on his feet.

The pastor continued to call regularly to monitor his progress.

With the months passing the weather brightened. On good days Corry was able to sit outside in a chair. With the summer coming, the cress was more plentiful but she only made half what she made when she went out with Annie. Passing the baker's shop one morning she saw a card in the window. It read: '*Staff Required, must be honest and able to count.*' Hettie went in.

"You're one of the watercress girls aren't you?" the baker said with a smile.

Hettie nodded.

"Well," he said. "Selling's selling I suppose. Five shillings a week and all the bread you can eat."

"It's a pity young Annie doesn't take a leaf out of your book," Dorcas said when Hettie told her she'd got a job. "That girl's trouble. Mark my words, no good'll come of it."

Hettie sighed. It was true Annie had changed since she'd given up the cress to go on the stage. She frequently returned home smelling of drink just as Hettie was getting up from the bed they shared, and it was well into the afternoon before she rose again.

Hettie knew Corry worried too. He constantly asked after her. Sleeping downstairs he must have heard her coming in and, from the noise she made, Hettie guessed he'd have a pretty good idea of her condition too.

When Hettie confronted her she sniffed and put her nose in the air.

"You're not my mother," she said, grimacing. "Not that my mother would disapprove. Everyone does it," she said. "You've got to be sociable. Honest, anyone'd think I was on the road to ruin instead of earning a living doing something I enjoy. What's more I'm good at it. If I didn't know you better, Hettie Bundy, I'd say you was jealous."

There was no arguing with her. "I don't like what's happening to Annie," Corry said one day. "I'm not sure it's a proper thing she's doing. I'd like to know what she gets up to being out all hours of the night."

Hettie could see he was seriously worried and the fact he was unable to go see for himself only added to his frustration.

"I'm sure she knows what she's doing," Hettie said. "If you like, I'll go along and have a look. Would that put your mind at rest?"

Corry threw his crutches to the floor. "Help me up, Hettie," he said. "It's time I stood on me own two feet."

Hettie gasped. She wanted to help him, but what if he fell and made his injury worse? "I'm not sure…" she said, but it was too late. Corry had grabbed her arm and was lifting himself off the bed. He grinned as he stood upright.

"I knew I could do it," he said. "A few more days an' I'll be good as new."

Hettie's stomach crunched. If he found out what Annie was up to... She shuddered at the thought. Still, it was no good talking to Annie, she never listened.

After a week Corry was able to get out using only a stick. He could walk short distances, but each day he went further. Pastor Brown came to see him.

"My word, Corry, you're doing well. You've surprised us all."

"I wish I could do more, Pastor," Corry said. "I'll be needing to get out and find a job. It's about time I paid my way instead of depending on Annie to pay the rent."

"Ah," the pastor said. "I think I can help you there. I've had a word with the brewery foreman. They'll take you back in the office. I told them you've a good head on your shoulders. It's not heavy work and they owe you don't they?"

Corry beamed.

The next day he was out early and off to the brewery yard. Hettie walked part of the way with him as he had to pass the bakery. "Good luck," she said. "I'll be thinking of you."

Corry looked at her. "I'll be thinking of you too, Hettie," he said and for some reason Hettie had a smile on her face for the rest of the day.

Corry had been back at work a week when he asked Hettie about Annie.

"A bit of singing and dancing I think," Hettie said.

"And that keeps her out until all hours of the morning?"

"Well, she has to socialise a bit, you know, mix with the customers and that."

"It's the 'and that' I'm worried about," Corry said, a look of thunder darkening his face. "I think it's time I went and saw for meself."

Hettie tried to talk him out of it. She'd seen Annie's idea of acceptable evening activity when they visited Haymarket. She felt sure the music hall was only one step better. "It's a theatre, not one of those dens of iniquity," she said. "And Annie's right, she can look out for herself. She's been doing it since she was seven and started with the cress."

He shook his head. "It's different now. Annie's different and I want to be sure."

Hettie sighed. He was as stubborn as Annie when he got an idea in his head.

"I'm teaching at the school tonight. Why don't you wait until tomorrow, then I'll come with you?" She'd gone along herself one evening and was shocked by what she saw, shocked but not surprised. The evening's entertainment had consisted of scantily clad dancers performing in front of an audience of bawdy rowdiness and constant calling out of obscenities and lewd suggestions. All Corry's fears would be confirmed. He'd be livid. At least if she went with him...

She was late home that evening as she'd stayed at the school to help a young lad with his counting and arrived home just as Corry came barrelling along the road. Even taking his limp into consideration he was moving at quite a pace. He stopped when he saw Hettie. His face set like granite.

"What on earth?" Hettie said, heart racing.

He stared, breathing heavily, unable to move.

Hettie pushed him indoors into the parlour where he still slept. His hands were shaking. He sank onto the bed, a haunted look in his eyes. "I didn't mean it Hettie. It were an accident. I didn't mean to kill 'im."

Hettie's eyes shot wide. "What!" she swallowed. "Kill him? Who? Where? What happened?"

"At the theatre – well that's not what I'd call it." He trembled as he spoke. "Upmarket whorehouse more like." His face twisted in pain. He glanced up. "You should have seen them, Hettie. Girls prancing about the stage, showing everything they got. And the dancing! Not like any dancing I've ever seen."

Snakes writhed in Hettie's stomach. "What happened, Corry? What did you do?"

"I went there. Went to see the show." His voice got louder and his speech speeded up. "I went backstage to complain and see the man in charge. I wanted to get Annie out of there. Making an exhibition of herself she were. If you'd a seen her, Hettie, you'd have done the same." Anger simmered now in his eyes.

Hettie frowned. "So what happened?"

"I saw this bloke in a cutaway jacket and pin-striped trousers. Right geezer he was. He had a gold necktie with a jewelled pin. He seemed to be in charge, so I went to have a word. Then I overheard him talking to a young man in a morning suit. He looked like a toff and was offering the geezer money. Said he wanted to book the dancer with the flame coloured hair to come to his room for a private performance. Well, I knew what that meant, and who he wanted the private performance with – Annie."

Hettie's heart sank. "So what did you do?"

"I saw red. Snatched the money just as he were handing it over. The man in the suit tried to grab it back, we got into a struggle. The toff punched me and he were giving me a right battering but I gave as good as I got. Doubled him over with a gut punch." Corry's eyes shone with pride. Then his face collapsed into a grimace. "I swung a wild punch at the manager bloke and landed one right on his jaw. He dropped like a stone and hit his head on a plinth in the hallway." Tears filled his eyes as he spoke. "Oh Hettie, I think I've killed him."

Hettie gasped, her hands flew to her mouth, energy drained out of her. She stared at Corry. His life flashed before her eyes. There was nothing she could do or say. It felt unreal. She sank down on the bed beside him.

Corry sighed. "He were pimping Annie out. He shouldn't have been doing that."

It took Hettie several minutes to gather her thoughts. "Oh Corry," she said. "Surely you know Annie would never do anything like that? She might have a drink with a man or even dance for him, but it'd never go any further. What were you thinking?" Hettie knew exactly what he'd been thinking.

Corry sat with his head in his hands. Then he jumped up and started to gather his belongings, cramming them into a bag. "I can't stay, Hettie," he said. "I need to get away. I'll not stay to be hanged for killing a man who was taking advantage of Annie."

"But where will you go? Wherever you go they'll find you and it'll be all the worse for you having run away."

"I can't help that, Hettie."

"No, Corry. You can't ..." Hot tears burned Hettie's cheeks. She wished she could turn the clock back and make everything all right, but she couldn't. If only she'd gone with him...

He hoisted the bag onto his shoulder and picked up his coat. Breathing heavily he glanced around the room and then at Hettie whose heart dissolved at seeing him so distraught. "No, Corry, please no..."

"I'm sorry, Hettie," he said. He put his hand on her shoulder. "It's for the best. I can catch a ship in the docks and be well away before they come for me." The anguish in his face wrung her heart. "Say goodbye to Annie for me. Look out for her, Hettie, please. She's all I've got."

Hettie stared at him. The look that passed between them stretched time. She tried to press the image of his face into a permanent memory in her mind.

She threw her arms around him. It was foolish to cling on to him or to any hope he would change his mind. If he'd ripped her heart out of her chest it would have been less painful.

He pushed her away. "I'm sorry, Hettie," he whispered, then he was gone.

As helpless as a feather spinning in a storm Hettie watched him limp away with his head bent, dragging his left foot, until he was no more than a speck disappearing into the darkness of the night.

Tears stung her eyes as she closed the door, then, as though a dam had broken, a storm of tears ran unchecked over her cheeks. She collapsed sobbing on the bed. It was all Annie's fault. Why did she have to be so promiscuous? Couldn't she see what it was doing to Corry, or didn't she care? Suddenly she hated Annie. Hated the girl who'd become like a sister to her, the girl she'd always envied for her looks and lively good humour. Her jaw clenched. Could she ever forgive her?

Dawn was breaking, its pale sunlight dappling the walls when Annie came storming in. "Where is he? Where is that idiot brother of mine? You won't believe what he's done, Hettie. Where is he?"

Hettie's face hardened as she looked at Annie. Suddenly she looked like a stranger. This was not the Annie she knew, the kind-hearted, fun-loving Annie she'd grown up with. This was the harridan from hell Annie, clearly bent on turning on the one person in the world who'd die for her. How could she?

"He's gone," Hettie said.

"Gone? Where?"

"Just gone," Hettie said. She wasn't about to let on to Annie that he'd gone for good and it was all her fault.

Annie paced the room shaking her head. "Did he tell you what he did – stupid fool?" She glared at Hettie. "Made a right fool of me he did. I could've lost me job and got thrown out thanks to him. You wait 'til I find him. I'll give him what for."

Hettie took a deep breath. "Your job? Thrown out? Is that all you care about, Annie Flanagan?" White hot rage flared inside Hettie. The built up emotion of years of caring for Corry and looking out for Annie welled up and threatened to explode in Annie's face. "The fact that your brother may hang doesn't worry you then? May hang for trying to protect your virtue – something that's probably long gone anyway?" Hettie's face burned and she felt like slapping Annie to bring her to her senses.

Annie sank down on the bed, puzzled. "Hang Corry? Why would they want to hang Corry?"

Hettie relaxed. So Annie didn't know. "He said he'd killed the manager of that theatre where you work. That's why he's gone. He didn't want to be convicted of murder when it was an accident. Surely you knew that? He said you were there."

"Yes, I was there, in the theatre. I heard about the fight. That's what nearly cost me my job – but murder?" She glared at Hettie. "You mean he thought... Oh no." She stood and paced the room as though running the scene through her head. "He knocked him down, yes. Gave him a right good punch. Knocked him out – that's all." She blinked as a sudden thought came into her head.

"He left before Archie came round." Her eyes widened. "You mean he thought...oh no...surely he didn't think...how could he have thought...but he must have known?"

She sat down again. "We have to find him. Catch up with him and bring him back. Tell him it's all right." She jumped up. "Archie'd never bring proceedings. He won't want the authorities to know about his little sideline." She frowned. "And Corry should have known I'd never go along with it. I don't need him to protect me, Hettie. I can look out for meself." She glared at Hettie. "Where is he? Come on let's go after him."

Hettie looked at the clock. Corry had been gone for hours. He'd be at the docks by now.

"It's too late," she said, fresh tears stinging her eyes.

"Come on. It's worth a try," Annie said pulling her out of the door, but when they got to the docks it was only to learn that Corry had caught a ship and was on his way to America.

Chapter Nine

The house felt empty without Corry. Hettie missed him more than she thought possible. She'd become used to eagerly awaiting his arrival home from work. He'd tell her about his day, the horses and the lads at the stable. Occasionally he'd walk up to the pastor's school with her in the evenings before going on to meet his mates in their favourite watering hole.

Every day her heart ached, and it was all Annie's fault.

Jack helped Dorcas move Corry's bed back upstairs, then she gave the parlour a good clean.

Annie sulked. "What was he thinking, running off like that? He should have known we'd sort something out."

"He ran because he thought he'd killed someone and they'd hang him," Hettie said. "He wasn't to know the man was only knocked out."

"Well, he should have known. He's been in enough fights himself," Annie said. She eyed Hettie. "He's no angel. You're always sticking up for 'im and making out he's some sort of god. Well, he ain't."

Hettie knew that. He often used to come home covered in cuts and bruises from the scrapes he got into. Not so much since his accident, but still she sensed his underlying belligerence. Like Annie, he had a temper, but she seemed to bring out the worst in him. He was morose and tight-lipped when she was in the house, withdrawing into himself.

Why couldn't she have preserved her modesty? Why did she always have to show off her new clothes and brag about the people she met at the theatre?

"Real toffs," she said. "An' so generous." She never came home without flowers or chocolates or some other trinket. When Corry questioned her about how she'd earned them, she'd laugh and call him an 'old stick in the mud' jealous of her success. She said the same to Hettie when she asked. The atmosphere between them soured.

She did little to help in the house these days either. "I pays me rent, that should be enough," she said when Dorcas asked for a hand.

The only day they spent any time together was Sunday. Annie had stopped going to church, preferring to stay in bed on a Sunday morning after being out all Saturday night.

"Too grand to sing in the choir now," Dorcas said. "She'll get her comeuppance, you see if she don't."

During one particularly vicious row Annie said, "You're no better than me, Hettie Bundy. You was always goggling after Corry, and making up to him." She pulled a face. "You're so clever, Corry. Well done, Corry. Thank you in bunches, Corry," she mimicked. "You're only jealous because he paid me more attention than you." She tossed her head making her dark copper curls bounce like springs. "Can't blame him neither. Who wants to look at a miserable sad-faced cow like you when I'm around?" Then she'd stalked off in another huff.

Hettie never spoke to her after that. She made sure she was up and out in the mornings before Annie woke and even moved her things into the box room Corry had vacated when he had his accident.

Annie sniffed at that, saying it was as though by moving into his room Hettie somehow hoped to bring him closer. But all Hettie wanted was to remove the possibility of running into Annie every day. The rift between them deepened. Hettie didn't know what to do, all she knew was that things were different now that Corry had gone and it was all Annie's fault.

One evening, after school, Hettie spoke to the pastor about Annie and how she'd changed. After all, he'd known her since she was a child.

"I expect she misses Corry," he said. "As we all do. A most unfortunate misunderstanding." He shook his head. His face creased into a frown. The depth of his sorrow at Corry's leaving surprised Hettie. She hadn't realised they were so close. True, the pastor showed more favour to Corry than any of the other boys, but Hettie had thought it because he was brighter and more likely to get on.

"I've been to the docks and made enquiries as to his possible whereabouts," he said. "As far as I can make out he'll be docking in New York or Boston." He shook his head sadly. "If I could only contact him I could explain the situation and persuade him to return." The fact that he couldn't obviously upset Pastor Brown. Hettie had never seen him so distraught.

"I'm worried about Annie," she said. "I fear she's fallen into temptation and got in with the wrong crowd. Can't you have a word, Pastor?"

He sighed as though lost in thoughts of times past, smiled benignly and said, "People must take their happiness where they find it."

Hettie sighed. He was no better than Dorcas who'd taken to muttering, "Like mother, like daughter," whenever Annie's name was mentioned.

The months passed, the weather worsened. That Christmas was a dismal one; the atmosphere in the house one of tension and suspicion. Annie dressed in her best midnight blue gown and put a spray of matching feathers in her hair. "Don't make dinner for me," she said, "and don't wait up for me neither."

Hettie could only guess at the sort of friends who'd invited her out and what type of party it was. Even the benevolent presence of Pastor Brown couldn't cheer Hettie up. She recalled past Christmases when Corry had been there which only served to deepen the void in her life. In her heart she still blamed Annie. Still, what could she do?

The following summer Annie came home one evening full of excitement. "You'll never guess what's happened," she said. "No, you'll never guess. I'll have to tell you."

Hettie watched her spinning around the room. "The Prussians have been driven out of Paris and Madame Galiouse is going home." She clapped her hands as she danced around the room. "She has asked for some of the dancers from the theatre to go with her. Guess who she has chosen?"

It was clear from Annie's energetic animation that she'd been included. "I'll be dancing at the famous Folies-Bergère." She did another twirl. "Oh Hettie, isn't it exciting?" Her eyes shone brighter than the midday sun, the animosity between them forgotten in an instant.

Hettie, who didn't know who Madame Galiouse was, had never heard of the Prussians, nor the Folies-Bergère for that matter, quickly got caught up in her enthusiasm, despite herself. "Who is this Madame Galiouse?" she said. "When are you going? How are you travelling? Who else is going?" Hettie's questions bubbled out of her mouth as the excitement bubbled inside her, or was it relief at the fact that Annie was leaving?

"Madame Galiouse is the dancer from Paris I told you about. She left when the Prussians invaded but now she can go home and I'm going with her. Oh Hettie, I'm so happy I could burst."

Hettie wished her all the luck in the world, but part of her wondered if her relief at hearing that Annie was leaving had anything to do with the fact that she'd no longer be reminded daily of Corry's departure and how much she missed him.

Annie was due to travel the following week so Hettie helped her pack her things, carefully folding her dresses in tissue paper and wrapping her spare pair of shoes in a muslin cloth. She managed to fit everything into a small trunk. It was agreed that Annie would leave her personal belongings behind, to be sent on if and when she got settled.

As the time for her departure neared, memories of their days selling watercress filled Hettie's mind. They'd been good friends then. She recalled Annie's lively conversations, her cheerful exuberance and how she was always getting into scrapes and just managing, through charm or shrewdness, to escape Dorcas's displeasure. Losing Annie would be as much like losing a limb as losing Corry had been.

A dull ache filled Hettie's heart as she watched Annie climb into Jack's hackney. The sight of her hoisting the skirts of her smart new burgundy suit, worn over a high-necked candy-striped blouse and her unruly copper curls escaping in ringlets beneath her pert be-ribboned hat would be forever imprinted on Hettie's mind.

Annie turned to Hettie to wave. "I'll write," she called as the hackney drew away. Hettie's heart crunched. With Annie and Corry both gone her life would be very dull indeed.

Dorcas stood with Hettie watching the hackney drive away. "Well, that's both of them gone," she said. "Don't let anyone say I didn't do me best for 'em."

"You did all you could, Ma," Hettie said. "No one could have done more."

"Aye. You're right," Dorcas said. "Now they've both gone out in the world to find their own futures." She sniffed, brushed her hands together and went inside. "I've a gentleman coming to view the room," she said. "Make sure it's good and tidy, eh?"

Hettie smiled. So it was 'business as usual'. No change there then, she thought.

That evening Hettie moved her things back to the room she'd shared with Annie, the room that held so many memories. Dorcas decided to move downstairs to the back room next to the kitchen. "It'll be better for me legs," she said and lodger can have the bigger room."

The large front room where Dorcas used to sleep was taken by a young solicitor's clerk who worked in Shoreditch. A Polish sailor moved into the room that used to be Corry's. Dorcas provided breakfast and evening meals and charged them each five shillings a week.

"You can help serve breakfast in their rooms before you go work," Dorcas said. "And Mrs Mackie's daughter Sarah's going to come in for a couple of hours a day to help with the washing and cleaning. Pastor Brown says as how she's a good little worker." She gave a satisfied smile. "Yes. I think we'll do very nicely thank you," she said.

In the evenings Hettie helped with the evening meal before she left to help out at the pastor's school a couple of evenings week, although the pastor had long since stopped being able to pay her.

She gave her mother half her wages towards the rent and saved the rest to put towards the nursing course she was determined to take. She'd heard that Florence Nightingale, the nurse famous for her work in the Crimea, had opened a school of nursing at St Thomas's Hospital, across the river. As soon as she could afford it Hettie intended to enrol.

Despite her promise to write, Hettie heard nothing from Annie, not even at Christmas or her birthday. Corry hadn't written either and some days Hettie wondered whether she'd ever see either of them again. They'd been close when they were growing up but it seemed that counted for nothing.

The only reminders Hettie had of her friends were an old coat Corry had left behind and Annie's box that she hadn't had room to take with her when she went. Hettie felt they were a piece of her life that had slipped away with her childhood, leaving only the memories of their having been part of it. She kept their things in her room and hoped one day they could all be together again. As time went by this felt like a very forlorn hope.

Chapter Ten

January 1875

Snow lay on the ground, the air crisp with frost. It had been a long hard winter and the weather showed no signs of letting up. Annie's telegram came out of the blue. Hettie had been about to serve breakfast when it arrived and sent all thoughts of toast and marmalade flying from her mind. Whatever could it be? It must be trouble. What on earth could have happened? The young telegraph boy looked half frozen, his hands red with cold as he handed Dorcas the envelope. She gave him sixpence for his pains.

She huffed as she opened it, her hands shaking. She'd never had a telegram before but knew it could only mean bad news. As soon as she saw it was from Annie she pushed it into Hettie's hands. Hettie's heart pounded. Annie'd been gone over two years without a word. Now she'd sent a telegram. It read, *'Coming home Arriving Kings Cross pm Annie'*.

Hettie stared open mouthed at Dorcas. "Annie's coming home," she said.

Dorcas shook her head. "I always knew telegrams meant bad news," she said. "She must be in some sort of trouble to come back here. Probably have her tail between her legs if I know owt about our Annie."

Ma was probably right, but Hettie wasn't going to admit it. "You're wrong, Ma," she said. "She'll be coming home to show us how well she's done and I for one will be glad to see her." Hettie hoped this was true and Dorcas wasn't right that it was trouble bringing Annie home.

She studied the paper more closely. "This was sent from Dover so she'll be here this afternoon." She glanced at Dorcas. "We'd better get a room ready. I'll go to the bakery and tell them I'll not be in today." She smiled. "There's a turn up," she said. "Annie coming home after all this time."

Dorcas wasn't so pleased. "I suppose she'll be expecting us to provide room and board for nowt," she said. "Well if she thinks we'll be dancing attendance on her she's another thought coming. Always did think too much of herself that one." She rolled up her sleeves and stomped out to take her ire out on the copper full of washing in the back yard.

Still, Hettie noticed that when Sarah arrived Dorcas sent her upstairs to move their one remaining lodger into the smaller back room and give the upstairs front room a good clean ready for Annie when she arrived.

Hettie sent a note to Jack to meet Annie at Kings Cross Station that afternoon. It was the least she could do to make Annie feel welcome. Then she hurried to the bakery hoping they'd let her off for the afternoon. All the way there she thought of Annie. What would she be like? Had two years in Paris changed her, and if so, for the better or for the worse? And what would she think coming back to the tiny terraced house in a run-down Wapping street after the glamour of Paris? Hettie shivered and it wasn't only because of the cold.

Hettie glanced out of the window when she heard the hackney draw up outside. She ran to open the door just as Jack was unloading Annie's travelling trunk and several bags. When Annie stepped out of the carriage Hettie hardly recognised her. A heavy muffler covered her head and face wrapping her up against the bitter cold of the day.

Jack carried her trunk on his broad shoulders and some bags in his other hand. "Morning, Miss Hettie," he said. "I've brought Miss Annie home and she's got a little surprise for you an' all."

Hettie looked past him to see Annie coming up the path carrying a large wicker basket over her arm. Inside the house she placed the basket carefully on the hall table. She removed the scarf, reminding Hettie again how small and delicate she was. Hettie rushed to greet her but stopped short as Annie glared at her, defiance in her eyes.

"Hettie, I'm so glad to see you," she said. She indicated the basket. "This is my son, Billy." A broad smile spread across her face. "I hope you will be happy to see him too."

Hettie gasped. She couldn't have been more surprised if a bat had appeared out of the wall and flown over them.

"A son!" she said. "You have a son?" She stared at Annie. Thoughts raced through her brain: How? When? Who? But she knew better than to ask. She quickly gathered her wits and grinned. She stepped forward and took Annie in her arms, hugging her wildly. Emotions swirled inside her. "It's been so long," she said, "and not a word. Now you come home out of the blue with a baby. What am I expected to say?" She stood back to take in the sight of Annie returned.

"You're expected to say you're delighted to see me and thrilled to see him," Annie said. Her gaze never left Hettie's face.

Hettie leaned over the basket. As soon as she saw the tiny scrap of humanity curled asleep in the basket her heart melted. "What a darling," she said. She paused. "I don't know what Ma will say."

Annie bridled. "She'll say the same as she always does, Hettie. As long as the rent's paid we'll be welcome to stay."

Hettie sighed. Annie was right of course. The rent the rooms brought in made the difference between living well and merely surviving. Money was always tight and Dorcas made a virtue out of squeezing it even tighter.

"You must be tired from the journey," Hettie said. "Let me show you to your room and once you're settled I'll make some tea. Follow me."

Annie picked up the basket and bags and Jack carried the travelling case upstairs to the room on the first floor over-looking the road. He swung the case onto the floor. Annie paid him and, from his broad smile as he left, Hettie guessed gave him a generous tip.

"Anytime you need anything you know where to find me," he said.

Annie glanced around the room as she took off her heavy cape revealing her exquisitely tailored magenta suit and cream high-necked silk blouse well-trimmed with lace.

Hettie ran her hands down her own plain blue cotton day dress and immediately felt drab. "I hope the room is to your liking," she said.

"This is perfect," Annie said. "The best room in the house. I'm honoured."

"When you're settled come down to the kitchen. Tea'll be ready," Hettie said. "And if there's anything else you need please let me know."

Annie laughed. "It's good to be back, Hettie," she said. She sighed. "It's very different from Paris."

Hettie grimaced. "I'm sure it is," she said. She left Annie to unpack and went to make the tea. So, this was Annie come home. Apart from new clothes and a baby she hadn't changed a bit. She'd been dying to hear all her news about Paris, but a baby was the last thing she'd expected. It didn't look as though there was a man included in Annie's plans either. What on earth would Ma say about that?

Over tea and scones, freshly baked by Hettie that morning, Annie told Hettie about her life in Paris, the grandeur and glamour of dancing at the Folies, the men she had met and the extravagant lifestyle she had lived.

Hettie told Annie about Ma's lodgers and her job at the bakery.

"I meant to write, Hettie, honest I did. But things happened so quickly I got carried away with it all."

Hettie could well imagine how easily Annie would be distracted from her life back home and how quickly she would want to forget it. She wasn't stupid enough to think that Annie wouldn't attract the kind of male attention respectable women tried to avoid, but she'd seen Annie turn male attention to her advantage in the past so felt confident she been able to do the same in Paris.

"And the baby's father?" she asked, eyebrows raised.

Annie's face clouded over. "All you need to know is that I loved him madly."

That sounded just like Annie, rushing into things without thinking about the consequences.

"Oh, I suppose I was swept away with the romance of it all. Paris, the dancing, being in the spotlight. But he said he loved me too, Hettie." She took a sip of tea and paused as though biting back a painful memory. She sniffed. "He was an English gentleman, a toff, would you believe? He left before I knew I was pregnant. I wrote to him but he didn't reply." She bit her lips together and glanced up at Hettie. "I can't believe he's abandoned me – honestly Hettie – he loved me too, I know it."

Hettie reached out and touched Annie's hand. "I'm sure he did," she said. "Who wouldn't?"

"I suppose you think me terribly foolish?" Tears welled in Annie's eyes.

How must it feel to be so swept away by love, Hettie wondered. A stab of envy pierced her heart. Annie had always had it all; the looks, the figure, the admirers and the confidence to do whatever in life she wanted. Still, she didn't deserve to be left with a child no matter how recklessly she lived her life.

"No, not foolish," Hettie said. "Just terribly unlucky."

They sat in silence for a while, each lost in their own thoughts until Hettie asked, "Did you ever hear from Corry?" She said it as casually as she could manage, not wanting Annie to see the depth of her concern.

"Corry?" No never, but then I didn't expect to. He wouldn't have known my address." She frowned. "Did he write to you?"

Hettie shook her head. "Not a word," she said.

That evening Annie fed Billy and put him upstairs to sleep. Hettie was washing up and Dorcas was in her room doing her books. In the kitchen Annie sidled up to Hettie. "Billy's asleep," she said. "He won't wake up until morning."

Hettie smiled and wiped her hands.

Annie grinned. "Would it be alright if I popped out for a while?" she said in her most wheedly voice. "Just to have a look round, see the old place. I've been away so long I've almost forgotten what it was like."

Hettie gazed at her. She'd been hoping they could spend Annie's first evening back either going out together or staying in if the weather was bad. She hadn't reckoned on Billy...

"You're such a love," Annie said before Hettie could speak. "Just look in on him now and then and listen out, although he hardly ever cries. If he does there's a bottle of milk by his basket just needs warming up." She jumped up and kissed Hettie on the cheek. "Thanks," she called from the hall as she grabbed her coat and muffler. Hettie heard the front door slam shut.

"What time did madam get in last night?" Dorcas asked Hettie the next morning. She was making porridge for the lodger's breakfast. Hettie didn't reply. Dorcas huffed. "Nowt's changed then? I suppose she'll be expecting us to do for her and her baby as well." She huffed again. "Not under my roof we won't," she said.

Hettie sighed. "Give her a chance, Ma. It must be strange coming back here after all that time.

She'll want to see her old friends, what's changed and how she can fit back in."

"Fit back in! I'll give her fit back in. I haven't forgotten when she was here before. Out drinking and coming in at all hours. Well, she's got a baby now. Can't fit back in with that."

Hettie didn't see Annie again until she got home from the bakery but Dorcas was quick to tell her about her day, and with some disgust. "Still in her bed at eleven when I went out," she said.

Hettie sighed. "Where is she now?"

"Out," Dorcas said. "Out and took the baby with her. I expect she'll be home in time for supper though."

Dorcas was right. Annie came home with Billy in a pram she'd bought in the market. She'd bought him clothes and toys as well. "Oh, it's good to be back," she said to Hettie as she took off her coat and muffler. "I'd forgotten what fun it is going round the market. The shopkeepers and stallholders in France aren't half as friendly. Everyone here has a cheery word and they all adored Billy, didn't they cherub?" she said leaning over the pram. She gave Hettie a beaming smile. "It's good to be home," she said.

Chapter Eleven

That evening Hettie went to the pastor's school to help the young boys with their reading and writing, so she didn't see much of Annie or Billy, but Dorcas was eager to fill her in on the details the next morning.

"She put the little lad to bed, helped herself to bread and jam for tea and took it up to her room. Didn't see owt of her after that," Dorcas said. She sighed. "I heard the baby crying 'til well after midnight, so she didn't get much sleep. Don't suppose we'll be seeing her this morning either." Hettie grimaced. She was hoping to at least spend a little time with Annie, but Dorcas was right. Hettie had to leave for work before Annie was up.

"I'll catch up with her this evening," Hettie said.

"If she doesn't go out and leave us to look after the sprat," Dorcas said.

Hettie took a breath. "He's not a sprat, he's a baby, and a bonny one at that. I'm sure he's no trouble." Even as she said it Hettie wondered if Dorcas wasn't right. Annie had come home for free babysitting and to allow her to get back to her old life.

Sunday was the first day Hettie could spend at home with Annie. After breakfast had been cleared away Hettie looked forward to spending the day with Annie and getting to know Billy.

Annie had other ideas. "Can you look after him for a while, Hettie?" she asked, pleading in her voice. "I want to go to the church and visit Ma's grave. Now I've a little one of my own I think I understand her better." She twisted her lips into a pout. "I must have been a terror when I was little," she said. "I never gave Ma much credit for all she did for us. I'd like to go to see her and say sorry."

Hettie couldn't refuse. "I could come with you," she said. "Put Billy in his pram…" but Annie said no, it was too cold, so Hettie spent the morning playing with him until he fell asleep, then she got out her sewing box and got on with her mending.

Over the next few weeks, on evenings when Hettie wasn't at the school teaching, she was indoors babysitting Billy while Annie went out 'renewing old acquaintances'.

"She's making a fool of you," Dorcas said. "Running around town every night, up to who knows what. All the same if you wanted to go out gadding about isn't it."

"Ma," Hettie said. "If I wanted to go out I'd go. As it happens I don't, so where's the harm in me helping out a friend? Anyway, he's no bother and I rather like spending time with him. He's a joy."

"Hmmph," was all Dorcas could say.

Hettie did get to spend time with Annie at the weekends, and some days after work. On those evenings, when they were both in, Annie talked about her time in Paris, showed Hettie the latest fashions in the magazines she'd bought and helped Hettie put her hair up in the latest Paris styles. "You should dress up a bit, have your hair done differently, put on a bit of glam," she said to Hettie. "You're a young lady, not an old maid, you shouldn't dress like one."

Hettie laughed. "And what would I have to dress up for?" she said. "Working in the bakery and at the school's not mixing with the height of society is it? Not likely to run into the Prince of Wales am I? No, I'll stick to my comfortable but practical outfits. I wouldn't know myself if I got all dolled up."

"Well, a bit of colour wouldn't go amiss," Annie insisted.

Another time, in her room where Billy was sleeping, Annie showed Hettie the pieces of jewellery she'd collected on her travels. She had an emerald pendant necklace, several brooches, a pair of earrings and a bracelet that made Hettie's eyes pop out. Surely they couldn't all be diamonds, emeralds and sapphires. She also noticed a man's signet ring, but Annie quickly hid that away.

"Try them on," Annie said.

So Hettie did and gazed in the mirror hoping she'd be transformed like Annie, but somehow the jewellery looked out of place on her. "They don't suit me at all," she said. She laughed. "Just as well, I'd never be able to afford anything like these."

Annie smiled. "The men in France are generous to a fault," she said, then her eyes misted over as though in memory and she put the jewellery back into the box Corry had made for her and closed the lid.

"What was he like?" Hettie asked, toying with a piece of lace Annie had bought to sew onto a blouse she was making.

"Who?"

"Billy's father."

"Oh." Annie grimaced and took a breath. "His name was Charles. He was tall and handsome, kind and, well, he said her loved me. I believed him." She shook her head and put the jewellery box back on the table next to her bed and came and sat with Hettie. "We met at the Folies-Bergère," she said. "He waited for me at the stage door. He bought me flowers, red roses and this." She lifted the chain around her neck to show Hettie the locket that hung from it. She opened it and inside Hettie saw a picture of Annie in a feathered headdress on one side and a man wearing a top hat on the other.

"Is that him?" she said. "He looks so handsome."

Annie smiled and gazed at the portrait. "We had the pictures done by an artist sitting on the banks of the Seine." She gazed at Hettie. "It was so romantic, Hettie. The Seine is just like the Thames, only much cleaner and brighter. No mudlarks there, or people living in slums..."

She tailed off as her face hardened. "So many people living on the breadline though, desperate, lonely people." She jerked her head up, suddenly bright again. "Come on, Hettie, let's go out. I want to walk by the river. We'll take Billy in his pram and I'll show him where Uncle Corry used to scrabble around in the mud to make a ha'penny or two to pay our rent." Hettie didn't miss the bitterness in her voice.

It was on one of their walks that Annie told Hettie of her financial situation. "I have a little money," she said. "Enough to pay the rent for now, but with buying things for Billy, his food and toys, clothes he grows out of in a week and everything, it won't last for ever." She pulled a face. "I could sell some of my jewellery, that'd help but..." she shrugged. "I'll have to find work. I can't expect Dorcas to look after Billy and I can't afford to pay anyone else." She rocked the pram. "I wouldn't leave him with just anybody." She looked at Hettie. "I could earn enough for the rent if I do a turn at the music hall a few nights a week."

Hettie stopped in her tracks. "Do a turn? What exactly do you mean?"

Annie sighed. She glanced around as though trying to avoid what she was going to say next. "You know, sing, dance, act on stage, just like I used to. It'd only be four nights a week, including Saturday..."

Hettie filled her lungs with the good fresh air. "Just like you used to?" she said. "Just like when Corry ran away?" Her heart was racing now. A tidal wave of bitterness washed over her. The memories were too painful to bear.

She breathed out slowly. She still felt an ache in her chest when she thought of Corry, somewhere across the ocean. How was he getting on? What was he doing? Was he still alive even? She bit her lip and jerked her head up. It was easy to blame Annie, but it wasn't really her fault, well, not entirely. If only Corry had waited...

"It sounds as though it's all settled," she said. "Like you've already made arrangements." She turned to Annie. "Have you?"

Annie had the grace to blush. "Well, I told them I may be able to," she said. "Nothing definite. I couldn't with Billy, unless..."

"Unless I babysit, four nights a week," Hettie said. Her heart burned with indignation.

"I could pay you, not much, but something, and it'd only be temporary, until I find something better. What do you say? Please say yes, Hettie. I don't know what else I can do."

Hettie sighed. It was true Annie had no money coming in and her savings wouldn't last forever. Without work she couldn't pay her rent and Ma would put her out, sooner or later, probably sooner if she knew Ma. Ma depended on the rent money and the lodger had recently talked about moving out, so without money from Annie...

"I suppose it'll be all right," Hettie said. "But you don't need to pay me. I have enough from working at the bakery and I don't need much. Billy's no problem. I'll happily look after him."

Annie hugged her. "Hettie, you're a treasure," she said. "I don't know what I'd do without friends like you and your ma." Hettie wondered if Ma could really be called a friend, but in hindsight she thought, yes, she could.

When Hettie told Dorcas about the arrangement she was pleasantly surprised at her response. "At least she'll be earning," she said. "Hard enough with a baby and no income. You have to to give her credit for making an effort." So

Hettie stayed in looked after Billy when she wasn't needed at the pastor's school.

As the weather brightened and the cold wind turned to a warm breeze Hettie and Annie took Billy out each Sunday to walk in the park or sit by the river. Hettie felt their closeness returning. They had a history between them, growing up together. Annie may have changed on the surface, but underneath Hettie believed she was same spirited, head-strong, obstinately determined girl she'd always been.

One Sunday Hettie and Annie were both home, Hettie intended to catch up with her stitching. Outside the early May sun shone and the air felt fresh and clean.

"Come on, Hettie," Annie said. "It's too fine a day to stay in. I'll treat you to tea in the park and we can see the roses coming into bloom."

Hettie's brow creased into a frown. She'd finished clearing away the breakfast things and was about to settle down to work on a new blouse she was making, but Annie was right, it was too fine a day to be sat indoors. They'd had heavy rain for a week. Every day Hettie had dodged the raindrops bouncing off the pavement but she still ended up with her skirts drenched and heavy with water. Today the air would be fresh as it always is after rain and a walk in the park would be a treat.

Still, it wasn't like Annie to suggest it. Especially after her having been out so late the night before, and up again in the night with Billy, so Hettie wondered what she was after now.

She put her sewing away and put her coat on while Annie sat Billy up in his pram with his colourful rattle and a stuffed lion he was particularly fond of. It was a bright day but there was still a chill in the air and Hettie was glad to get inside when they reached the tearooms. By then Billy was asleep in his pram.

Annie ordered tea and cakes which were soon brought over by a young waitress.

"I have something to say," Annie said. "A favour to ask." Her lips twisted into a pout. Hettie poured the tea. Suddenly all became clear. A favour for Annie could only mean something Ma would disapprove of. She sighed. "Just say it," she said.

Annie hunched her shoulders as though she knew what she was about to say would not be well received. "When I was in Paris, after Charles had left, a friend gave me the card of a lady who lives in Belgravia. She is a society hostess, very grand."

"Yes?" Hettie raised her eyebrows. She couldn't work out where this conversation was going.

"Well, I went to see her."

"And?"

"She has asked me, no, not asked, suggested... no I mean... invited me, to stay with her." Annie paused, waiting for Hettie's reaction. There was none, save for a slight tightening of her jaw.

"And you're going to stay with her?" Hettie's eyes widened. This was the last thing she'd expected Annie to say.

"She lives in a grand house and entertains the cream of high society. It'll be a chance to meet wealthy and famous gentlemen, escorting them to parties, the opera, the theatre. This will be a real opportunity for me. Please say you're happy for me, Hettie."

Hettie put the pot on the table. She blinked. It sounded highly dubious to Hettie. "Well, I assume she's not going to ask you for rent," she said. "These men you meet, what would they be expecting?" She stared at Annie, eyebrows raised. She knew very well what they would be expecting.

Annie laughed. "Honestly, Hettie. You and your English morality. Everyone knows what goes on and how most of the women working in London earn their living. You'd think no one ever did it. Anyway I'd be working as a hostess not a prostitute. I'd escort gentlemen who need a pretty girl on their arm to impress their friends and are willing to pay generously for the privilege. There's nothing sinister about it. In Paris this is an accepted way of life. I came to London to search for Billy's father. This is where I may find him."

Annie had told Hettie that Billy's father had left Paris unaware that she was with child. It was only natural that she'd want to find him, but Hettie wasn't sure that Annie was going the right way about it. The establishment Annie described sounded like a high-class brothel to her, but perhaps Annie was right. She knew nothing of how these things worked in high society and she had no other suggestions. Annie knew more about that sort of thing than she did, so she said nothing. It seemed that Annie had made up her mind anyway.

Annie replaced her teacup on its saucer. "I ask you because I need you to look after Billy. I know he'll be safe with you. Please say you will."

So, she wasn't taking Billy with her. Hettie glanced over at the sleeping child and her heart fluttered. Suddenly she realised how much she'd miss him if Annie took him away with her. She'd become attached to him in a very short time, how much worse must it be for Annie? She saw the depth of concern in Annie's eyes. She didn't want to refuse. Looking after Billy would be a joy, but Ma would never agree to such an arrangement.

"What about Ma?" she said, "and my job at the bakery?"

Annie pouted and huffed. She let out an enormous sigh. "I'll pay," she said. "Double what they're paying you in the bakery. Your ma will agree to anything as long as there's cash involved."

Hettie smiled. Staying at home and looking after Billy would be a lot easier than being on her feet all day working in the heat of the bakery. But she still wasn't sure.

She shrugged her shoulders. Ma would never agree anyway, she thought. "If you can get Ma to agree, I'll be happy to look after him. He's no trouble and I'll enjoy it more than standing in the bakery for hours on end."

"Thank you," Annie said. "But it must remain our secret. This lady would not have offered me a place if she knew I had a child. In France this would not matter so much, but here, in England phew..." Annie turned her eyes to the ceiling.

Hettie smiled. She knew about the double standards held by the English aristocracy. They often had children out of wedlock, but rarely were these mentioned or acknowledged. Different if you were a servant or shop-girl though. Very different.

Dorcas wasn't happy about it either.

"No good'll come of it," she said shaking her head. "Ideas above her station that one. It'll end in tears, mark my words." Only the promise to pay and the fact that Annie's room could be let out again, persuaded her.

Hettie helped Annie pack her things. In the six months she'd been living with Hettie she hadn't unpacked all her dresses. "I won't be taking my everyday clothes," she said. "I'll just take the Paris dresses. They may be useful." Hettie nodded. Annie obviously thought her 'everyday' clothes unsuitable for the elevated circles she'd now be moving in.

All she was taking was packed into her travelling case. She left everything else with Hettie. "I won't be needing these either," she said.

She sent a note round to Jack asking him to collect her and her belongings and take them to an address in Belgravia.

Hettie helped Annie move Billy's cot, his basket of clothes, toys and blankets into her room. "He likes this in bed with him," Annie said, handing Hettie his stuffed lion. "And don't forget to warm his milk last thing. And oh, he's still teething, so he's got a ring to chew." She handed each item to Hettie then picked Billy up and hugged him so tight Hettie thought she'd never let him go. "I'll be coming back as often as I can," she said, cradling him in her arms and watching his face as though committing it to memory. "I'm going to find your daddy so we can be together like a real family," she whispered. Hettie saw Annie's cheeks were wet with tears before she hurriedly brushed them away.

The pain on Annie's face squeezed Hettie's heart. "I don't know what else to do," she said. "Look after him for me, Hettie. He's all I've got."

"I'll love him like my own," Hettie promised. She took the weight of his tiny body in her arms and felt the soft warmth of his breath on her neck. A moment later Annie was gone. Holding the child close she remembered last time Annie left. Then vivid memories of Corry's leaving brought a lump to Hettie's throat. A big empty void opened up inside her.

Chapter Twelve

Looking after Billy brought Hettie more joy than she could ever have anticipated. He'd greet her with a smile each morning when she lifted him from his cot. "Good morning, my precious," she said. "How are we today?" His answering gurgle filled her heart.

Each morning she fed him and sat him in his chair while she prepared breakfast.

Dorcas let Annie's room for a good rent to a married couple who took their evening meals out so she didn't need to cook for them. After breakfast Hettie put Billy in his playpen with some toys while she helped Sarah with the cleaning and Dorcas with the washing.

In the afternoon he had a nap. If the weather was fine she put him in his pram and ran errands for Dorcas, or sometimes just took him for a walk to get some fresh air.

One day she was with him in the park when he threw his rattle out of the pram. A young man passing bent to pick it up. "What a sweet child," he said handing the rattle to Hettie. "And a pretty mother, too."

Hettie blushed as he walked away. She supposed that was what everyone thought when they saw them. She realised she wasn't at all unhappy about that.

Annie was as good as her word. She visited Billy as often as she could. The first time she visited she brought biscuits for him and a teacake for Dorcas and Hettie. "Oh, you shouldn't have," Hettie said. Dorcas said nothing, but Hettie noticed she put the teacake out with their tea.

Annie played with Billy, bounced him on her knee and made a great fuss of him. "I'm sure he's grown," she said. "He's looking so well. You're doing a grand job, Hettie. It's as though you were made for it." She pouted. "I wish I could keep him with me, but I can't so it's no use even thinking about it."

When it was time to leave she reluctantly handed him back to Hettie. "I miss him so," she said. "But at least I know he's in good hands."

Every time she visited she brought a treat for Billy. She brought him a push along horse on wheels and another time a pull along wooden duck. "You'll spoil him," Hettie said astounded at her generosity.

"That's what mothers do," Annie said, but Hettie couldn't recall either of their mothers spoiling them.

"I have certain benefactors," Annie said when Hettie asked how she could afford such treats. She never said who they were or talked about them but she did tell Hettie about the parties and balls she attended, the fabulous gowns and exotic hairstyles she'd seen and the stunning jewellery.

Another time she brought him some chocolate. "You'll make him sick," Hettie said.

"Oh, don't be such a fuss-pot," Annie said. Hettie bit back the stab of envy she felt for the child's obvious pleasure in the gifts and the affection in his eyes when he saw his glamorous mother. Then she was overcome with guilt for feeling jealous of something so natural.

Annie worried about him too. "Is he eating all right?" "Does he miss me?" "Look how big he's getting," she said whenever she saw him. The emotion on her face fluctuated between intense pride and overwhelming anxiety.

"His smile would light up the darkest corner of Newgate's cells," Hettie said. "He grows bonnier every day." She put him on the floor. "Look, he's trying to pull himself up. He'll be walking before we know it." They both glowed with pride at the little lad's achievements.

The only one who wasn't seduced by his charm was Dorcas. "He's a baby," she said. "Nice enough now but wait till he grows up." Still, she agreed to sit with him in the evenings when Hettie went to the school, but Hettie was convinced it was more to please the pastor than any other reason.

Over the summer Annie visited every Sunday and Hettie and Annie took Billy out to either the park or to walk by the river. On the rare occasions when Annie couldn't visit she sent a boy with the rent she'd promised Dorcas and money for Hettie. Hettie kept a record of the things she'd bought for Billy, clothes, shoes, toys, medicine etc. and Annie would pay her for those too. She never seemed to be short.

It was the end of summer, the leaves on the trees in the park beginning to turn to gold, when

Annie missed the first payment. Hettie thought nothing of it. She's too busy to visit so she'll pay the next week, she thought. The following week she still heard nothing but Dorcas said, "Annie's rent's late. I hope she hasn't done a runner and left us in the lurch."

"Of course she hasn't," Hettie said but when Friday came and there was still no word she began to worry. Another week went by and then another.

"Annie's not sent her rent," Dorcas said.

"Oh, I forgot," Hettie said. "Annie sent this round." She delved into her purse and paid Dorcas out of her own money. She was sure Annie would come soon; Billy's first birthday was only a week away.

That week, despite the drizzling November mist and rain, Hettie went out and bought Billy a spinning top. She couldn't wait to see what Annie would bring. When Dorcas commented on Annie's non-appearance Hettie brushed it off. "I expect she's saving it for Christmas," she said.

Christmas came and went with no word from Annie. Now Hettie was seriously worried.

Her heart fluttered every time Dorcas mentioned the cost of his food or clothes and riled at the amount of time Hettie spent looking after him. She heard Dorcas tutting whenever she left her chores to see to him. He was toddling now and into everything. Hettie feared taking her eyes off him but it was difficult as she still had her chores to do, helping Sarah with the cleaning and cooking as well as helping Dorcas with the laundry.

Billy spent more and more time in his playpen and grizzled whenever Hettie left him. Times when Hettie could be spared to take him out over the park or to the river to feed the ducks became rarer and rarer. Without Annie's money coming in Dorcas demanded more and more of Hettie's time.

"I thought you said you'd pull your weight around the house," Dorcas said on more than one occasion. "Seems to me you're spending more time and money on that child than need be. It can't go on forever. I'm not a charity you know." She'd taken to thumping out the washing in the copper and berating Hettie while she hung it out. "Some of us 'as to do a fair day's work," she said. "We can't all spend our time mollycoddling bairns."

Hettie was at her wits' end. Since she'd left the bakery to look after Billy, Annie's money was all she had coming in. The rent from the lodgers barely covered the food and Sarah's wages, even though Dorcas had cut her hours back since Annie's money stopped.

Hettie sighed. She picked Billy up, cuddling him in her arms. "I'll never let you go," she said. "If you have to go I'll go with you. I'll look after you just like I promised your ma. I'll not let you down." Deep rooted fear coiled in her stomach. How on earth would she manage? She didn't care; she'd do anything... just as Annie had done. Holding Billy close she suddenly understood how Annie must have felt. She'd been driven to work in what Dorcas now referred to as 'that place' for Billy's sake. She too would do 'whatever it took' if Billy's welfare was at stake. How could she not, when he greeted her with that magical smile and arms held wide every morning? His wellbeing and happiness depended on her. Yes, she too would do anything...

Annie wouldn't willingly abandon her child, Hettie was sure of that. Something must have happened to her. "Don't worry, sweetheart," she said to Billy now chortling in her embrace. "I'm going to find her and sort things out once and for all."

That evening Dorcas agreed to watch over Billy while Hettie went to call on Pastor Brown. Hettie had to smile when she saw how Dorcas's demeanour changed at the mention of his name. "See if he can find a place for the bairn," she said. "He'll know what to do."

Hettie had no intention of asking the pastor to find a home for him. She wanted to know if the pastor had heard anything from Annie, or any rumours about her whereabouts. Pastor Brown knew everyone, from the highest to the lowest. If anyone had heard anything it would be Pastor Brown.

She recalled the day she came to see him after Corry's accident, how he'd visited Corry, often bringing books and lifting his spirits. How Dorcas glowed with pleasure every time he called. That brought a smile to her face. She wondered what he thought of Annie's shenanigans. Did he think 'like mother like daughter' as Dorcas did, or even 'blood will out', another thing Dorcas kept saying? She couldn't believe that was the case. Pastor Brown had compassion and understanding oozing out of him. He wasn't one to condemn sinners; he did what he could to reform them but always without judgment. He knew the hardship of their lives and that honesty wasn't always rewarded. What would he say about Annie, she wondered.

The answer came soon enough. The pastor hesitated as she entered the room, then smiled. "Good evening, Miss Hettie," he said. "I wondered who could be calling at this time of night. Mrs Mackie said she'd shown someone in as they were in such a state. I'm sorry if I've kept you waiting."

"It's Annie Flanagan I've come about. I don't know what to do." She wrung her hands in a gesture of helplessness. "You know about her coming home with a child and everything." Hettie blushed at what she guessed the pastor must know. He knew more about people's lives than anyone gave him credit for. He heard all the gossip and rumours, people confided in him. If anyone knew of Annie's whereabouts it would be Pastor Brown.

She carried on, "I don't suppose you've heard from her have you? It's been months now and no word. It's not like her, I'm worried sick." As she spoke Hettie's deepest fears for Annie came rushing to the surface. It was all she could do not to burst into tears. The worries of the last few months had formed a ball inside her and threatened to explode. She glared at the pastor. "Have you heard anything? Anything at all?"

Pastor Brown shook his head sadly. "Regrettably not," he said. "I heard that she'd left you and your mother for greener pastures." He raised his eyebrows. "Or so she thought, but I fear it may all have ended badly as these things often do." He handed Hettie a handkerchief. "I'm afraid not everyone in the world has the same high moral standards as you or your mother. Friends can be cast off like yesterday's socks if they fail to live up to expectations. I fear that may have happened to Annie." He shrugged.

Hettie nearly hit the ceiling. "My mother!" she said. "High moral standards? She wants to put Billy out onto the streets. Imagine, Annie's child on the streets." She dabbed away the tears now trickling over her cheeks. The pastor may think what Annie was doing was akin to being on the streets and she regretted the suggestion. "Well, not exactly on the streets," she said, "but put him into the workhouse which is just as bad. You know it is."

The pastor looked shocked. "My dear," he said. "I had no idea." He shook his head and stared at his boots. After a few deep breaths he led Hettie to a chair. "Please be calm," he said.

"She's always had it in for Annie," Hettie said. "Always willing to think the worst of her, and Annie's not like that, really she's not."

The pastor walked round and sat behind his desk. "You have to have patience with your mother, Hettie. It may be just seeing the baby..." He shrugged. "You probably won't remember, you were only a toddler, but she lost a baby boy shortly after your father's accident. Two losses in such a short time..."

Hettie's head shot up. "Ma had another baby? Apart from me?"

"Yes. She never speaks of it of course, but at the time..." He sighed heavily. "She was inconsolable. Perhaps Annie's happy, healthy boy...

She may not trust her instincts. It was a long time ago but memories hidden deep can surface and bring untold misery."

Hettie's heart twisted. The pastor looked at her. "He was only a few weeks old. Dorcas did all she could for him, but he was very sick. There was nothing anyone could do. I know she felt guilty about it. Felt she should have been able to save him, but it was God's will." He leaned back in his chair for a few seconds before leaning forward to look at Hettie. "She'd be livid if she knew I'd told you, but I hope it helps you understand. Taking Corry and Annie in was Dorcas's act of atonement, a way of trying to make things right. She thought if she helped them God would forgive her. Of course, when Corry ran away and Annie was so wayward..." He frowned. "Your ma may have thought she'd failed again and was being punished. Now Annie's abandoned her baby..." He shrugged.

A torrent of rage flowed through Hettie. "Annie hasn't abandoned him," she said, staring at the pastor. "She left him with me. I promised to keep him safe. Now Ma wants to have him put away, it's not fair."

"Life is seldom fair," he said. He gazed at the ceiling as though remembering an injustice in his past. He shook his head to dislodge it. He blinked and looked at Hettie. "Your ma struggled to keep body and soul together after your father died. She may rattle and moan, threatening all sorts of things, but rest assured she would never put a child out. Not your ma." He smiled as he mentioned her and Hettie's heart relaxed.

He stood up. "Now," he said, all brisk efficiency again. "I'll put the word out among the street boys to see if they've heard anything. Other than that I don't know what I can do. I fear Annie has turned her back on her old friends and may have moved on."

Hettie's jaw tightened. Even the pastor thought badly of Annie. "No," she said rising from her chair. "I'll never believe that."

The pastor looked as though he was about to say something and then thought better of it. "I'm sorry," he said eventually and showed Hettie out.

Chapter Thirteen

The next morning Hettie rose early, washed and changed Billy and sat him in his highchair in the kitchen with his milk while she made tea and toast for Dorcas. All the while she was feeding him and preparing breakfast her mind filled with worries about Annie and Billy's future.

She watched him spoon porridge into his mouth, dropping it over his chin and onto the tray in front of him. His happy smile and obvious joy at seeing her each morning tore at her heart. What was to become of him?

After breakfast had been served and eaten Sarah arrived. Hettie put Billy in his playpen in her room with some toys and with Sarah cleaned the grates, made the beds and tidied the room let out to lodgers. Visions of Billy's warm smile and bubbly cheerfulness were never far from her mind. Her sweeping became more and more energetic as deep fear swirled inside her.

When the cleaning was finished it was almost time for luncheon and they could take a short break, before they began the laundry and dinner preparations. Hettie went to fetch Billy to bring him down to play. As soon as he saw her he chuckled and held out his arms to be lifted. She picked him up and held him close, feeling the soft warmth of his cheek on hers. She breathed in the smell of him and kissed the plump fold of skin around his chubby knees, which made him giggle and chuckle all the more. Her heart turned over.

"What's to become of you?" she said. "Poor mite."

He gurgled. She sighed. "I'll do all I can for you but it's not much. I'm afraid Ma may be right. We can't offer you the sort of lifestyle your mother was hoping for."

She thought about what Annie had said when she came back from Paris. Her hopes of finding Billy's father and that he would provide for them. This now seemed like a distant dream. She knew nothing of Annie's life in France or who Billy's father might be. When Annie returned she seemed to be comfortably set up. She dressed well and her manners were more refined than when she left. If, as Annie had said, Billy's father was an English gentleman, she couldn't deny him his heritage. His father's family could surely offer him more than an impoverished upbringing in the poorest, roughest part of London, if he could be found.

What should she do? She should at least report Annie to the authorities as missing, but then they'd take the child away and put him in one of those dreadful institutions. She couldn't bear that. She needed to find Annie for Billy's sake. But Annie had been adamant. Billy's existence must remain a secret. In fact she'd said it would be best if no one knew anything about any of them. She'd say she'd come directly from Paris, it would be better that way.

Everything had been fine as long as she paid her rent. Now Hettie was beginning to wonder if she'd planned to leave him all along. No, she'd never believe that, but a niggling thought deep inside reminded her that Annie hadn't always told the truth.

There was only one thing to do. Find Annie and confront her.

Hettie put Billy back in his playpen and went to the basket Annie had left behind. It contained the things she said she wouldn't need where she was going.

She took a deep breath. "I'm coming to get you, Annie," she whispered. "Ready or not." It was what she used to say when they played hide-and-seek around the market. Hettie closed her eyes, just like she used to do. Funny how Annie was always the hider and she was the seeker. Perhaps Annie hadn't changed that much after all.

She opened Annie's basket and rummaged through her personal belongings. It brought her no pleasure, but she needed to find any clues to her whereabouts.

Folded on top of the basket Hettie found Annie's plain blue woollen skirt, the bottom flounce torn loose where Annie had caught her heel in it. That was the day Hettie had gone with her to the market to buy a bigger cot for Billy. Then there was the blouse Annie had worn when they walked along by the river in the early spring sunshine. Hettie recalled her catching the sleeve on a bramble.

There were stockings and a petticoat, all in need of stitching. The afternoons they would sit in the warmth of the kitchen when it was too cold or wet to go out played in her mind. They'd each get on with their mending while talking about the latest fashions and the high jinks in society over a cup of afternoon tea. Annie was full of stories about the people who worked in the music hall and sometimes the antics of the audience.

Hettie paused. Beneath a lace-trimmed petticoat she found the embroidered muff she'd made for Annie that first Christmas. Annie had worn it that winter and the next. How tiny her hands must have been, Hettie thought, looking at it now. There was the hairbrush and comb from Dorcas and the song book Hettie had given her the following year. Memories flooded her mind. Memories of happy, carefree days selling watercress when they'd become close friends. Annie would never have let her down or left Billy if she could help it. No, something terrible must have happened.

Determination clenched Hettie's jaw.

Under the pile of mending Hettie found an array of brightly coloured hair ornaments, combs and clips. A picture of Annie's glowing auburn locks and unruly curls appeared in her mind. She recalled the afternoon Annie had shown her how to put her hair up in the latest Paris style. How they'd laughed and tried different styles, having fun. She couldn't carry off the sensational styles nearly as well as Annie who oozed glamour from every pore.

Hettie put the hair ornament to one side.

Next were the programmes and advertisements for the Folies-Bergère. She'd used the name 'Angelique'. There were some for the Variety Theatre where she'd worked for nearly two months before moving to Belgravia.

Hettie put the programmes to one side.

Among Annie's other mementos Hettie found a bundle of letters tied with pink ribbon. They were address to Annie in Paris. Hettie decided that reading them would be a step too far. She put them on one side.

Next she uncovered an album. It looked old and fairly worn. It smelled of stale perfume. Hettie lifted it out and opened it, gently turning the pages. There were pictures of babies who could only have been Corry and Annie. Then the same children as toddlers, growing up. It must have been Annie's mother's album, a precious keepsake of better times. The pictures stopped when the children were small. There was a picture of a house with a garden in front, a pony in a field and a man dressed in plus-fours and a shooting jacket, holding a double-barrelled shotgun under his arm. He wore a flat cap and was smiling.

Hettie shivered. This was Annie's family history. She closed the book and hid it under the clothes. She never realised she would feel so intrusive as she looked through Annie's things. She put the rest of the papers belonging to Mary Flanagan on one side.

That left only a folder of papers in French, a small black notebook and some loose photographs. Hettie picked up a photograph of Annie standing in front of what could only have been a palace. Dressed in a smart suit and hat Annie was smiling for the camera. Who could have taken such a picture, Hettie wondered.

There were drawings and sketches of Billy as well as a more recent studio photo of Annie that Hettie thought might come in useful in her search. Annie kept a picture of Billy in a silver frame beside her bed but that was gone. Would Annie take his picture if she intended to abandon him?

A small blanket lined the bottom of the basket. Hettie lifted it and saw a velvet pouch. Intrigued, she pushed her fingers inside and lifted out a gold crucifix. She recognised it at once as the one Annie said her mother used to wear. Annie wore it, until she moved away. She must have left it behind because it didn't fit in with her new life. Hettie sighed and put it back.

She rifled through the papers in the folder. Annie had said her new home would be in Belgravia. If Hettie could find the address she'd have somewhere to start. She picked up the notebook and flicked through it until she found what she was looking for. It wasn't actually an address, just a name, Sylvia de Vine, and the word Belgravia. Hettie wasn't sure how much help that would be, until she remembered Jack.

Jack had driven her there. Would he remember the address after so long? It was months ago. She put the notebook and the most recent picture of Annie in her bag. That evening, after school, she'd go to the Kings Cross yard where Jack stabled his horses. He might just remember.

That night, after school, Hettie set out. It was early January and snow still lay on the ground but Hettie didn't feel the cold as she pressed on. Glad of the amber glow of the street lamps she made her way to Kings Cross. Her heart leapt when she saw the ragged beams of light coming from the stable yard ahead of her. She hurried on. When she arrived she saw Barney, one of Jack's horses. For a moment she feared she may have missed him. Then she spotted him cleaning the mud off the wheels of his hackney carriage. Relief flooded over her.

"Jack," she called. "I'm glad I caught you."

He glanced around. "Why, it's Miss Hettie," he said. "What brings you to the yard? You could have sent a lad. I'd have come to you."

"No need. I was just after some information."

"Information? Well if I can help, I will, but I can't think as how I knows anything you don't."

Hettie laughed. "It's an address I want. The place you took Annie when she left us to live in Belgravia."

Jack frowned. "Belgravia?" He stroked his chin. "I'm not sure I rightly remember."

Hettie's heart sank. "It was early summer," she said. "You remember. Annie had a travelling case. You collected her from our house."

Jack shook his head. "Don't get much call to go to Belgravia," he said. "Most of 'em's got their own carriages or they take a hansom. Mostly I stay around these parts."

"But you took Annie there. Please say you remember." Doubt filled Hettie's mind. Of course Jack would make thousands of journeys all around London. Why should he remember one which was months ago? It was hopeless.

"Well," he said. "I can't rightly remember an address but if I took you there I could maybe recall a street I've been to afore."

"Could you? Please? Tomorrow?"

Jack laughed. "If it means that much to you I expect I can," he said.

Hettie arranged to meet him in the afternoon for a drive to Belgravia to see if he could remember where he took Annie. At last Hettie thought she had a lead. Tomorrow she'd find where Annie had moved to and remind her of her responsibilities.

Chapter Fourteen

The following afternoon, after all the chores were done, Hettie gave Sarah sixpence to take Billy to the park and buy an ice cream. Then she walked to Hackney End where she was to meet Jack. As they travelled to Belgravia the narrow cobbled streets became wider and cleaner. Street boys swept the paths and carriages and hansoms replaced the carts and barrows of the East End.

They drove through twisting streets, the buildings lining the roads becoming taller and more impressive as they went. When Jack stopped outside an imposing building in an equally imposing street she blanched. Surely this couldn't be the place?

"Well, this is where I took her," Jack said opening the hackney carriage door for Hettie. He pointed at the black front door at the top of some steps. "She went in there."

Hettie couldn't imagine Annie going into the building, it was so grand, but that was where Jack said he'd taken her. She squared her shoulders and prepared to walk up the stone steps.

"Do you want me to wait?" Jack asked.

Hettie shook her head. "No. Thank you. I'll be all right now. I can find my own way back." She glanced at the building and grimaced. "You're sure this was the place?"

Jack nodded.

Hettie didn't know quite what to expect when she banged the brass knocker as hard as she could. Her hands shook, but she gritted her teeth and stood tall. She was taken aback when the door swung open and a portly man in a black coat over a blue waistcoat stood on the threshold, his eyebrows raised in question.

"Erm." Hettie swallowed as her courage slid away like butter off a hot spoon. "I've come to enquire after Miss Annie Flanagan," she heard herself say in a voice several octaves higher than usual. "I believe she resides here."

"There must be some mistake," the man Hettie realised was the butler, said. "There's no one of that name living here." He stepped back and attempted to close the door.

Panic set Hettie's heart racing. Jack had said she'd gone in here and this was the only link she had to Annie. If she didn't live here they must know where she'd moved to or at least have some hint of her whereabouts.

She lunged forward and stopped him closing the door. Heat flushed her face and tears threatened to spill from her eyes. The dread and torment she'd been feeling over the past weeks rolled into a ball in her stomach and pushed bitter bile up to her throat. She wasn't about to give in to her deepest fears and these people weren't going to stop her from finding out what had happened to Annie and why she'd stopped visiting her son. It must have been something so terrible that Annie couldn't face it. She would never have lost contact otherwise.

She reached into her reticule and took out Annie's most recent likeness. "Look, this is Annie Flanagan. Please tell me if you've seen her. Has she visited perhaps? She's missing and it's of the utmost importance that I find her. You must help me, please." She had a sudden idea. "She may have called herself Angelique," she said.

The butler stared at the photo. A hint of recognition lit his eyes. He glanced up at Hettie and, seeing the depth of her pain and worry, his face softened. "You'd better come in," he said.

Hettie followed him through the dimly lit hall to a side room. "Wait in here," he said. "I'll see what I can do."

Hettie glanced around the room. A huge marble fireplace dominated one wall. A fire crackled in the hearth, but still Hettie felt a chill run through her. A large aspidistra stood on a mahogany table in the bay window. Elaborate red flocked wallpaper covered the walls and heavy brocade curtains shut out most of the January sun leaving only the flickering firelight to illuminate the room. The pictures on the walls made Hettie blush. Not the sort of thing one usually found hanging on the walls of gentlefolk, she thought. Her stomach turned over. She had a faint idea of the sort of live-in position Annie had obtained but was unprepared for the reality of it.

Annie had spoken of it as being an adventure, with fun, frivolity and unrivalled opportunities for advancement. She would be escorting high ranking and wealthy gentlemen to parties and balls. Hettie had turned her mind away from whatever else may have been involved. Now she had come face to face with it. She shivered and not only because of the cold.

After a short while the butler returned. "Miss de Vine will see you now," he said. "Please follow me."

Miss de Vine? Hettie remembered the name from Annie's notebook. She followed the butler up the grand staircase, averting her eyes from the pictures on the wall which appeared to become more risqué the further up the stairs she advanced. She trembled at the thoughts running through her mind.

She took a deep breath to steady her nerves. She owed it to Annie to do all she could to find her no matter how unpleasant it may be. If the girls working here could shed any light on her disappearance Hettie's revulsion would be eased and her visit well worthwhile.

The butler showed her into a room very different from the parlour below.

Pale winter sunlight streamed in through the large windows. Blue and silver paper covered the walls; a matching rug covered the floor. A chaise longue and two comfortable chairs were grouped around a coffee table in front of the elaborately decorated fireplace. A fire, protected by a large wire fire-screen, roared in the hearth. The overall effect was of light, cosy elegance and style.

The woman who rose from behind a light-wood desk by the window to greet Hettie also exuded restrained elegance and style. She held herself erect, showing off her slender frame. Her ash-blonde hair was neatly styled and her dress exquisitely-tailored. She moved with grace and, although her smile beamed warmth, Hettie felt out of her depth. What on earth was she doing here?

"Good afternoon. I'm Sylvia de Vine," the woman said moving towards Hettie. Chadwick tells me you're here on a mission."

"Hettie, er, Henrietta Bundy," Hettie said resisting the urge to curtsy. "I've come looking for a friend. I believe you may know of her whereabouts." She took Annie's picture out of her bag and passed it to Miss de Vine.

"Please," Miss de Vine said, indicating the chaise longue.

Hettie smiled and took a seat.

Miss de Vine sat beside her and gazed at the photograph. "Ah yes, Angelique," she said. She grimaced and handed the picture back to Hettie. "I'm afraid you're too late – she has gone."

"Gone?" Hettie swallowed. "Do you know where she has gone? Please, it's imperative I find her."

"Indeed I don't," Miss de Vine said. "I wish I did. She left without so much as a 'by your leave'.

In fact she's left me in somewhat of a difficult situation as regards her – erm – benefactors – shall we say. Some of them are quite upset."

Hettie blushed. She realised Miss de Vine meant 'clients' but let it pass. Miss de Vine looked quite put out in any case.

"That's the thing you see," Hettie persisted. "She's left me in some difficulty as well and it's not like her, not like her at all. I'm worried that something untoward may have happened to her."

"Something untoward? Well, my dear, I can't imagine what that might be." Miss de Vine looked at Hettie, sadness filled her eyes. "She's not the first young girl in my care who's latched on to someone she thinks can provide a better living. These girls, they meet a young man who turns their heads with promises they have no intention of keeping. Although, I must admit I thought Angelique far too clever to be taken in in that way."

Hettie's eyes brightened. "That's just it," she said. "She wouldn't be." Hettie bowed her head and chose her words carefully. "I believe she's too wise in the ways of men to be taken in by false promises." Her face reddened as her anxiety mounted. "She wouldn't leave ..." she almost said 'her child', but recalled that his existence must remain a secret and changed it to: "...without some sort of word."

Miss de Vine's face hardened. "I don't know what kind of a pickle Angelique has left you in and quite frankly I don't care. It's enough that she's gone without a word to anyone, so I'm afraid I can't be of any help to you." She rose as though to see Hettie out.

Hettie didn't move. Tears stung her eyes. Her last chance to find a link to Annie was fading fast. She clenched her hands and said, "She has a child. She may have left me and indeed you, but she'd never leave him. She just wouldn't."

Miss de Vine sat down again. "A child?"

"Yes, a son, Billy."

Miss de Vine gazed heavenwards. "Oh, my dear."

She gazed sadly at Hettie. "Do you know how many children are abandoned in London every day?" she said. "Hundreds. More than the Foundling Hospitals can cope with. They have a ballot to choose which of the unfortunates they are able to take in."

She stared at Hettie. "Sadly, even then, many die. How do I know this? Because I am a Patron of one such place." She sighed. "It's the least I can do." She touched her hand to Hettie's arm.

"There are many girls like Angelique who seek a lifestyle free of such encumbrances. When they see such a possibility they seize their chance and care not for those they leave behind." She removed her hand and smiled at Hettie but concern still clouded her eyes. "I can see from your face and demeanour that you are a person too soft-hearted for your own good. Angelique has taken advantage of your kind nature and left her son with you secure in the knowledge that you will look after him and do him no harm." She shrugged her elegant shoulders. "I am sorry, there is nothing more I can do or say."

Miss de Vine rose from the chaise longue again to show Hettie out.

Hettie's mind raced. She didn't – couldn't believe that Annie could be so heartless. She recalled the times she had visited on Sunday afternoons, taking him to the park or just to walk by the Thames. Over the weeks she marvelled at how he'd grown and how clever he was when he did the simplest thing. She'd brush his blonde hair until it shone, then she'd pull him up on his chubby legs and tickle him to make him laugh. Hettie saw the tears she wiped away when she had to hand him back. She'd never voluntarily leave him; Hettie was a sure of that. Miss de Vine was wrong, very wrong but Hettie saw no point in telling her so.

Hettie remained seated. She held back a sob and bit her lip. "Do you think I could see her room?" she said. "She may have left something of use – something I can keep for the child. Even a small memento of his mother would be precious beyond measure."

Miss de Vine smiled. "Of course," she said and moved to pull a bell-rope by the fireplace. Seconds later the butler appeared. "Could you ask Chloe to come here please," she said. The butler bowed and backed out of the room."Chloe was friends with Angelique. She'll be able to show you whatever belongings she left behind."

A few moments later, moments in which Hettie gathered her thoughts, a young girl, no more than sixteen from the look of her, entered the room. Hettie guessed the dress she was wearing cost more than half-a-year's rent for Dorcas's house. Had Annie's head been turned by the availability of such luxury and a lifestyle of ease and comfort? There'd be no lack of funds for whatever trinkets or clothes one wished to purchase or anything one's heart desired. Perhaps Miss de Vine was right after all.

Chapter Fifteen

"Chloe, this is Miss Henrietta Bundy, a friend of Angelique's. Please show her Angelique's room and allow her to take whatever of Angelique's things she thinks may be of use."

Chloe nodded and showed Hettie to the room Annie had occupied. "This is kind of you," Hettie said. "Did you know Anne- I mean Angelique well?"

Chloe smiled. "We became close. Angelique was lively and fun to be with." Her face clouded over. "I have missed her since she left."

"Did she give you any idea at all where she might be going or who she might be with? I would dearly like to find her." Hettie held her breath. If Annie had confided in anyone it would have been this young girl with the open face and trusting eyes.

"Indeed she did not. She said not a word, which surprised me greatly. We'd become such good friends, sharing everything in the short time she was here. She appeared to me to be quite genuine." Chloe sighed. "If you do find her, I'd love to see her again," she said.

Hettie's heart lifted. So, she wasn't the only one who found Annie's disappearance strange.

"This is where she kept her things," Chloe said indicating the bed next to a small cabinet and wardrobe. "I haven't moved anything. I was hoping she'd return."

Hettie stood by the bed Annie had occupied. There was nothing unusual or special about it, but Hettie felt Annie's presence in the colourful counterpane and cushions laid casually at the head of the bed. The side table contained nothing that gave any indication of sudden departure, although Hettie supposed the maid would have cleared anything away in any case.

She opened the drawer, conscious that Chloe was watching her. Annie had left a few trinkets but nothing of any value. Next Hettie opened the wardrobe and gasped. The array of magnificent dresses hanging there took her breath away.

"Did Angelique take any clothes with her?" she asked. From the number of dresses and shoes in the wardrobe it certainly didn't look as though any might be missing.

"No." Chloe shook her head. "That's what's so odd about her going. She loved those gowns. She wouldn't have left without them."

"But she did – didn't she?"

Chloe's face reddened. "It would appear so," she said.

Hettie noticed a pile of neatly folded petticoats at the back of the wardrobe. She gently pushed her hand underneath and felt something hard hidden there. Excitement buzzed through her as she lifted out the wooden jewellery box Corry had made for her. Inside she found her emerald pendant necklace, locket and the ring she'd seen in the box when she returned from Paris. Alongside those she saw an emerald bracelet, a string of pearls, earrings and some other obviously expensive pieces.

Chloe gasped. "I can't believe it," she said. "She's left her favourite necklace behind."

Another reason to think something untoward had happened to Annie, Hettie thought. She pushed her hand under the pile of petticoats again and this time withdrew a black leather-bound book with the word '*Journal*' embossed in gold on the front.

She flicked it open. Annie's spidery handwriting filled the pages. A journal – Annie had kept a journal. Tucked inside between the pages Hettie saw the photo of Billy that used to stand on Annie's bedside table at home. She'd hidden it from view while she was here but Hettie knew Annie would have gazed lovingly at it every single day.

"Tell me about Angelique," she said. "Did she have other friends, or – er – benefactors – she may have gone to? What were they like? Was there anyone special?"

Chloe's brow creased into a frown as she sank onto the bed. "Angelique had many admirers," she said. "She was the most popular girl here but I never got the impression she was particularly taken with any of them."

Hettie flicked through the journal. Most of the pages contained notes of appointments, parties and functions she was to attend but Hettie noticed that every Sunday was blank. Of course, she visited Billy on Sundays whenever she could – before she'd stopped coming, but she'd hardly write that down.

Hettie took a breath and, heart hammering said, "What did she do on Sundays?" She made the question sound as casual as she could.

"Sundays?" Chloe thought for a moment, puzzlement in her soft hazel eyes. "Oh, you mean the church she went to. Yes, Sundays she always went to church."

Hettie tried to stay calm but blood rushed through her veins. If she went regularly to church someone there may know of her whereabouts and if she'd been going there for the past six weeks why had she not visited Billy or sent money for his keep?

Hettie managed to screw her face into a frown. "Oh yes, the church. St Peter's in Eaton Square wasn't it, the one she used to attend?"

Chloe laughed. "You'd think so wouldn't you, but no, she didn't go to church locally. She travelled to Bromley by Bow to a church over there." She looked a little sheepish as she whispered, "I think she met someone there. I offered to go with her once but she said she'd rather go alone. I never said anything. After all, we are allowed to have friends aren't we? We don't have to give them all up just because Miss de Vine pays for..." Chloe blushed furiously and her voice faded as she said, "...everything." Hettie had no doubt Chloe had already said too much, but she had the sweet sensation of having been told a shared secret that should go no further.

"Well, I must say you have been most helpful, Chloe," she said. "If I may, I'd like to take Angelique's journal and her jewellery. It will bring me some comfort to read her words and who knows, with what you have told me I may even be able to find her."

Chloe's look of relief and happiness stayed with Hettie all the way home, but her over-riding thoughts were about the church Annie had attended and when she could go there.

Chapter Sixteen

Sunday morning Hettie set out early to walk to Bromley by Bow. She took Billy in his pram, having no one to look after him. When she arrived she looked around to see if she could see any reason Annie would come here instead of going to the nearest church, coming home to go to the pastor's church or even not go to church at all. Something must have drawn her to this run down part of the city.

During the service she glanced around the congregation while Billy fidgeted beside her. She wasn't sure what she was looking for. There was only the slightest chance that she'd see Annie or anyone she recognised, but she felt she had to make the effort.

After the service she joined the rest of the congregation in the church hall for tea. The vicar was a rotund, be-whiskered man who held court in a corner of the room, surrounded by matronly ladies simpering in his presence. She settled Billy in his pram and parked it at the side of the hall where she could keep an eye on him. A young man with sandy hair stood near the door. Dressed in clerical garb and standing alone she thought him approachable. Everyone appeared to be ignoring him in favour of the portly vicar so she picked up a second cup of tea from the long white-clothed table and wandered over to him.

"You look parched," she said, holding out the cup and saucer.

Blue eyes regarded her. Then he smiled. "Indeed I am," he said taking the tea. "That's very kind of you. I'm invisible to most people who only see the great and good." He indicated the crowd around the vicar. "What chance does a humble curate have?"

"Oh, I don't know," Hettie said. "I'm sure a great many people would be interested in your opinions if you cared to express them."

A pink flush crept up his face. He studied her more closely. "You're new here aren't you? I can't recall having seen you before and I'm sure I wouldn't forget someone so kind."

Hettie seized her chance. "I'm looking for a friend," she said, placing her cup and saucer on a nearby ledge. She thrust a hand into her bag and brought out Annie's picture. "Annie Flanagan. I know she attended this church. I wonder whether you may have seen her." She handed him the picture.

A smile of recognition flashed across his face. "Annie Flanagan?" he said. "But this is Angelique Bouvoir surely?"

Hettie's hopes soared. "Yes, Angelique. Have you seen her? Do you know where I may find her?"

The curate frowned and shook his head. "I haven't seen her since..." He paused in thought. "It must be a couple of months now. She used to come to the service and then we'd chat for a while. I knew her in France, that's why she came here." He gazed again at the photo. "She was beautiful and so very popular. She had many admirers. Perhaps she's gone off with one of them."

Hettie grimaced. Why did everyone, including this curate, always think the worst of her? "She wouldn't do that," Hettie said vehemently. "Not and leave without a word. I know she wouldn't."

The curate shrugged, then, seeing Hettie's distress said, "I'm sure you're right. I only met her briefly. You probably know her better than I."

Hettie sighed. "That's the problem," she said. "Sometime I wonder if I ever knew her at all." Sadness welled up inside her. She reached into her bag to find a handkerchief but the curate beat her to it, handing her a freshly laundered one from his pocket. Hettie took it just in time to catch the tears rolling down her cheeks. She sniffed. "Now it's you who's being kind," she said.

He grinned. "That's my job." He glanced around the hall as the rattle of cups and saucers being replaced on the table and the general movement of people edging towards the door increased. He stepped to one side, pulling Hettie with him. "If there's anything I can do to help you find your friend I'd be happy to help, but to be honest I knew little of her."

Hettie saw kindness in his eyes. "It's the child," she said. "I could believe she'd gone off of her own free will if it wasn't for her having left Billy with me."

"Billy?".

Hettie indicated the pram parked along the wall.

"Oh," he said. He walked up and gazed into the pram at the sleeping child. He stood entranced for so long Hettie had a fleeting moment when she wondered if he could be Billy's father. She watched as he touched Billy's cheek. "How old is he?" he asked.

"Fourteen months," Hettie said.

The curate's brow creased. "She never mentioned having a child," he said. "Whenever she came here all she spoke about was our time in Paris. She often asked if I recalled the people she was with, how well did I know them, had we kept in touch?" He shrugged. "As I said my time in Paris was brief. I recall very little."

He shuffled his feet and glanced around the room. Hettie had the distinct feeling he was looking for an escape to avoid saying any more. He glanced back at Hettie. "She wouldn't have had him then, it was over two years ago now and she's never mentioned him." He looked perplexed. "I'm sorry, I don't think I can help at all. She never spoke of her life since she returned – only about her time in Paris. I am very sorry."

Hettie's hopes faded. "Well, at least I know why she came here," she said. "She was looking for Billy's father and contacting anyone who may have known him."

"Someone she met in Paris?" he said. "Not someone here? No, that would make sense."

Hettie's hopes rose again. "Was there anyone she was especially fond of? Anyone she spent time with? Anyone she asked about in particular?"

The curate's eyes narrowed. He bit his lip as though trying to decide what to say. He took a breath. "I wouldn't like to accuse anyone or suggest..." He shrugged.

"Please," Hettie implored him. "If you can think of anyone."

He straightened up and his whole demeanour changed. "I don't know," he said. "I really couldn't say. I'm sorry – there's nothing more I can do."

Hettie's heart sank. She'd had such high hopes of this young man. She pulled a notebook and pencil from her bag, wrote her name and address on one of the pages, tore it out and handed it to him. "If you hear anything of Annie or have any other thoughts please be so kind as to let me know. I am so dreadfully worried."

"Of course," he said, his face softening again as he took the paper. "If I hear anything."

As she walked away Hettie had a feeling that the curate knew more than he was prepared to say. There was nothing she could grab hold of and deal with, nothing tangible, just a feeling. What could she do? She couldn't press him further – not right away, but perhaps, over time, if she returned he may recall something, something he'd hardly reveal to a stranger. She vowed to make sure she came to know him better, after all, he knew Annie in Paris, he would have known her friends and even, Hettie hesitated to think of it, her lovers.

Having got nowhere with the visit to the church Hettie turned again to Annie's journal. Turning the pages slowly she noticed the number of appointments and parties Annie attended. It was a very different life to the one she'd been living with Hettie and Dorcas.

Who wouldn't be seduced by the ease and comfort that comes with money and status? Annie loved meeting people, her grace of movement, eloquence and comportment had been polished in Paris and Hettie could see how easily she would fit into the social whirl. No wonder she loved it. She might have been made for it, if she didn't have Billy.

Hettie winced as she recalled Annie saying her move was a 'step up'. Had she now decided to move on and leave them all behind?

She shook her head, determined to put her doubts behind her. Annie would never do that – would she? Flicking through the diary Hettie read – *Party at TJ's* or *Appointment with RH*. All the entries used initials which weren't much help in identifying the people she met. Then again Hettie wondered how many of them used their real names anyway.

The journal had not lived up to Hettie's expectations. In fact it was no use at all, except to show Hettie what a busy and fulfilling social life Annie was leading and how many admirers she had, which Hettie was well aware of anyway. Disheartened she closed the book.

She was at a loss what to do next. It was possible that Annie's disappearance had more to do with her life in France than recent events. Or perhaps it was nothing to do with anything other than Annie's desire to be free of any encumbrances and make her own way in the world. Maybe everyone was right and she had moved on to greener pastures.

She gazed at Billy, sitting on the mat in front of the fire. His tiny fingers clutched the toy Sarah had brought him. Every day he learned something new. This morning he'd played peek-a-boo, pulling his blanket over his head, then pushing it down and giggling. She shook her head. No, she thought, Annie wouldn't leave him. She really wouldn't.

The next day there wasn't much to do in the house. The married couple had left and been replaced by a single gentleman who wasn't due to move in until the following evening. Hettie wrapped Billy up warmly and put him in his pram for his morning walk. She slipped Annie's journal under the bedding and set out to walk to Belgravia. The air was cold and fresh, but thankfully it was dry and the streets deserted except for the occasional costermonger with his barrow calling out his wares. As she neared the wealthier end of town street sweepers stood idle awaiting a carriage or a pedestrian who might be willing to part with a ha'penny to cross the road without getting mud and horse manure on their shoes.

Judging from the entries in Annie's journal not many parties or appointments took place before noon. If she caught Chloe at about that time perhaps she could decipher the initials. Chloe might give Hettie an idea who Annie was seeing, which could lead to her whereabouts.

Hettie wasn't holding out much hope, but at least she felt she was doing something. Chloe seemed like a good person with a genuine fondness for Annie. Hope springs eternal, Hettie thought, as she strode along. Some hope anyway.

Hettie arrived at the Belgravia house just as Chloe was making her way to a waiting hansom. She pushed the pram across her path.

"Oh." Chloe stopped in her tracks. She turned as though to admonish the interloper. A puzzled expression crossed her face when she saw Hettie. "Don't I know you?" she said. "We've met before haven't we?"

Relieved, Hettie said, "Yes. I'm a friend of Ann... Angelique. You remember. I was looking for her."

"Oh, yes of course." Chloe stared into the pram. "This isn't... no it couldn't be... surely not?" She gazed at Billy. "Angelique's child? What on earth are you doing here? You didn't think Madam would take him in did you?" Her brow creased. "She won't you know. She'll want nothing to do with him."

Hettie laughed. "No, of course not. I came hoping to see you but I see I've caught you on your way out."

Chloe grimaced. "A long standing appointment I'm afraid. I fear you have had a wasted journey."

Hettie shook Billy's rattle in front of his face to make him chuckle. "And we've come such a long way too, haven't we, precious?"

Chloe relented. "Well, perhaps not entirely wasted," she said. She reached into her reticule. "Here's my card. I'm to visit the dressmaker in Wigmore Street tomorrow at noon. Afterwards I will take tea in the tearooms in Cavendish Square. Perhaps we could meet there at, say, two o'clock. How would that suit? Then you can tell me how I can help."

Hettie gladly took the offered card, confirmed that she would be at the tearooms by two o'clock and then watched as Chloe got into the hansom and was driven away.

"Well, that wasn't a complete waste of time," she said to Billy who lay back in the pram ready for sleep. A feeling of deep gratitude flowed through her. She chuckled at her good fortune in meeting Chloe and happily pushed the pram all the way home.

Chapter Seventeen

The next morning Billy woke Hettie with his crying. He'd been coughing in the night, despite the cloth spotted with eucalyptus oil she'd hung over the lampshade to gently scent the air. Hettie was afraid his crying would wake the lodger who'd returned the previous evening. If he complained about it Dorcas would have more reason to want to find a place for him.

She leaned over, lit the lamp beside her bed and got up to see to him.

Poor mite, she thought. She shushed him to try to quieten him and lifted him gently from his cot. Horrified she stared at his face, bright red and glowing. She felt his forehead. He was hot and clammy. His breath came in hoarse rasps. She loosened his clothes and quickly dampened a cloth from the jug on the dresser. He was wheezing badly and still felt hot to the touch even after she'd bathed his head and chest.

Hettie raced down the stairs. "Ma, Ma," she called. She rushed into the kitchen where Dorcas was already preparing breakfast. "Billy is sick — please come and look. I'm so worried about him."

Dorcas turned and stared at her. Then she dropped the saucepan she was holding and pushed past Hettie. She moved fast. By the time Hettie got upstairs Dorcas had the child on her lap, soothing him and running her hands over him to check him out. She opened his mouth, looked down his throat and examined his ears and eyes. He was still having difficulty breathing.

Quick as a flash Dorcas stood and carried him downstairs. In the kitchen, holding Billy in the crook of her arm she put the kettle on the stove. "Fill a couple of saucepans," she said to Hettie, "and put them on to boil as well. The steam will help to clear his lungs."

When the water in the kettle was beginning to boil Dorcas poured some into a bowl, took a cloth from the airer, folded it lengthways and dipped it in the hot water. She wrung it out and wound it around Billy neck. Billy's breathing appeared to ease slightly. The kettle was now billowing out a good head of steam and Dorcas held Billy close enough to breathe in the steam but not so close as to scald him. Hettie stood by, wringing her hands.

"Run down to Mrs Judd," Dorcas said. "She'll have some willow-bark to sooth his pain and bring the fever down. Quick as you can."

Hettie didn't need telling twice. She was out of the door and down the road in no time flat, her skirts flying as she ran. When she returned Dorcas dripped two drops of the medicine into Billy's bottle of milk and, rocking him gently in her arms, fed him. After drinking half his bottle he dozed off. Hettie sighed with relief.

"Just a touch of croup and a chill," Dorcas said. "Nothing serious."

Hettie smiled. "It could have been if you hadn't been here to help," she said.

"That's as maybe," Dorcas said, but Hettie noticed the glow of pride on her face and how she held the child close to her bosom, watching him as she rocked him to sleep.

"Bring his cot down to the kitchen," Dorcas said. "It's warmer and the steam will do him good." She glanced at Hettie. "I'll see to him. You get on with the breakfast. Lodger'll faint with hunger if we don't get it dished up and served."

Hettie grinned. She happily left Billy in Dorcas's care while she got on with her work. Despite all she said about turning him out, Hettie saw that possibility fading faster than a half-remembered dream. Dorcas held him in her arms and cooed over him.

That afternoon Hettie was due to meet Chloe in the tearooms in Cavendish Square. For once Dorcas was more than willing to look after Billy.

"Leave him with me," she said, her face softening as she looked at the sleeping baby. "He's still a bit off colour but a good sleep and he'll be right as rain."

Hettie's heart warmed at the change in Dorcas. Now all she had to do was persuade her to change her view of Annie. Without Dorcas's help she couldn't go on looking for Annie in all the places she may have visited. At least now it would make things easier.

She dressed in her best blue suit, well, her only blue suit, and put on her best felt hat. Annie had left the muffler she'd worn to travel home from Paris so Hettie wrapped that around her shoulders. She took an omnibus to Cavendish Square.

As soon as she entered the tearoom Hettie saw Chloe sitting at a table near the front. A teapot with two cups set out on saucers and a three tier stand of cakes were already on the table. Hettie removed the muffler and eased herself into the vacant chair opposite Chloe. Her cheeks burned and not only from the bitter wind outside.

Chloe's face brightened. "I was hoping you'd come," she said. "It's not often I meet people outside of Sylvia's circle and I'm so looking forward to our conversation."

Hettie laughed. "In that case I hope I don't disappoint," she said.

Over tea and cakes Hettie told Chloe about her early life with Annie selling cress on the streets and

Chloe talked about her childhood in Liverpool. "The prospects for a girl growing up near the docks are not good," she said. "I didn't want to end up on the streets or married to a man who'd beat the living daylights out of me every night when he had a tank on." She poured Hettie a second cup of tea. "When my mother died I went on the stage. Sylvia saw my potential and here I am. It appears that Angelique and I had much in common." She glanced at Hettie. "If there's anything I can do to help you find her please let me know."

Hettie took Annie's journal out of her bag. The initials meant nothing to her but they might to Chloe. Chloe took the journal and looked through it.

"Oh, I remember that party," she said pointing to one particular entry. "We both went. It was fun." Then on another page she pointed out where they had both been to the opera. "*Don Giovanni*," she said. "It was a bit dull for me but Angelique enjoyed it."

Apart from being able to tell Hettie which parties and events she had attended with Annie there was little else she could say. She handed the book back to Hettie.

"What about these initials – RH, JP, and SM – do you know who they might be or what the initials might mean?" Hettie said.

Chloe took the book again and looked more closely. "RH – that'd be the Right Honourable," she said. She chuckled. "Angelique said he wasn't honourable at all. She called him the Right Horrible. Said he had exotic tastes and liked what he called 'vigour'. Angelique said it was more like torture." She pouted. "Come to think of it I haven't seen him around since Angelique left." She turned and stared at Hettie. "Do you think that's a clue?"

She looked again at the other initials in the book. "JP – he's a Justice of the Peace, and SM, er," she gazed heavenward as though trying to place him. "Something in shipping I think." She handed the book back to Hettie. "I can find out more if you like, ask a few discreet questions. Would that help do you think?"

"It most certainly would," Hettie said, her eyes lighting up with glee. "If I had their names..."

Chloe thought some more. "Well, I haven't seen The Right Horrible since Angelique left. He hasn't been back to see any of the other girls." Her brow furrowed. "Has she gone away with him perhaps? Although I can't see why she should, she could hardly bear him."

The air punched out of Hettie's lungs. Everything Chloe said made it more and more likely that Annie had been taken against her will, but who was RH and where could he have taken

Annie? Hettie drew a breath. "Who is RH? Do you know his name? Where can I find him?"

Chloe shrugged her delicate shoulders. "As far as I can recall he was Lord something or other – Crenshaw, Cranshaw – no Crenshaw I think. I'm afraid I'm not much help."

"On the contrary," Hettie said. "You've given me something to go on at least and I'm grateful for that."

"Please let me know if you find anything or if I can be of any more help. I'd love to see her again." Chloe smiled a most beguiling smile. No wonder Sylvia thought she had potential, Hettie thought.

Hettie promised to keep in touch. Chloe said she'd look into the other initials in the journal and let Hettie know if she managed to decipher any. "It's very exciting isn't it," she said. "Like solving a mystery, although... I mean..." her face crumpled. "I do hope nothing bad has happened to Angelique. I hope we find her happy and healthy, but in this game..." she shrugged and Hettie saw tears forming in her eyes.

They said their goodbyes and Hettie left to make her way home along the darkening street. Her head buzzed with ideas. The Right Honourable Lord Crenshaw? She'd seen that name somewhere, if only she could remember where.

When Hettie got home she told Dorcas about her meeting with Chloe and how she was sure something had happened to Annie. "Chloe was friendly with Annie and she was surprised at her disappearance, especially as she left all her fine clothes and jewellery behind."

"Left her clothes and jewels behind?" Dorcas said. "Well she may leave her illegitimate child behind, but she'd sure as hell take her ill gotten gains with her when she moved on."

Hettie sighed. Would Dorcas never think well of Annie no matter what she did? Still at least she was beginning to acknowledge that her disappearance may not have been intentional. "Chloe gave the name of a man she'd been seeing..." Was that the right way to put it? He was obviously one of her 'clients' but Hettie shied away from the actually admitting what Annie was doing for a living. "The Right Honourable Lord Crenshaw," Hettie said. "I'm sure I've seen his name somewhere. In the papers I think." Then it came to her. She'd seen it on the news-stand where Jimmy the boy stood calling out the latest news and selling his papers. If he was in the papers Hettie could find out all about him and possibly his relationship with Annie.

Dorcas smiled. "Lord Crenshaw? The one who's been in all the papers? If Annie's got mixed up with the likes of him she's in real trouble. Nasty piece of work from I hear and I hear a lot."

"Really, Ma? What do you hear? Where do you hear it? I'd like to find out all I can about him. He may be the one who's holding Annie against her will. Please, Ma, tell me all you know."

Dorcas sighed. "Well I know old Elsie's niece works for him. He's got a place in Bloomsbury as well as a country house in Devon. House parlour-maid she is. Been there a few years now. She knows all that goes on in that house. She could tell you a tale or two."

Hettie's spirits rose. "I'd love to see her. Do you think that's possible? I could go to the house…"

Dorcas shook her head. "No need for that. Biddy visits her aunt every Sunday afternoon. She's the closest relative she's got. Elsie brought her up when her ma ran off. I'll be seeing Elsie on Thursday. I'll arrange for you to go to tea on Sunday, if that suits. That'll give you a chance to meet Biddy and have a chat. Not sure how much she can help, but it's something."

Hettie beamed at her mother. "It's something all right," she said. "It's a chance to talk to someone who knows all about this Lord Crenshaw. I can hardly wait."

Chapter Eighteen

Sunday morning Hettie walked to St Leonard's in Bromley by Bow. She'd found out the curate was called Reverend Reginald Smythe and she took Billy in his pram hoping to stir his conscience by letting him know how much Billy missed his mother and the struggle Hettie was having to keep him with no news of Annie.

"There's been talk of the Foundling Hospital or the workhouse," she said to him in the church hall after the service. "I'm at my wits' end. If I can't find his mother soon the Lord only knows what will become of him." Hettie held Billy in her arms.

Reverend Smythe reached out and touched Billy's head. Hettie thought Billy's smile would melt even the hardest of hearts. He looked perplexed. "I don't know how I can help," he said. "I only knew Angelique briefly. She had so many friends."

"Do you know any of them? Perhaps if I could contact one or two of the people she knew in France I may find out where she would be most likely to go to look for Billy's father. From her account of him I cannot believe he would willingly let her down. She spoke so highly of him."

He smiled. "It's easy to make a good impression when one has nothing to lose but everything to gain," he said. "One can never be sure of another until put to the test. You may be right about his good intentions, but who knows?" He shrugged.

Hettie sighed. She was getting nowhere. "Things are looking very bleak for this poor innocent in that case," she said anger rising inside her. "Strange that someone with so many friends could so easily be forgotten and a child left fatherless because of it."

Reverend Smythe looked uncomfortable. Hettie pressed home what she saw as her advantage. "I suppose there's nothing for it but the workhouse then. Such a shame when he may be the son of a decent man who could offer him something better."

She turned to put Billy back into his pram. Reverend Smythe swallowed and said, "Look, I don't know how much help it will be but there was a girl, another dancer. I think she was good friends with Angelique. She gave me her name..." He blushed and Hettie guessed there was more to the relationship than he was prepared to admit. "I believe she also came home to London and is working at the Gaiety Theatre in the Strand. You may find her there. Her name is..." He paused, his face flushing even redder. "Veronique, or it was. Of course it may be quite different now."

Hettie smiled. "Thank you," she said.

Since Billy's illness and recovery Dorcas had become fond of him and he of her. He gave her an especially bright smile in the morning. He chuckled and held out his arms to her. She gave him a cuddle as she put him in his high chair.

Hettie left him with Dorcas after lunch and went to see Biddy and Elsie. She'd spent any spare time she'd had reading through the newspapers left by the lodger in his room and she'd even looked up Lord Crenshaw in the pastor's copy of *Debrett's*.

Elsie's house was much the same as Dorcas's, only Elsie lived in just the ground floor rooms. She spent most of her days sitting by the window overlooking the street watching the people going by. Those who knew her waved. If the light was good enough and Elsie saw them she'd wave back. Mostly she sat knitting or crocheting. On days when Elsie couldn't get out Dorcas collected a few things for her at the market.

A smiling face and watchful blue eyes greeted Hettie when Biddy opened the door. Slim and not much older than Hettie, Biddy's plain grey dress with white lace collar accentuated the paleness of her skin. "You must be Hettie," she said. "My aunt has told me all about you. Do come in."

She showed Hettie into the front room where Elsie sat near the fire with a woollen blanket wrapped around her legs. Hettie couldn't help but compare Elsie's parlour with Dorcas's. It was hard to believe they were the same size. Dorcas's parlour was spick and span, her table polished and her antimacassars always freshly laundered. Elsie's on the other hand was cluttered and crowded. An ancient horse-hair sofa stood among the ill matched, worn and stained tables and chairs. A large picture hung over the fireplace, haphazard ornaments and a clock adorned the high mantelshelf. The floor was bare, whereas Dorcas's parlour boasted a colourful rug in front of the tiled fireplace.

The room looked snug enough with the fire lit but Hettie guessed it was only lit for Biddy's visits. Elsie smiled and Hettie said, "Hello." She handed Biddy the tin of scones Dorcas had sent.

"How lovely," Biddy said. "I'll make some tea, then we can talk. Aunt Elsie said you are interested in hearing about my employer, Lord Crenshaw, though I doubt I can tell you any more than's been in the papers."

"Anything you can tell me will be a help," Hettie said.

Biddy disappeared into the kitchen. Hettie sat on the sofa and chatted to Elsie while Biddy made the tea. Biddy returned carrying a tray set out with cups, saucers, a pot of tea and Dorcas's scones with jam on a plate. She placed it on the table near the window.

"Thank Dorcas for the scones," she said. "Aunt Elsie doesn't do much baking these days and they look a treat."

She poured a cup of tea, added milk from a white china jug and handed the cup to Elsie. She put one of Dorcas's scones on a plate and put that on a small table next to her aunt.

Over tea Biddy told Hettie about Lord Crenshaw's London house. "It's not a large house as London houses go," she said, "but there's enough to keep me busy. Four good rooms on each floor with just me and Daisy to do." She pouted. "Lady Crenshaw lives most of her time in Devon. She only comes up for the season." She put her cup on the tray and took a scone. She pulled a face. "When she comes she brings her lady's maid, Vera. I have to move in with cook and she snores something terrible. Vera complains all the time about the cramped conditions, the crowded streets, the dirt and the noise. They don't stay long."

"What about visitors?" Hettie said. "Does he ever have guests staying?" If Annie had moved in with Lord Crenshaw Biddy would know.

"Visitors? No. Dinner guests sometimes."

"So, what's he like?" Hettie asked.

"Um, difficult to say," Biddy said. "We don't see much of him to be honest. I only see him when I help serve at table when he entertains, and that isn't often. When he does it's usually business acquaintances." Suddenly she smiled and turned to Hettie, her eyes shining with glee. "I did hear something the other week," she said with a conspiratorial grin. "Couldn't help but hear what with the discussions being so heated." She glanced down and tipped her head nonchalantly. "Over dinner it was."

She stared at Hettie, warming to her subject. "Rum company he had that night an' all. Not the usual sort. Lots of raised voices, shouting really. Someone mentioned a Government contract but I didn't hear all of it. Still, it sounded like he was being threatened. Truth to tell I've never seen anything like it. Red in the face he was. I thought he was going to burst a blood vessel the way he was carrying on."

She poured herself another cup of tea and added milk. "I dunno what went on after that 'cos I had to clear the dishes. Mr Pattison, he's the butler, sent me back to the kitchen. Still, Jenkins, he's the footman, he said as how they almost come to blows." She laughed. "He said they weren't the Master's 'sort'. People in trade or some such, he thought. 'Badly dressed in expensive clothes with shabby shoes', he said. When they left the Master, well he looked right put out. Didn't even finish his brandy he didn't and that's a right turn up for the books."

Hettie grinned. So all was not well in the Crenshaw household. Could that have anything to do with Annie's disappearance? "Shabby shoes? Whatever could he have meant?"

Biddy chuckled. "Tatty, you know. Not handmade. Stitching all over the place and not polished neither." She sipped her tea. "One of 'em had heavy boots too. Like workmen wear, or the men from the docks. I didn't like the look of 'im." She wrinkled her nose. "Smelled a bit an' all."

"Who else lives in the house?" Hettie asked. "Does he have any guests, friends, for example, maybe a lady friend?"

Biddy giggled. "Well, if he does he keeps 'em mighty quiet. The only ladies I see are the ones who come to dinner with their husbands. A right lot of dried up old harridans they be." She blushed. "Begging your pardon."

Hettie smiled. At least Annie wasn't being kept as a guest at his house. Hettie and Biddy chatted for a little longer, Hettie tried to find out as much about Lord Crenshaw as possible. She wondered what sort of man he was and what the argument was over. He worked in the Treasury so it must have been important, but all Biddy could add was that he was a 'right stickler' who bullied his staff at every opportunity and 'you kept out of his way as best you could if you knew what was good for you'.

After visiting Biddy Hettie decided she'd like to visit Lord Crenshaw and see what sort of man he was for herself. She'd have to come up with a believable pretext for her visit though. Something he wouldn't question; nothing to arouse suspicion.

Back at home Hettie looked through Annie's journal again. What did she know about the men who visited her? Only what Chloe could tell her. One was a Lord working in the Treasury, another probably in shipping. All were wealthy and influential, most were probably married. There must be some connection, Hettie thought, but she couldn't fathom out what it could be. Biddy said it was as if Lord Crenshaw was being threatened. Could Annie's disappearance have anything to do with it? How damaging to his reputation and thereby his business interests would it be if their association became public knowledge? Was someone using knowledge of it to bring pressure to bear on Lord Crenshaw? He may have something to hide, but there was no shame attached to men who could afford to pay for the privilege of being seen with a well turned out woman, schooled to meet every demand and fall in with every whim. If you had enough money you could live your life in any way you pleased, free from public censure.

Biddy had mentioned that his dinner guests were 'badly dressed in expensive clothes with shabby shoes'. Could they have been from the docks? Hettie knew a lot of things that weren't talked about went on behind the backs of The Port of London Authority. Her father had worked on the river before his accident. Everyone knew you could get anything you wanted if you kept in with the right people. Perhaps that was something she should look into. If the men who'd shared a table with Lord Crenshaw were also Annie's 'clients' her disappearance could well be connected to their business.

The next day, after breakfast had been served and cleared, the rooms swept and dusted, the grates cleared and fires re-laid it was eleven o'clock. Hettie decided the best way to contact Veronique at the Gaiety Theatre would be to walk along the Strand and leave a note asking to see her at a convenient time. "I can go that way to the market," she said to Dorcas. "Save you going out later."

"Thanks," Dorcas said. "And don't worry about Billy. I'll keep me eye on 'im."

She wrote out a list and gave it to Hettie. "Don't forget to watch the butcher when you gets the meat. I swear he leaves his thumb in the scale when he's weighing it up."

Hettie grinned. Since Billy's illness Dorcas had watched him more and more often, even sending Hettie out so she could stay in with him.

"Well, he's a little darling," she said. "It's not his fault his mother's left him. If I had a little 'un like Billy I'd never let him out of my sight."

Another dig at Annie, Hettie thought, but at least Billy was in good hands.

She made her way to the Strand and, sure enough, as she walked past the Gaiety Theatre the posters advertising the shows included a reference to '*Veronique – fresh from Paris performing exotic dances first performed at the famous Folies-Bergère*'.

Hettie couldn't help a chuckle escaping her lips. She'd overheard the older boys at the school talking about what they termed 'erotic dancing'. Annie had described it as 'a form of Art', but the boys had obviously missed the artistic nature of what they referred to as 'scantily dressed bints kicking their legs in the air so high you could see everything they had to offer'.

She handed the note to the surly guardian of the stage door. "Please could you see Veronique gets this as soon as possible," she said. "It's very urgent."

He grunted. "I'll give it to her when she arrives. Don't know when that'll be. Can't say fairer than that."

"I'll call again tomorrow then," Hettie said. "For her reply." She hoped she'd made it clear that she expected some response.

"Oh aye, I'll tell 'er," the doorman said.

Hettie walked on to Covent Garden Market where she saw Eliza surrounded by palettes of fresh watercress. "My, you look busy," she said.

Eliza grinned. "That's the way I like it an' all," she said. "Since you and Annie left I bin supplying the hotels regular." She put a basket of cress on her stall. "You should have stayed with the cress, I'm bringing it up from the country now. One day I'm gonna sell cress to all the hotels in London."

Hettie smiled but she wondered if Eliza wasn't right. They would have been better off staying with the cress. Annie would have been for sure.

The next morning she walked to the theatre again, hoping that Veronique had responded to her note. Her spirits soared when the doorman handed her an envelope. Her fingers trembled as she opened it and read:

'*Your note intrigued me. I take luncheon regularly at Ellis, the chop house in Covent Garden at one o'clock if you care to join me. I'll be wearing a black cloak over a purple suit and a hat with roses in the brim. Veronique.*'

Her anxiety eased, the weight on her shoulders lifted. At last someone who knew Annie well in Paris. She put the note in her pocket and hurried to the restaurant.

The clock in the market struck the quarter hour as she was passing. She glanced up. It was quarter to one. She arrived at the chop house just as the clock struck the hour.

On tiptoe she peered over the heads of the crowd standing around the door. The windows were steamed up and she could see nothing inside. She took a breath and squeezed past the queue waiting at the serving window for their pies to take with them for their lunch. She pushed the door open and stepped into the shop. It felt like walking into a furnace. Her face glowed and her eyes stung.

She saw Veronique sitting at a table at the back of the room. She hurried over to join her.

"Ah!" Veronique said as Hettie got to the table. "The mysterious person who is a friend of Angelique. It's been so long I hardly remember, and so much has happened since Paris, but if there's anything I can do for a friend of Angelique please, you must tell me."

Chapter Nineteen

Hettie eased herself into the chair opposite Veronique. She smiled. "I'm Hettie Bundy," she said. "The girl you knew as Angelique was in fact Annie Flanagan. We grew up together in Wapping. I understand from Reverend Smythe, the curate at St Leonard's in Bromley by Bow, that you knew her in Paris. I'm trying to find her and hoped you could help."

Veronique smiled and nodded. Her grey eyes twinkled. She was older than Hettie had expected but still slim with an air of vivaciousness.

"Please join me for lunch," Veronique said. "I usually dine alone, but today interesting company would be most welcome." She spoke with a slight accent but Hettie couldn't decide whether this was genuine or a theatrical affectation.

Hettie said she'd be delighted to join her and Veronique ordered them each a bowl of stewed lamb. "This is my only meal of the day," she said. "I won't eat again until after the performance and then it's often too late." Once it had been served Veronique said, "Now, you must tell me all about yourself and... erm... Annie was it?" She laughed. "Many of the people in Paris are not who they pretend to be." She shrugged. "So, Annie... Angelique... it makes little difference. What has she done that makes you seek me out after all this time?"

Hettie hesitated. "I don't know what she's done, that's the problem. All I know is she's disappeared and I'm trying to find where she may be."

"And you think I may know?" Veronique raised her eyebrows.

"Well, Reverend Smythe told me you were a dancer in Paris like Annie. You may know who her friends were then and who she was likely to see when she came home."

"Ah!" Veronique said. "I was a dancer in Paris, yes. But not like Angelique. I danced in the Corps de Ballet. Now in London I dance as the Prima Ballerina. Very different from Angelique's dancing which was more, how should we say, flamboyant."

Hettie smiled. That explained Veronique's wiry frame which radiated a sense of inner strength only gained through years of strict discipline. The Gaiety Theatre boasted a programme of entertainments ranging from opera and ballet to circus performances and the latest 'exotic' dancing, so Hettie wasn't at all surprised Veronique was a ballerina.

She explained to Veronique about Annie's return from Paris, how she'd left Billy in her care when she moved in with Sylvia de Vine in Belgravia. "I think she was hoping to find Billy's father," she said. "She used to visit Billy regularly but suddenly she stopped coming. Something must have happened to her. You knew her friends in Paris, what do you think?"

Veronique pushed a piece of stewed lamb around her bowl and took a breath. "Ah, poor Angelique," she said. "I fear she was badly used."

"Badly used?" Hettie stared at her. "She told me it was marvellous, all glamour and excitement, men, jewels, extravagant living. She said she'd fallen in love with a wealthy Englishman who loved her madly. Do you mean it wasn't true?"

She recalled how Annie could make up stories at the drop of a hat. Once, when she was picking up the flowers dropped from the market stalls she told the flower girls she wanted them for her mother's grave. "It would have been her birthday today," she'd said. Hettie still didn't know if that was true. It had gained her a substantial bunch of flowers though.

Annie had enough imagination to talk her way out of any situation. Had she been stringing Hettie along so she'd look after Billy and Annie could get on with the life she'd always wanted?

Veronique shook her head. "Sometimes we believe what our heart wants us to believe. Even someone as headstrong as Angelique can be fooled. She may have believed everything he said and at the time he may even have meant it, but sometimes men say only what is expedient to get them what they want."

A well of sadness formed inside Hettie as she saw how Annie's dreams must have crumbled into dust. "So there was no English gentleman eager to marry her and make her an honest woman?"

"I'm not saying that. Yes, there were many gentlemen and one in particular. Angelique was very much in love but it was always destined for disaster." She gazed at Hettie. "His future had been planned for him from birth and it certainly didn't include a dancer from the Folies-Bergère. To these young men a trip to Paris is just a pleasant interlude before their real lives of responsibility begin."

"Tell me about her life in Paris," Hettie said. "I want to hear it all. Perhaps there's something that may help find her."

So Veronique told her. "We both worked hard. A dancer's life is demanding and often punishing. The customers at the Folies expect a professional performance for their two francs. We danced every night and shared a room in the Boulevard Montmartre. We worked hard and played hard too. Life as an artiste is short you have to make the most of it." Her eyes glazed over as though in reflection. "Angelique was petite, pretty and popular. She had many admirers." She smiled at Hettie. "Angelique danced with feathers, you know, a magnificent fan made of ostrich feathers." She laughed. "Smaller feathers strategically placed on her costume preserved her modesty, if she ever had any that is." Veronique took a sip of the lime cordial she'd ordered with her lunch. "At first she managed to brush off the most persistent of her admirers, accepting gifts, enjoying their hospitality and perhaps a little dalliance now and then, nothing serious, until she met Charles. He was a captain in the Guards and very handsome. They became close and even..." She stopped as though she was about to say more but feared it would reveal too much. She shrugged. "I know little of their liaisons. I had my own." She smiled. "I too had many admirers."

"Charles?" Hettie said. "Charles what? He must have had a surname."

"If he did I never knew it," Veronique said and continued to eat her lunch. Hettie took a bite of hers and pushed the rest around the bowl.

"And Billy?" she said eventually. "Did you know about Billy?"

Veronique sighed heavily and gazed at the pictures on the wall. She looked at Hettie. "Of course I did. Everyone did. A thickening of the waist, a heaviness in your step, sudden fatigue – not an easy thing to hide when you dance in the Folies-Bergère."

"So, what happened?"

"What happened? She lost her job of course. Turned out to earn her living the only way she knew how. Even that became impossible in the end. Not many men will pay for a woman in that condition." She waved her fork at Hettie. "We all helped as much as we could, but it was tough for Angelique."

"And the man, Charles?"

"Oh, he was long gone."

"She said she'd come home to find him. Is that not so?"

Veronique pouted. "After the baby was born we lost touch, but I heard rumours. Angelique sold most of her jewellery before the child was born. She kept only the small pieces that meant the most to her. Things Charles had given her. She moved to a room in Saint Germain, the 6th arrondissement. I think that's where she gave birth. Afterwards she worked where she could, cleaning, waiting on tables, anything to save enough money to return home. It was where she thought she'd be looked after and seeing you here, so concerned about her, proves she was right." She patted Hettie's hand. "You have been a good friend. She's lucky to have a friend like you. In Paris people were not so nice."

Hettie swallowed. So Annie's tales of a life of glamour and high living were untrue. She wondered about the rest of Annie's stories. Had she simply come home with Billy so she could leave him with Hettie and go back to the sort of life she'd led before she had him?

"Thank you for telling me," Hettie said. "It seems I've got Annie wrong. She only came home to find someone to clean up after her mistakes and find a home for him."

Veronique looked aghast. "Oh no," she said. "In Paris there are lots of ways to get rid of unwanted embarrassments, shall we say. No, Angelique's decision to keep him would have come from the heart. It was a hard decision to make. There were easier options. No, Angelique had the child from choice and worked hard to keep him and make a home for him. She must have loved him beyond reason."

After the meal Hettie said goodbye to Veronique and thanked her for her honesty telling her about Annie.

"I'm happy to have helped, if indeed I have. I liked Angelique. She had fire and passion. We had good times together and when you find her I'd like to see her again. Please tell her to get in touch. You know where to find me."

"Thank you, I will," Hettie said. Then, as she was leaving, Veronique caught her arm. "Go back to see Reverend Smythe," she whispered. "Ask him about the church in Le Peletier." She put her finger across her lips in a sign that she'd say no more.

Hettie walked home more confused than ever.

A few days later, before she could visit Reverend Smythe, Hettie received a note from Elsie's niece Biddy. In it she said Lord Crenshaw's visitors had returned. She'd overheard them having an angry exchange with her master. She hadn't heard it all but Hettie might be interested to know that they were arguing about a ship waiting to be unloaded at the docks. She hoped this would help.

Well, Hettie thought, at least now I know Lord Crenshaw's visitors are in shipping, but whether any of them has any connection to Annie is another matter.

That evening she went to the pastor's school as usual. She looked at her class of young boys, all come in straight from the river or by the docks. She knew many of them would watch ships moored along the bank waiting to go into the Pool. Often men from the ships would give them a ha'penny or two for directions to a receiver who'd take merchandise off their hands with no questions asked. Then there were the dark shadowy ships that moored on the far side of the river, between Gravesend and Rotherhithe. Their cargoes were unloaded onto lighters and ferries before they reached the docks. Who knew what they carried? She decided that this evening she'd ask them to talk about their experiences and she'd help write them down.

"Ain't we gonna copy the letters off the board, Miss?" one lad asked when Hettie handed out the slates with nothing on the board for them to copy.

"No. Tonight we're doing something special," she said. "We are all going to write about something we've seen in our own words."

The boys looked apprehensive. "What – make up words ourselves?" one incredulous lad asked.

"With my help, yes," Hettie said. She began by asking them to talk about things they'd seen and done. Soon the classroom came to noisy life. Some of the tales were taller than the highest ship's mast, everyone vying to be the most outrageous, but Hettie learnt an awful lot about what went on around the docks. Some of the boys crept alongside the boats to grope for bits of tin, copper or coal dropped over the side. Dredger men would throw stolen items overboard and come back later to pick them up while pretending to search for coal. Lumpers unloaded ships and smuggled small items, like watches, braces, money clips, silk ties or tiepins, ashore. Then there were the pickpurses, petty thieves, cut-throats and ruffians. The boys couldn't wait to tell Hettie their lurid tales, although Hettie wasn't sure she believed all of them.

The boys were let out at nine o'clock, pushing and shoving each other through the door, bursting onto the street like peas released from the pod.

"They seemed to enjoy your lesson this evening," the pastor said to Hettie as she was clearing up ready to leave. "From what I heard you had a somewhat lively debate."

Hettie laughed. "They're all rascals and scallywags. I don't believe a word they said." She put the slates in the cupboard. "But some of them were very enlightening."

It was the beginning of February and although the days were lightening, at night an inky blackness descended on the narrow streets. Hettie walked home thinking about what the boys had said. On an impulse she decided to take a detour through Limehouse. One of the boys had said he'd seen opium dens there by the cut. He'd described filthy houses and Chinese people like the living dead wandering the back alleys until they collapsed senseless in a fog of smoke. Hettie didn't believe a word but even allowing for the inventiveness of the boy the picture he'd painted was grim.

The other boys agreed they'd seen it too. She'd heard talk in the market of the addictions some people fell prey to from the drug that was freely available in medicinal form but had a hallucinatory effect when smoked. She couldn't imagine why anyone would want to do that to themselves.

Shivering in the chill wind, she turned from the main road into a side road which led to an alleyway running through to Limehouse basin. In daylight it would be an easy walk, but now, in the deepest darkness Hettie could ever remember, it felt intimidating.

She looked this way and that but saw no one. No pallor faced Chinese sailors staggering about until they fell in a stupor to the ground. No opium dealers hanging around on doorsteps, in fact no one at all. She was beginning to think the boys' stories, each more fantastic than the last, were nothing more than juvenile fantasies invented to liven up a dull class at school, when she became aware of footsteps behind her. It's nothing, she thought, a dockworker or sailor on his way home most likely. She speeded her step all the same. The footsteps also quickened and drew closer.

The menacing presence behind her sent a chill down her spine. She chided herself for her foolishness and hurried on, her heart hammering and her pulse racing. Stupid, stupid, stupid, she thought. She could have come in the morning when it was light or anytime. Why had she decided to come tonight?

The footsteps came closer, heavy boots ringing on the cobbles. She turned to look behind her. The grotesque outline of a head loomed near. A powerful arm grabbed her around her waist and, before she could utter a sound a hand closed over her mouth. A foul odour filled her nostrils, rank breath burned her cheek and a face rough with stubble, pressed against her head.

She tried to wriggle from his grasp, kicking back with her heels but missing his shins. She clawed at the arm that held her head back against his shoulder, but he was stronger than her and held her firm, breathing in her ear.

"You ask too many questions," he said in a hoarse whisper. "You know what curiosity did to the cat."

The arm around her waist tightened. The hand over her mouth slid to her neck and, before she could scream, squeezed.

Chapter Twenty

She was about to pass out when someone shouted, "Hey, you!" Startled, her attacker loosened his grip. Fresh footsteps raced towards her. The man holding her spun round, gasped and threw her into the road before running off. Her head hit the cobbles. A wall of darkness engulfed her.

A noxious smell under her nose brought her sharply to sickening consciousness. She became aware of voices that must have been near but sounded distant. Her head pounded, she couldn't recall where she was. The air around her felt cold and damp. She shivered. When she opened her eyes a man's face peered down at her.

"She's coming round. Thank the lord for that," the woman standing next to him said, sending a waft of warm alcohol laden breath across Hettie's face. "We thought you was a gonner." She replaced the cap on her bottle of smelling salts.

"Are you all right?" the man said.

"Course she ain't all right," the woman said. "She could've been killed. Where's the rozzers when you need 'em. Never one about then is there?"

Hettie blanched at the mention of the police.

"Should I call a doctor, or take her to the hospital?" the man asked. "She looks very pale."

Hettie swallowed the sickness rising in her throat. The cold from the stone cobbles seeped into her body. She shivered. Every part of her ached. She wondered if she'd fainted but why would she? Then she recalled the man who'd attacked her. Terrified she glanced around but that made her head thump even more.

"I saw it all," the woman said. "You was attacked by ruffians. It ain't safe for decent people to be out on street. It's about time someone did somat about it."

Hettie saw how angry and shaken the woman appeared just from having witnessed the attack. She guessed she'd thought 'there by the grace of God', but Hettie knew it wasn't a random attack. Her assailant had made it clear why she had almost been strangled – abundantly clear.

"The hospital then?" the man said. "I'll send for a cab. We'll have you there in no time."

Hettie struggled to speak. "No. No really. I'm fine." Her voice came out as a hoarse whisper. Her throat ached from the effort.

"Well you don't look fine to me," the woman who had recovered enough to air her views said. "The gentleman's right. You should go to hospital. Get everything checked out. You could've broken somat. Best be on the safe side."

"No. Really. I just want to go home." Hettie swallowed, the taste of fear still sour in her mouth. Her insides had turned to jelly and tears were beginning to fill her eyes. If she didn't move soon she'd turn into a quivering heap and then they'd cart her off to hospital and Dorcas would kill her for sure. How could she have been so stupid?

"Nonsense," the woman said. "You've had a shock. There's no telling what after-effects you may have. I knows a man collapsed and died from shock an' it were a week after he'd been attacked. I think the gentleman's right. Hospital's best place for you."

Hettie took a deep breath. This was getting ridiculous. All she wanted to do was go home. "No, honestly. I'll live," she said. For now, she thought as she said the last words. Whoever she'd upset by asking questions meant business. She'd been saved this time but this was unlikely to be the end of it.

"Thanks to the pair of you I've suffered nothing worse than a muddy skirt and a few bruises," she said. That would be a bit more believable if I wasn't sitting on the pavement all of quiver, she thought. She struggled to get to her feet but her legs were shaky. The man caught her as she wobbled ready to fall and sat her gently back on the ground.

"If you really think you'll be better at home I'll fetch a cab and take you," he said. "But I insist on coming with you. I won't leave until I'm sure you're safe."

"That's very kind of you," Hettie said, relieved.

The woman, who told Hettie her name was Freda, stayed with her until the man returned with a hansom. Her constant complaints about it not being safe to walk the streets these days made Hettie feel even worse about taking the detour through Limehouse. By the time the man returned with the cab a fresh wave of relief washed over her.

Together the two Good Samaritans managed to get Hettie into the cab and the man climbed in beside her. She thanked Freda who said she'd be looking out for her again, gave her address to the cab driver, settled her thudding head against the cushioned backrest and closed her eyes. Now all she would have to do was explain to Dorcas how she came to be in Limehouse. She shuddered. She hoped that explanation could wait until morning.

The man's voice, coming over the rattle of the cab as it hurtled along, interrupted her thoughts. "My name's Tobias Ebbs. My friends call me Tibbs."

Hettie turned her head, causing it to throb even more. She'd fallen badly on her side when she was spun into the road and her arm and back ached. The jarring movement of the cab over the cobbles didn't help. She opened her eyes slowly. "How do you do?" she said. She took a breath. She really must try harder, after all if it hadn't been for him... She swallowed. "Hettie, Hettie Bundy," she managed to say. She looked down at her mud soaked clothing and decided not to offer him her hand which was black with dirt.

"I do hope you haven't broken anything," Tibbs said.

"I'm stronger than I look, I'll be all right once I get home. My mother will look after me."

He looked relieved.

"This is very kind of you. I'm profoundly grateful," Hettie said.

"It's nothing, I'm only glad I was there."

"Me too," Hettie said and sank back to rest her body against the padded upholstery. She wished her stomach would stop churning and she could drift off to sleep.

Dorcas had the front door open before Hettie could alight from the hansom. She smiled to herself. The arrival of a hansom cab in the street would be the talk of the neighbourhood for weeks. Tibbs helped her down and asked the driver to wait.

Dorcas stood wide-eyed in the doorway. "What on earth?" She stared at Hettie and the man with her, then wiping her hands on her apron ushered them into the house. "I don't know what you've been up to," she said to Hettie, "but whatever it is we don't need the whole street talking about it."

"Mother, this is Tobias Ebbs. He's been kind enough to bring me home. I think I need to sit down." She made her way into the front room and sank into a chair.

"Well... Look at the state of you an' all," Dorcas said, following her into the room. She glanced at Tibbs. "I'm sure it's very good of you to bring her home, sir. I can't think what she's been up to."

"Your daughter was attacked on her way home tonight," he said. "I'm afraid she's in a bad way. I should have taken her straight to the hospital but she insisted on coming here."

Dorcas stared at him. "Attacked? Hettie, what on earth happened? Where were you? Should I be sending for the police?"

Hettie sighed. "No really, Ma. Don't fuss. I'll be all right. Just a few bruises. Nothing worse than if I tripped and fell." Even as she said it she knew it wasn't true. It was a vicious attack and for a reason but she was too tired to think about that now. All that mattered was that she was home and safe. She'd think about everything else tomorrow, when she felt better.

"I'd say it was a lot worse than a fall," Tibbs said. "You were brutally attacked. Calling the police wouldn't be out of order. I could do it for you."

Hettie's eyes widened. Calling the police would entail a lot of explanations she wasn't prepared to give. Why she was in Limehouse, what had she hoped to find and worst of all, why she hadn't reported Annie as missing? Not that the police would do anything about it. A woman in her profession wouldn't be at the top of their list and they'd only believe like everyone else that she'd run off with some wealthy gent who could offer a better lifestyle than they could.

"There's no need for that," she said. "Freda was right. I was attacked by a ruffian who hoped to steal my purse and anything else he could get his hands on. If the police investigated every street attack they'd have their hands full in no time. No. I'd best put it down to experience and be more careful where I go walking at night."

"Well, if you're sure," Tibbs said. "I'll leave you to the care of your mother, but I do hope I may call again tomorrow to see how you are. I won't sleep tonight for worrying."

"Of course you may," Dorcas said. "We're both right glad of your help, aren't we Hettie? Don't worry, I'll look after her."

Dorcas saw Tibbs out. By the time she returned Hettie had removed her damaged bonnet and was taking off her cape.

"Here give 'em to me," Dorcas said. "I'll give 'em a good brushing when mud's dry. They'll be good as new. Pity I can't say same about you." She glared at Hettie.

Hettie's eyes filled with tears as the full realisation of what had happened and how much worse it would have been had Tibbs and Freda not been there dawned. She began to shake. It was all she could do not to vomit. Holding her hand over her mouth she rushed to the kitchen where she was violently sick.

Dorcas tutted and muttered about the gangs getting out of hand and how they should call the police.

"Not now, Ma," Hettie said. "All I want is to get to bed. We can talk about it in the morning." Dorcas huffed but made her a nightcap with cocoa and brandy.

All through the night Hettie tossed and turned as memories of the man's face pressed against hers filled her mind. She saw Freda and Tibbs but they appeared distant and remote. Time and again she woke up bathed in sweat. Then she remembered Annie. The more she thought about it the more convinced she became that the attack had something to do with Annie's disappearance and the more determined she became to get to the bottom of it.

The next morning, still groggy from the attack, she forced herself to get up and see to Billy. At least being with him brought some comfort. His warm as sunshine smile and chuckling laughter healed her quicker than any medicine.

She winced as she lifted him out of his cot and carried him down to the kitchen. Dorcas insisted she take some willow bark and rub arnica on her bruises. "So, you gonna tell us what 'appened last night then?" she said. "I weren't born yesterday and didn't come down in the last shower of rain neither. What was you doing going through Limehouse? Not your usual way 'ome is it?"

So Hettie told her what the lads at the school had said and how she wanted to see for herself. "I'm sure Annie's disappearance has something to do with the docks. That attack proves it."

Dorcas shook her head. "Proves you should keep well away and mind your own business more like. What was you thinking of? It's police who should be looking into the goings on around the docks. Not you."

After breakfast the morning air was still chilly. Hettie stayed in the warmth of the kitchen to play with Billy. When Tibbs knocked on the front door memories of the previous evening came rushing back.

Dorcas let him in. He wore a heavy topcoat over a navy three-piece suit. The high collar of his pristine white shirt was pressed into wings. A blue and green silk tie circled his neck. His blonde hair was smoothed back, his thin moustache neatly trimmed and he had a smile on his fine featured face. He held his crown derby hat in slender fingers. She realised for the first time how well dressed he was. He had an air of dignity and intelligence about him which surprised Hettie. She hadn't remembered that. She could understand Freda walking the streets of Limehouse in the evenings. The cut of her dress and her brightly coloured shawl made it clear how she earned her living, but it wasn't often you saw a gentleman dressed as well as Tibbs in those streets at night, not unless they were up to no good anyway.

Dorcas took his hat and coat and showed him into the parlour. "I'll make us some tea," she said. She picked Billy up and carried him into the kitchen with her.

Hettie indicated a chair for Tibbs but he remained standing. She smiled at him, noticing how blue his eyes appeared in the dim morning light. "It's still quite cold, should I light the fire?" she said.

"Please don't bother on my account," he said.

Hettie felt his gaze assessing her. She reddened. "Please take a seat," she said.

"After you," he said.

She sat. Her heart beat faster.

"How are you this morning?" he asked, his face creased with concern. "I hope you are at least a little better."

"I'm quite well, thank you," Hettie said. "Thanks to you and Freda."

Dorcas came in carrying a tray loaded with a pot of tea and three cups. She poured the tea handing them each a cup.

"Hm. Yes, Freda," Tibbs said taking the cup and saucer from Dorcas. "I quite understand why she was roaming around Limehouse last night, but it's an area well known to be – shall we say, not the most salubrious. I can't think why a respectable young lady such as yourself should be there. What on earth took you to Limehouse cut of all places?"

Dorcas stared at Hettie. "Go on – tell him," she said.

Hettie sighed. He'd saved her life but it didn't give him the right to patronise her. She pulled herself up to her full height. "I'd heard there were opium dens around there. I was curious. I wanted to see for myself," she said as though delving into the evil dens was the most natural thing in the world.

"Good heavens," Tibbs said, sitting back in shock. "That was beyond foolish. You know what curiosity did to the cat."

Cold sweat ran down Hettie's spine. The memory of the man's voice in her ear, his stubble grazing her cheeks and the smell of his breath filled her mind. His words struck her sharper than a blow. Her hands trembled. The teacup tipped from its saucer and fell, spilling hot tea down her skirt as it smashed on the floor.

Tibbs jumped up, his own cup wobbling on its saucer. "Oh lord," he said. "You're obviously not as well as I had hoped. It's not too late to call a doctor if you need one. I should have insisted you see one last night." His face was a picture of contrition.

Hettie tried valiantly to retain her composure. "No. It's all right. Just a fleeting fear of what may have befallen me had you not happened along." She brushed her skirt with her hand. "It's nothing. Really."

Dorcas tutted as she bent to retrieve the broken cup. "No surprise she's shaken," she said. "Who wouldn't be a nasty thing like that? Good job you were there and kind enough to help. We're both grateful."

He looked relieved but Hettie still wondered if his fortunate appearance had been as coincidental as it had seemed. She did her best to smile but her heart wasn't in it. She felt sick.

Chapter Twenty One

It took Hettie over a week to find the strength to go out at night again. She wasn't afraid of walking out in the daytime, taking Billy over the park or to the market where she bought groceries for Dorcas. She stopped to chat to people she knew, but at night the memory of the man's hand around her throat and his voice in her ear kept her indoors.

When she did at last decide to go back to the school and resume lessons for the boys the pastor sent her a message to come and see him. Had he heard something about Annie? He knew everyone in the area, if anyone could find out where she'd gone he could. Hettie dismissed the boys and hurried to his office.

Rushing along the familiar hallway a tide of memories engulfed her. Her mind spiralled back to the day Corry had his accident. When was that? It must have been over five years ago. Annie had been away for two and back for one. How things had changed since then. She sighed. She still thought of them as happier days, with Annie and Corry at home. They'd felt like a real family then. Now there was only her, Billy, Ma and the lodger.

She knocked on the door, waited for the call to enter and walked in. Pastor Brown sat behind his desk. A warm feeling of familiarity fell over her. At least here she felt safe.

"I've got some news," the pastor said indicating a chair for her to sit.

"News?" Hettie's heart leapt. "News about Annie? You've heard from her? Is she all right?" Please let it be good news she prayed.

The pastor smiled. "No," he said. "It's not about Annie, although I wish to God we had heard from her. No, it's about Corry. I've found Corry." He waited for Hettie's reaction.

It took several seconds before she realised who he was talking about. Her brow puckered. "Corry? Corry Flanagan?" She stared at the pastor and saw the truth of what he was saying dancing in his eyes.

He chuckled. "Yes. Corry Flanagan."

A chaos of conflicting emotions assailed her. Shock, disbelief, and pure joy swirled in her head. "How? When? Where?" She couldn't get the questions out fast enough.

"He's living in America and, from what my contact tells me, he's doing rather well."

Hettie couldn't believe what she was hearing. Questions chased through her brain. "Is he coming home?" Her voice squeaked. Her heart hammered. She tried to imagine what it would be like seeing him again. Had he changed? Would she even recognise him?

The pastor laughed. "So many questions," he said. "Let me tell you from the beginning." He steepled his fingers like a man about to tell his life story. Hettie grinned as the news that Corry was alive and well and the pastor knew where, slowly sank in. Warmth, like stepping out of shadow into sunlight, washed over her.

"A few months ago I dined with the Bishop and several friends. The Bishop knew I'd written to an archdeacon who'd travelled to America asking him to look out for Corry Flanagan." He smiled. "It was a long time ago and I thought he'd forgotten, but that night he'd invited a minister recently returned from America to dine with us. Well, this chap had met a young man from these parts over there and wondered whether I might know him. He gave me his name but it didn't sound familiar so I said I doubted he was one of my flock." He paused. "I pride myself on my memory for names," he said looking directly at Hettie.

"Yes," she said. "I'm sure you have an excellent memory. Please go on."

"Oh. Well, he was quite insistent. Said this fellow talked about the mudlarks and the river. He said he was sure I should know him as it's part of my parish. I asked him to describe this person, which he did, but it still didn't ring any bells. Then he said the man had mentioned that his sister used to sell cress." The pastor's hands flew apart. "Of course!" he said. "It must be Corry." He looked exceptionally pleased with himself. "I still wasn't sure so I suggested I write to this man and ask him if he was indeed Corry Flanagan and if so..."

"And was he?" Hettie asked her impatience at melting point. "What did he say?"

The pastor grinned and placed his hands flat on the table as if bracing himself. "To cut a long story short – yes. He sent word back that he was Corry and asked about you and Annie and even Dorcas. I wrote again and explained about the misunderstanding that sent him away and assured him that if he'd consider returning home, he'd be welcomed with open arms." His eyes glinted with mirth. "I hope I did right."

Hettie could have kissed him. She drew in a sharp breath and let it out slowly to regain her composure. She couldn't help grinning. "Of course you did right," she said.

She sat back in her chair relief flooding over her. Corry was safe. He was as distant as the moon but at least he was alive and well which was more than she could be certain about with Annie. At that thought her swell of relief evaporated like water on a hot stove. Corry didn't know about Annie going to Paris, the baby or her connection to Sylvia de Vine and her nefarious trade. Now she'd disappeared and Corry wouldn't even know about that. A heavy stone of dread formed in her stomach. What use was it knowing where Corry was when he was so far away as to be unreachable? America was an ocean away and the pastor hadn't even said if he was coming home. "So is Corry's coming home? Has he said?" Her heart pounded. If only... she thought.

"I had another letter a week ago," the pastor said, "but you were in no condition to be worried so I left it until you recovered. He said he was catching a steamship so he should arrive in

Liverpool any day now. He'll be home in less than a week."

Hettie's heart swelled fit to burst. At least he'd care about Annie no matter what she'd done or what sort of trouble she'd got herself into. "I'd best get home and get a room ready for him then," she said rising from her chair. "Although I don't know what Ma will say." She chuckled. What Ma would say was the least of her worries.

She couldn't wait to tell Dorcas the good news. Her joy was short lived.

"I suppose he'll be wanting to stay rent free an' all?" Dorcas said when Hettie told her. "That's all we need another mouth to feed with nowt coming in."

Hettie sighed. It was true things had become tight without Annie's money for Billy. Dorcas had let Sarah go and Hettie now had to cover all the cooking and cleaning as well as looking after Billy. But she wasn't about to let Ma put a damper on Corry's return. She took a breath. "Pastor Brown says he's done well for himself," she said. "Might be best to wait and see before we rush to judgement."

Just as Hettie thought, the mention of Pastor Brown's part in Corry's return deflated Dorcas. "Hmmph. Let's hope he's right," she said. "Pastor Brown always did have a soft spot for Corry."

Then Hettie had another thought. The only room available was Corry's old one, recently vacated at the back of the house, with hardly space for anything but the bed. "He can have my room," she said. "I'll move me and Billy."

Dorcas huffed. "Don't go making sacrifices for 'im before he arrives," she said. "He mightn't be staying long."

"What do you mean not staying long? Surely..." But Dorcas was right. Corry may be coming home but how long he'd stay was a different matter.

"Small room'll do for 'im for a start," Dorcas said and Hettie had to reluctantly accept her decision.

Corry was coming home. Hettie gave the room a good clean and made up the bed with the best sheets she could find. She took Billy to Covent Garden and bought a posy of flowers to put in a vase on the window ledge. There were hooks on the wall where Corry could hang his clothes and a small bookcase for personal items. She glanced around the room pleased with her efforts. It was cramped, but at least the bed was comfortable. Next, while Billy slept, she pulled out Annie's basket. There would be things in there that would bring back memories of Corry's childhood and she wanted to go through them with him when he arrived.

Although the weather was brightening it was still cold enough in the evenings for the fires to be lit. Hettie was in the middle of cleaning out the grates and re-laying them in the lodger's room when she heard a knock on the front door. Dorcas had taken Billy with her to the market to buy him some shoes so Hettie ran her hands down her apron and rushed to the door. She gasped when she saw the pastor standing there, dressed in his topcoat and hat with Jack's hackney in the road behind him.

"I had a telegram from Corry this morning," he said, grinning. "He's getting the train from Liverpool. He'll be here this afternoon. Do you want to come with me to the station to meet him?"

Despite wearing her oldest skirt and not having combed her hair, Hettie whipped off her apron ready to go. She grabbed her shawl. "Just let me leave a note for Ma," she said. Her hands trembled as she wrote. Suddenly it seemed so real. Corry coming home. Before now she'd hardly believed it, but the thought of seeing him in a few hours...

As she tied the strings of her bonnet under her chin she remembered the last time they'd had a telegram. It was to tell them Annie was coming home. Now Corry was coming home but Annie had gone. What would Corry think? Would he blame Hettie?

Carriages, horse-drawn omnibuses, drays, wagons and carts packed the road to the station. They were forced to a standstill so often Hettie despaired of ever getting there. When they eventually arrived vehicles clustered around the building, their horses champing at bits. Jack pulled over to the side of the road for Hettie and the pastor to alight.

Inside the station impatient travellers milled around, pushing their way toward to the platforms. A hubbub of noisy confusion surrounded them as they made their way to where the trains came in. A porter trundled past, his wooden trolley piled high with leather trunks. A loud whistle, a blast of steam, a maze of platforms and frenetic chaos reigned beneath the high span of the railway shed.

Hettie scanned the crowds, standing on tiptoe to see over the heads of the arriving passengers. An emotional turmoil of anxiety and excitement raged inside her at the thought of seeing Corry again. Had he changed, or was he just as she remembered?

The pastor also looked about him. Hettie was the first to see him. She called out and waved her hands in the air. He was taller than she remembered and broader in the shoulder. He raised his wide brimmed Stetson when he saw her. A curl of black hair fell over his forehead. Her heart beat faster than humming birds' wings as he rushed towards her.

He dropped the case he was carrying and hugged her. Suddenly, in his arms all her worries faded away. He held her close for what felt like minutes, but was probably only seconds. Then he held her at arms' length. Her face reddened as his gaze washed over her. Golden glints of warm appreciation danced in his soft brown eyes and his lips stretched into a most disarming smile.

"Hettie," he said. "It's good to see you. I can't tell you how often I've thought about you." Hettie's blush deepened. He had a quiet energy and emotional intensity about him. Resolution and courage shone in his face. She'd never seen him looking so handsome.

He glanced around. The pastor shook his hand. "Welcome home, son," he said.

Corry glanced around again. "Where's Annie? Didn't you tell her I was coming? I expected her to be here."

The anxiety twisting Hettie's stomach increased. "Come back to the house," she said. She looked at the case he'd dropped. "Where's the rest of your luggage? Is it coming on later?"

Corry chuckled. "This is my luggage," he said picking up the case. "It's all I'll need for a short stay."

Hettie's heart dropped to her boots. She'd convinced herself that he was coming home for good.

"Will Annie be at home? I can't wait to see her and tell her all about America."

Hettie's hopes dived.

"We'd better get along," the pastor said. "Jack's waiting and we don't want to waste any more of his time."

Soon they were rattling over the cobbles to Wapping. In the carriage Hettie couldn't help staring at Corry. She noticed how well he looked. His unbuttoned top coat, perfect for the time of year, parted to show a well fitting three-piece suit, the jacket cut short in the latest fashion. With shiny brown leather boots he looked every inch the successful businessman. He no longer limped either, Hettie noticed. When Pastor Brown said he was doing well Hettie had never imagined him as anything other than the gangling, frightened youth he was when he left. He was nineteen then. Now he'd be in his twenties, a full grown man. Something inside her thrilled at the notion.

Dorcas greeted them at the door when they arrived at the house. She held Billy in her arms. "Corry Flanagan," she said. "As I live and breathe. Well, you'd better come in and meet your nephew, Billy Flanagan."

Part Two
Corry

Chapter Twenty Two

Corry stared at Billy. Nephew? Billy Flanagan? What on earth was Dorcas talking about? Then realisation dawned. His face softened. "Annie's child?" he said, eyebrows raised.

Dorcas took a breath.

"I'll take him," Hettie said, stepping forward before Dorcas could speak. "She left him in my care."

Corry noticed how Billy's face lit up and he chuckled as Hettie took him.

"Here, let me," he said. He put his hat on the table, his case on the floor and held out his arms. "My nephew, ay? Must have been away longer than I thought." He grinned at the child in his arms. "Happy little blighter isn't he?"

He turned to Hettie. "So, where's Annie?"

"I'll get us some tea," Dorcas said. "Unless you'd like something stronger, Pastor?"

"Tea will be fine," Pastor Brown said. "I'm sure we're all gasping."

Dorcas tutted as she left the room.

"After you left, Annie went to Paris to dance at the Folies-Bergère," Hettie said. "When she returned she brought Billy with her. I don't know more than that, except she loves him beyond measure and would never have left him if she didn't have to." Corry saw tears glistening in her eyes. "She went to live with a society hostess... lady... person... in Belgravia."

He took a breath. So, wild, head-strong, obstinate Annie had had a child and then run off and left him with Hettie. How typical, he thought. Then the words – society hostess, living in Belgravia – began to sink in. Anger churned in his stomach. She'd gone upmarket and left her friend and her offspring behind. He bit his lip. He looked at Billy. "So, your ma's on the game and no daddy to speak of? Poor little chap." Furious with Annie he turned to Hettie. "Left you to clear up her mess as usual, did she?"

Hettie's eyes blazed. "If you mean to look after Billy, yes. And I was happy to do it. She told me she was hoping to find his father. They met in Paris and Annie thought the house in Belgravia gave her the best chance of finding him again."

Trust Hettie to defend her, Corry thought. But she couldn't have made it plainer. Annie was working as a high-class tart and the reason she gave was highly dubious. Corry put Billy on the floor to play with a pile of bricks at his feet. "Is that where I may find her?"

Hettie looked aghast, as though she thought he might go there to drag her out and bring her home. "No," she said. "I don't know where she is. She's disappeared."

"Run off you mean?" Corry said. "Run off to a better life leaving her mistakes behind. How like Annie." He shook his head.

"No," Hettie said. "Why does everyone judge Annie so harshly? It isn't her fault men lust after her and it doesn't make her a bad person. I don't believe she's gone of her own accord. I've been to the house in Belgravia. She left all her dresses and jewellery behind. If she'd left for a better life she'd have taken them with her."

Corry frowned. Upsetting Hettie was the last thing he wanted to do. "What do you think has happened to her?"

"I wish I knew," Hettie said, looking more distressed than ever.

Pastor Brown stepped towards her and put his arm around her shoulders. "Hettie's been making enquiries," he said. "No one could have done more. And I agree with her. Annie may have been a bit wild but she loved that child and wouldn't have left him voluntarily."

Dorcas returned with the tea and handed a cup to the pastor. "I've been to the police," he said, "but as Annie is an adult and free to go where she pleases, failing the finding of a body they have no interest in her whereabouts. As for the child, as long as he's in Hettie's care they'll take no action."

Dorcas handed Corry a cup of tea and glanced at his case. "How long are you planning on staying?" she asked. "Only I've lodger to think about and we're a bit cramped."

Corry hadn't expected much of a welcome from Dorcas but it was worse than he'd feared. "Lodger?"

"Yes," Hettie said. "We've a gentlemen in the best room. I've made up a bed for you in your old room." She swallowed. "I hope you'll be comfortable."

Corry immediately grasped the situation. Dorcas hadn't changed and Hettie felt bad about such a poor reception for someone who'd been away so long and was once part of the family. She was still fighting Annie's battles. Now she'd fight his as well. He immediately felt sorry. When he found Annie he'd make sure to let her know how he felt about her treatment of Hettie.

"I'm sure I'll do well enough," he said. "I'll pay the going rate as long as I'm here and I'll make up anything Annie owes. I don't suppose she expected you to have Billy for nothing."

"It's six months' rent she's owing, including the extra for looking after Billy," Dorcas said. "She's lucky we've managed to keep him, what with his food, clothes, and that. Anyone else'd have put 'im in the workhouse."

Hettie paled. Corry's insides twisted with rage. His jaw clenched. "Like I said, I'll make up anything she owes."

Pastor Brown stepped in. "Now, Mrs Bundy, I'm sure Corry appreciates all you've done, you being a Christian woman with high morals and a charitable nature. No one could have done more. We're all thankful for your generosity, aren't we, Corry?" he said.

Corry nodded silently. Inside he was seething. Some 'welcome home' this was.

"So," Dorcas said, sitting down with her tea. "Pastor says you're doing well in America. You going to tell us all about it or are we to sit here all night discussing the comings and goings of your wayward sister?"

Corry's eyes narrowed. Despite Hettie's obvious protestations, Dorcas still hadn't changed her opinion of Annie. He let it pass. His lips curved into a smile; a smile that didn't reach his eyes.

"Yes, Corry," the pastor said. "Tell us all about America. You've done well by all accounts."

Corry relaxed and the tension eased. There'd be plenty of time to talk about Annie. "Yes, I've done well," he said. "There's opportunities for those prepared to work hard. It wasn't always easy. When I arrived I struggled. I did all sorts of jobs, mostly labouring. Moved around a lot too, at first." He put his cup on the table and leaned forward. "New York's a great city and growing fast. There are amazing buildings, theatres, shops... Eventually I got a job looking after the horses for a chap named Silas Granby who owns a timber mill outside of town. We got on well. There's a huge demand for timber, what with the new buildings going up everywhere. I found places near the river, knew we could transport timber that way and saved him a lot of money. I went on to Boston and helped set up a mill near there. He made me a partner in his business. I'll be talking to people here to expand our exports." He grinned. "Not much else to tell."

"You always did have a good brain," the pastor said, his face glowing with pride. He stood up and patted Corry on the shoulder.

Hettie grimaced. "I'm sure there's more to it than that," she said. "It can't have been as easy as you make it sound."

Corry grinned. Of course Hettie was right. "Well, perhaps not," he said. "But I don't want to bore you with the details."

"I have to be off now and about my duties," the pastor said. "But I hope we can get together again soon and have a proper chat."

"You can depend on it, Pastor," Corry said.

Dorcas showed the pastor out.

Corry gazed at Billy and then at Hettie. "I'm really sorry I left the way I did," he said. "Perhaps if I'd stayed…"

"If you'd stayed things wouldn't have been any different. Annie always had a mind of her own. Can't blame her for that. Now, come on, I'll show you to your room."

"I think I can find me own way, Hettie," he said. "Then you can tell me all about Annie."

It was several hours before Corry could sit down to dinner with Hettie and Dorcas. Hettie had to put Billy to bed and help make dinner for the lodger. After the meal was eaten and the plates cleared away he said, "I'd like to go out and see the old place again." He glanced at Hettie. "Perhaps you can show me around."

Dorcas huffed, but Hettie smiled. "I'd love to," she said, her eyes lit with pleasure. "If Ma'll watch out for Billy."

Corry looked at Dorcas. She sighed and nodded. "Don't keep her out all night," she said. "Young un wakes early and she's a day's work to do tomorrow."

He watched Hettie put on her bonnet and cape. He was surprised how much he was looking forward to walking out with Hettie. It would be just like the old days before he left; only now they were both older and wiser.

Outside light drizzle dampened the air and glistened on the cobbles. Corry gazed up at the sky and grinned. "Dark, damp, drizzly London," he said. "It's what I missed most."

Walking down the familiar road his heart swelled. It was early evening and several children played in the gathering gloom. Gas lights hardly lit the narrow street, the buildings either side grimy with soot and dirt. The litter-strewn road reeked of horse dung and rotting vegetables. As they neared the docks the sky darkened. How must Hettie feel, walking these damp dark streets at night to go to and from the pastor's school? He had a sudden desire to protect her but knew it was stupid. She was far more determined and resilient than most people realised.

"I expect this is a come-down after America," she said.

Corry smiled. "Not especially. True, the buildings are newer and more impressive and in the city the roads are wider. There seems to be more space – but I did get homesick for dark alleyways, damp foggy nights, cold drizzly air and the muddy river with its ever changing tides."

They walked on stopping now and then to watch the procession of boats making their way to the docks. Ferries and barges passed, the light from their lamps dancing on the slate water. The air smelled of rotten fish and salt. Corry breathed it in. It was the smell of home. A smell you'd not get anywhere else on earth. He'd missed the sounds and smell of the river.

"It looks smaller than I remember," he said staring out at the wide expanse of water. "You forget how busy the river is." He looked at Hettie. "And the kindness of the people you've left behind."

A kaleidoscope of memories spun through Corry's brain as they walked, stopping at places he knew so well: the stone stairs, the wharves and warehouses where the boats used to unload, the quays, piers and jetties and the mudflats. Corry gazed out over the water where he spent his childhood delving in the sludge for copper nails and bits of wood, iron and coal. At the time they thought they were getting something for nothing – how wrong they were. The price turned out to be a lot higher than many of them suspected.

While they were watching a young lad, aged about ten, walked up the steps carrying his bucket of 'finds'. Barefoot, with his short trousers rolled up and dark curly hair falling over his grubby face he reminded Corry of himself at that age.

"Evening, Miss," the lad said to Hettie, tipping his cap.

"Good evening, Mugger," Hettie said, smiling. "Mugger is one of my occasional students. I keep telling him he'd do better if he came to school more often."

"Aw, Miss!"

"Corry used to be a mudlark just like you," she said to Mugger.

Mugger looked Corry over, obviously impressed with what he saw.

"Found anything useful?" Corry said peering into Mugger's bucket. He picked out a brass coat-hook covered in mud. "This looks like something."

"Two shillings," Mugger said. It was far more than it was worth.

"One," Corry said, digging a shilling out of his pocket and holding it in the palm of his hand.

Mugger nodded and took it.

Corry wrapped the brass hook in a handkerchief and put it in his pocket. It would serve as a reminder of where he had come from and how far he had travelled.

They walked on. "Not many mudlarks out these days," Corry said, watching two boys delving in the mud. "I guess death or the workhouse have taken the others."

"No," Hettie said. "They've opened a night shelter for the boys in Limehouse. A lot of them go there. And there's a home for waifs and strays where they teach them skills and a trade."

"Good," Corry said. "Mudlarking's not much of a life." They continued walking by the river and Corry resolved to keep an eye out for Mugger and the other boys. He wished there was something he could do for them.

"Do the girls still sell cress on the streets?"

Hettie smiled. "Hackney beds have gone," she said. "Gone to make way for the railway and houses for the workers. Eliza still has her stall in the Garden, but all the cress comes up by rail."

They stopped again to watch the boats. "There are a lot more pleasure steamers now and new docks along the river too," Hettie said.

Eventually they found a coffee shop, its windows misted from the warmth inside. Corry opened the door and showed Hettie in. Sudden warmth enveloped them.

Hettie found seats while Corry got them each a hot drink. He had coffee but Hettie chose hot chocolate. Once they were settled he said, "Now, tell me about Annie."

He noticed her reluctance and waited. Hettie took a deep breath. Even in the dim light of the café he saw her face turning pink. Any other time he'd have thought it most fetching.

"After you left she stayed on at the music hall for a short while, then a group of them went to Paris to dance at the Folies-Bergère." Hettie paused. "She said it was a great opportunity." Doubt shadowed her eyes.

"Opportunity for what?" he said.

Hettie shrugged and went on. "We didn't hear from her again until she telegraphed to say she was coming home. Then she arrived with Billy."

"And?"

"It was fine at first, but she couldn't afford not to work so I started looking after him in the evenings while she went to work back at the theatre." She glanced up and a warm smile spread across her face. "It was no trouble, he's good as gold. Anyway," her face fell. "One day she tells me she's had this offer to go and live in that place in Belgravia." Hettie paled but pressed on. "She said it was where she hoped to find his father."

"In a whorehouse? Is that where she met him in Paris?"

Hettie looked aghast. "No, I don't believe so. I think he was a gentleman admirer. One of many," she said casting her gaze down. She took a sip of hot chocolate, then glanced up. "I met a woman who'd known her in Paris. She told me."

Corry still couldn't find it in his heart to forgive Annie for leaving her child, apparently to pursue a better lifestyle. "So she upped and left the baby with you and you haven't heard from her since?"

"No. It wasn't like that. It was fine at first, she paid us well and visited regularly. I swear she'd have done anything for Billy. She would never have left him if she'd had a choice."

"But she did leave him..." Corry saw the anxiety in Hettie's face. She was pleading with him to believe her. He was Annie's brother. If he didn't believe in her..."So, what do you think has happened to her?"

Hettie stared at him. "I think she's been taken by the gangs around the docks," she said. "I can think of no other explanation."

Corry frowned. "You mean for the white slave trade?" It was something he'd heard about but believed to be more rumour and legend than reality, but now...

Tears again filled Hettie's eyes. Corry handed her his newly laundered handkerchief.

He shook his head. "I do so want to believe you, Hettie, but how can you be sure?"

Anger flushed Hettie's face. "Because I know Annie," she said as a crimson glow climbed up from her neck to colour her cheeks. "And you know her too, Corry, in your heart." She glared at him daring him to deny it. "She stood up for you when you was taken in, she worked to keep Ma off your back when you were ill and she wouldn't turn her back on Billy any more than you'd turn your back on someone you loved." She lowered her voice. "She loved that boy more than I've ever known anyone love a child. She wouldn't leave him, she just wouldn't."

Corry put his hand over Hettie's. A lump of misery formed in his chest. "I believe you Hettie and I'm sorry. Sorry I wasn't here to help Annie when she needed it. If anyone's to blame it's me for leaving like I did." He lowered his gaze. "I was a stupid, hot-headed, arrogant fool," he said. "Perhaps you were right, perhaps Annie wouldn't have done anything like that then... but now..." Anguish churned inside him. Memories of that night filtered through his mind...

It had been early evening, the stalls were filling up with lads from the market and the docks come to see the show. Upstairs in the balcony and the boxes the better off were filling the seats. Corry pushed his way through to the front. He'd never forget the first time he saw Annie on stage. She was in the chorus line kicking up her pink-silk-stockinged legs and smiling like a demented chicken. The chorus line moved across the stage then into a circle going round in an orgy of flesh and frilly petticoats held aloft. Then they formed a line across the stage, turned and bent over. A man sitting next to Corry yelled, "Give us a flash, love." Corry's eyes nearly popped out of his head.

As the dancers came off stage he made his way through to the offices and dining rooms at the back. It was there he saw the manager talking to a chap in a black frock coat with a white shirt and red cravat neatly tied to cascade from his throat. He overheard the conversation and, when Annie was mentioned and he saw money changing hands, he saw red. The anger that churned inside him then was starting to churn inside him now. Only now it was directed at Annie.

Hettie smiled. "You weren't to know and the important thing is that you believe me now."

He smiled. "You're right as usual, Hettie. I don't know what I'd do without you, or what Annie would have done either." He squeezed her hand. "You've been a good friend, Hettie, one of the best."

Fighting to regain his composure he picked up his coffee cup and took a sip. "So, what do we need to do to find Annie?"

Chapter Twenty Three

By the time they finished their drinks Hettie had given him details of all she'd found out. She told him about her visit to the house in Belgravia, her meeting with Chloe and learning of the church in Bromley by Bow.

"Why would she go there?" Corry asked, puzzled.

"Apparently the curate there, Reverend Smythe, knew her in Paris."

"Oh."

Then she told him about finding Annie's journal.

"I'd like to see that," he said.

"Well, I needed Chloe to decipher it for me," Hettie said. "The entries were all initials, but Chloe thinks one is Lord Crenshaw and another a shipping merchant. A third is a Justice of the Peace."

Corry frowned. It was obvious that her clients were men of influence. Annie had a look that turned men soft and stupid, but he doubted they'd have anything to do with her disappearance. If any of them had made her an offer she couldn't refuse, she'd still send money for Billy's keep. In fact she'd probably send a lot more. "What would they have to do with her disappearance?" he asked.

Hettie shrugged. "I don't know." She frowned. "For all my efforts I have to admit I know precious little."

"I'd like to meet Chloe myself and ask her a few questions."

"Well, I suppose you could always pretend to be a client," Hettie said.

Corry laughed. "What a preposterous idea. She'd be out of my league and price range no doubt." He shook his head. "Anyway, even if I could afford it it's not something I'd want to spend good money on."

Hettie looked relieved. "I'll send her a note asking her to meet with us," she said. "She's usually free on Sundays."

"Good."

Hettie suddenly became serious. "I asked the boys at the school about the goings on along the river," she said. "They spend time in and around the docks. You'd be surprised at the things they told me."

"I doubt that," Corry said. "Remember, I was one of them once."

Hettie went on. "They mentioned the smuggling then they said there were opium dens in Limehouse. I only half-believed them, so I went to see for myself."

Corry stared. "You did what?"

"Yes, I know it was foolish beyond measure, and so it proved. I was attacked by a man intent on strangling me. He said I asked too many questions. If it hadn't been for..."

"Attacked!" Corry almost jumped out of his chair. "Hettie, you should have said. This is terrible. You shouldn't be putting yourself in danger. Next time you go asking questions I'll go with you. I insist."

"Yes, but don't you see? What the man said links the attack to my search for Annie. There's no other explanation."

No, Corry didn't see. All he saw was Hettie, dear, sweet, innocent Hettie, being attacked in the street. It was beyond reason. Even he knew those streets were havens for brigands and gangs at night. "Honestly Hettie, you should have had more sense."

She sighed. "I see that now. But what I'm trying to say is that the man specifically targeted me. He followed me and made it clear that I should stop asking questions. He said something about what curiosity did to the cat." She stared at Corry. "The man who came to my rescue and insisted on seeing me safely home, said exactly the same thing."

Corry watched the blood drain from her face. Her chin quivered. She put her hand to her mouth.

It was as though speaking about that terrible night had brought it all back in clear focus and she suddenly realised the immensity of the danger she was in.

Corry's stomach knotted. "Hettie, what is it? You look like you've seen a ghost."

Hettie took a breath. "The man who saved me. His name was Tibbs. He's in it. I'm sure he is."

Corry stood up. "Come on. I'm taking you home. This has all been too much for you."

Hettie didn't argue.

Once out in the street, away from the muggy confines of the café, Corry took a breath. The drizzle had stopped and a light breeze blew in from the river. The cool night air refreshed him. If Hettie was right, Annie was in a great deal more danger than either of them supposed. Corry offered his arm. Hettie linked hers through it, leaning slightly against him. Under different circumstances this would be one of the happiest days of his life, he thought.

As they walked Corry tried to take her mind of the attack. He talked about America and feeling homesick. "That harmonica was a life saver," he said. "I'd play the old music hall songs in the bars and on the streets for nickels and dimes, until the police moved me on." He chuckled. "Then on long lonely nights I'd play the sad songs and memories filled my head." He turned to look at Hettie. "I often thought of you and Annie and the watercress. At one time I thought of starting a watercress farm but the water wasn't clean enough to grow it." He smiled. "I tried all sorts of things to survive, Hettie. But I always thought I'd come home to find you."

The next morning Corry rose early. He went to help Dorcas. The kitchen was warm and tidy, just as he'd expected. A kettle bubbled away on the hob. Dorcas had laid out slices of buttered bread and three mugs stood ready on the scrubbed oak table, next to the cosy topped teapot.

When Hettie came down with Billy he took him from her. "Here, let me," he said. "Come on little fella, see what Uncle Corry has for you." He gave Billy a wooden horse and cart.

"Oh, that's lovely," Hettie said. "Surely you didn't bring it with you?"

"Sure did," Corry said. "Carved it myself, just another of my sidelines."

"Sidelines?"

"Yes, wood carving. I started with animals, horses mostly. Sold a few to the lads at the wood yard for their kids. Then made a few boxes like the one I made for Annie, remember? They bought them for their wives' keepsakes. All I needed was off-cuts of wood and spare bits of board from the yard. The governor let me have them for nothing." He grinned. "I even made him a chess set for Christmas one year."

Hettie looked impressed.

After breakfast he played with Billy until Hettie finished clearing away the plates then they took him with them upstairs to Hettie's room. Hettie pulled out Annie's box. "Annie left this with me when she went to Paris," she said. "She was going to send for it when she got settled but she never did."

Corry looked at the box. It was the one he'd kept for Annie when their mother died. He opened it. Seeing Annie's things spread out in front of him made his stomach crunch. A swell of emotion washed over him, memories of their mother, Annie as a baby, and moving in with Dorcas flooded his mind.

He picked up his mother's old album. Inside were pictures of him and Annie growing up. He turned the pages slowly. Conflicting emotions battled inside him as he studied each one. A heavy stone of sadness formed at thoughts of what might have been. He put the album back and lifted out the gold cross on a chain.

"I remember my mother wearing this," he said. "It meant a great deal to her."

Hettie smiled. "Annie wore it when we were selling the cress," she said. "She left it when she started at the music hall. Said it didn't go with her costume."

Corry pulled a face. "Not much of a costume as I recall," he said. "That's when Annie started to change isn't it? When she gave up the cress and went on the stage." He sighed and put the cross back in the basket. He riffled through the various papers and bits of jewellery his mother had left. "Not much to show for a life is it?" he said.

Hettie bit her lip. Clearly she'd been thinking the same.

Next Hettie showed him the things Annie brought back from France. He fingered the clothes. "Annie brought these back from Paris?" he asked.

"Yes, she was there for nearly two years."

Corry nodded. He picked up the pictures, shuffling through them. Corry gazed long and hard at the programme from the Folies-Bergère trying to see his sister in place of the garishly displayed dancer depicted there. He opened the programme, glanced through it and turned it over before putting it back in the box with a sigh. Annie had been born to shine and the Folies-Bergère looked just right place for her extravagant, exhibitionistic nature.

The notebook was next. He flicked through the pages but there were only names of places to visit in Paris, recipes and shopping lists.

"So, apart from the letters and some papers in French there is nothing?" he said.

Hettie pulled out another box from under her bed. "These are the things from her box in Belgravia," she said, showing him the jewellery and the journal.

She lifted the emerald pendant, the locket and the ring to show Corry. "She was keeping these for Billy," she said. "I gather from her friend in Paris that she sold a lot of her jewellery to survive. The fact that she kept these must mean something."

He took the pendant. It looked genuine and expensive. Sadness squeezed his heart. Eventually he said, "So Annie's dream of fame and fortune never materialised? She had a tough time in Paris?"

"If what her friend Veronique tells me is true, and I've no reason to doubt it. Having a child without a husband is as bad in France as it is here."

Corry nodded. "So Billy's father?"

Hettie shrugged. "She never spoke of him, only to say they were very much in love." She handed him Annie's locket.

He opened it. "Annie and her lover?" he asked.

Hettie nodded. "I think that may be him," she said.

Corry put the locket down and picked up the journal. He flicked through it. "It is as you say. Only initials with dates for parties, events and functions. I'll take it and have a closer look, but at first glance…"

He picked out all the papers, notebook, letters and journal. "I'd like to have a closer look at these," he said. "I know a lawyer in London we do business with. He may be able to make sense of them." He smiled at Hettie. "You've done really well working on your own. It can't have been easy."

"It wasn't," Hettie said. Corry realised that had she been a man more doors would have been open to her and she'd have been taken a lot more seriously.

That evening Hettie persuaded him to talk to the boys at the pastor's school.

"After all, you were one of them once," she said.

So, to please Hettie, he agreed. He didn't know what to expect. Had anything changed since he'd been away? What were the boys like? It felt as though he'd been away forever, but when he walked into the classroom, it all came rushing back: the bare walls, the rickety desks and walking barefoot on the rough wood floor. He recalled the days he'd come to school straight from the river, still caked in mud and soaked through. Before lessons the pastor's housekeeper, Mrs Mackie, would let him and the other boys dry themselves in the kitchen. Then she'd dish out bowls of soup or stew and chunks of bread. They'd sit and eat while the pastor read them stories from the Bible. It all seemed so long ago now. Still, he hadn't forgotten the other bits either: Gander waiting outside until the boys came out of class, the fights and how they had to join in the thieving or it'd be the worse for them.

Gander ruled the streets, there was no doubt about that. Many of the boys lived in fear of him, but others could see no way of survival. Everything they stole had to be handed over to Gander in exchange for a few pennies, a hot pie, or sometimes nothing, just the avoidance of a thick ear. If anyone was caught they kept their mouths shut. That was the deal, everyone knew that.

He gazed at the boys in the class. All about ten they were dressed in shabby jackets and ragged trousers, scuffed shoes and threadbare caps. They looked a motley crew. Their clothes mirrored the misery of their lives, but he couldn't miss the enthusiasm in their bright little faces. His heart went out to these lads, now sitting where he had once sat, setting out on a journey that may or may not end happily. How many of them had fallen under Gander's spell? Was he still the Gangmaster, or had he moved on to bigger things?

He sighed and sat while Hettie called the class to attention and told them how he'd been one of them and had just returned from America having made his fortune. He shuffled his feet at that bit, feeling uncomfortable, but the pride in her voice made his heart beat faster.

Once Hettie had introduced him he told the boys about the opportunities waiting for enterprising lads like them on the other side of the ocean. "There they judge you by what you do, not by who your father was," he said. "Anyone willing to work hard can get on."

He told them about finding a job in a wood yard, looking after the horses and learning about the different properties of wood: which made the best kindling, which made the best furniture and which you should use for house building. He told them about playing his harmonica, selling his wood carvings and finally going out to find new customers for the wood and then being made a partner in the mill. "It's what you learn here that's important," he said. "Having an education will help you get good jobs so you don't have to work in the factories or on the streets. Schooling teaches more than reading, writing and counting. It teaches discipline and self-respect, essential to become the men you have it in you to be. The more you embrace learning the better men you will become. Listen to Pastor Brown and your teachers." He turned to smile at Hettie. "Especially Miss Bundy here. What they teach you will stand you in good stead for the future."

By the end of his talk every boy in the class wanted to go to America.

"If you do, come and see me," he said. "I'll give you a job and a good start." He chuckled and glanced at Hettie. A look of disappointment flitted across her face. Was it at the reminder of the temporary nature of his visit? Or had he misread it? Was it because that was how he felt? When he left America he hadn't expected to be so drawn to his home or the people in it, but being here tonight brought back memories of his own childhood and the gratitude he owed Pastor Brown, Dorcas and Hettie. Thanks to them things hadn't been nearly as bad as they might have been. Times were hard but at least they'd never gone hungry – not like some.

At the end of the talk he asked if the boys had any questions. A hand shot up.

"Yes," Corry said.

"Is Sir sweet on Miss Bundy?" the boy asked a picture of wide-eyed innocence.

Hettie jumped to her feet. "That's enough, Class," she said. "Let's thank Mr Flanagan for giving up his valuable time to come and speak to us." She started clapping. So did the class, although it wasn't quite loud enough to drown out the boy's disgruntled whine. "He didn't answer my question," he said.

Chapter Twenty Four

The next morning Corry went to see Pastor Brown. He smiled as he glanced around the pastor's study. It hadn't changed, except perhaps the carpet was a little more threadbare and there were more books crammed into the bookcase behind the pastor's desk. Corry's mind filled with happy memories of time spent in this room. The pastor allowed him and some of the other brighter boys to borrow books and sit in the quietness of the room to study. Corry realised how much he owed to this kind, gentle man. Without him his life may have taken a very different turn.

A fire was laid in the grate but not lit. Pastor Brown sat behind the desk. He rose as Corry entered. "Corry, my lad. It's good to see you looking so well." He pulled a chair up in front of the fire place opposite a large overstuffed armchair already placed there. "Refreshment?" he said. "Coffee perhaps?"

Corry grinned. He was being treated royally. "Coffee would be lovely," he said.

Pastor Brown rang a small silver bell on a side table and within a few minutes Mrs Mackie appeared. "Coffee for our young guest and one for me also, please Mrs Mackie," the pastor said. "See how well one of our young charges has turned out." Pride glowed in his eyes.

Mrs Mackie smiled. "Good to see you, young Corry," she said. "It's a pity more don't turn out like you."

Corry immediately thought of Gander and the other boys in his gangs. "Is Gander still around?" he asked. "Or has he moved on to better things?"

The pastor shook his head. "Sadly there are some lads we cannot reach," he said. "At the end of the day we must all account for our actions. I regret his accounting will take longer than most."

Sadness flitted across his face. "But what about you Corry? How long are you staying? What are your plans for the future?"

Corry took a breath. Suddenly all his previous ideas about using the visit home to further his business interests seemed futile and insignificant against the lives of people here and their struggles.

Finding Annie was now his priority; that and sorting out his feelings for Hettie, the depth of which had taken him by surprise.

"I'll stay as long as I'm needed," he said. "I'll not leave until I know Annie is safe and back home where she belongs." As he said it his resolve hardened and his options became clear. "I'll do everything I can to find her, even if it means moving heaven and earth to do so," he said.

"Yes," Pastor Brown said gazing up. "We were all devastated to hear of her disappearance. Hettie Bundy is most worried," he said. "I have come to believe she's right in her assessment of the situation."

"I was surprised Annie wasn't at the station to meet me but if what Hettie tells me is true she may be in serious trouble. I intend to make enquiries at the house in Belgravia where she was living as well as among the men who visited her there."

The pastor's eyes widened. "Do you think that wise? After all, that trade relies on discretion. You may be met with a great deal of resistance, and if the men are as influential as I suspect you may be putting yourself in danger too."

Corry smiled at the pastor's concern. "Don't worry, Pastor. There's none as discreet as I can be if Annie's safety is at stake, and Hettie's for that matter." He frowned at the thought.

The pastor nodded. "You must do as you think fit, my boy. My thoughts and prayers, as always, will be with you. Do let me know what you find out and if I can be of any assistance." He sighed. "The boys in the school are a rum lot, but they have heart of gold where wrongs inflicted upon one of their own are concerned. If you need them they'll rally to your call, I have no doubt of that."

"Thank you, Pastor," Corry said. If anyone knew about the underhand goings on around the docks it would the boys at the pastor's school: beggars, pedlars and petty thieves most of them. Mention of the school reminded him of what Hettie had told him.

"Hettie told me of the opening of a night shelter in Limehouse and the waifs and strays home. I'm glad to hear that someone is doing something for the street children as last."

"Yes," the pastor said, perking up. "It's all down to a chap called Barnardo. He wanted to train as a doctor and go to China I understand, but seeing the children sleeping on the street and on the roofs huddled against chimneys for warmth changed his mind." He smiled. "Not only has he saved lives he's given them hope and a chance to learn a trade. Man should get a knighthood, but I doubt he will."

"Do you still have as many boys here?" Corry asked.

"We do what we can," he said. "But his intervention, along with Lord Shaftesbury's backing, has made a real difference."

Mrs Mackie returned with the drinks and they talked some more about the changes that had taken place since Corry left. Corry told the pastor about his life in America and the people he had met there. It turned out that Corry and the pastor had quite a few mutual acquaintances. They spent a pleasant couple of hours swapping stories and laughing about their experiences. By the time Corry left his bond with home had deepened.

The next day Corry moved to a hotel in town to follow up his business interests. He'd brought a number of Letters of Introduction from business men in New York and Boston allowing him to conduct business on their behalf. Over the course of several days he saw bankers, city brokers, import and export company chairmen and shipping merchants. He managed to mention the house in Belgravia to them to see their reactions, hoping to find out more about the names in Annie's journal.

On Saturday he sent a young lad to find Jack so he could take him home. "Thanks Jack," he said, handing him a good tip. "I'll call you again when we need you."

"Whenever you want," Jack said. "Always happy help if it's about Miss Annie. She's as fine a lady as you're likely to meet in these parts."

Indoors Corry said he'd been talking to Jack about Annie. "He's been asking questions around the docks and he's willing to come with me if I need him. Depends what we find out, but if it's strong-arm stuff I'll not involve you, Hettie. It's far too dangerous."

"I suppose you'll be wanting tea?" Dorcas said.

"If you don't mind, Mrs Bundy."

Dorcas tutted as she went to the kitchen.

"Great welcome home for the conquering hero," he said.

Hettie laughed. "I don't think that's quite how she sees you," she said.

"No? Oh well." He sat down and opened Annie's journal. "I've been finding out about these events and functions and the people who attend them." He smiled. "It's handy being an accepted member of Boston society," he said. "It's amazing how many doors can be opened with the right credentials."

"So, what particular doors did you manage to open?" Hettie asked.

"I think I have a good idea who SM is."

Hettie gasped.

"Not only that, I've got us invited to a Gala Supper Ball at Somerset House. It's to celebrate Joseph Bazalgette's knighthood. I understand that Lord Crenshaw and this SM, whom I believe to be Miles Summerville, a well known merchant of shipping, will also be attending. It's too good an opportunity to miss."

Hettie's reaction was interrupted by Dorcas bringing in the tea. "I've put a couple of me fresh baked scones on an' all," she said. "Never let it be said as how I don't know how to make folk feel welcome."

Hettie jumped up and helped with the tea. Once the tea had been served Hettie looked at Corry. "What do you mean 'got us invited'? Who?"

"Me and you, well to be more precise, Mr James Fitzpatrick and partner." He grinned at Hettie. "It's what I called myself when I arrived in America. Didn't want the long arm of the law stretching out and pulling me back did I?"

She stared at him uncomprehending. "You mean me and you are going to a Gala Supper Ball?"

"Yes, that's exactly what I mean."

"But how? I mean... I can't go to such a thing. I've never heard such nonsense. What am I supposed to do at a Gala Supper Ball for goodness sake?"

Corry sighed. Hettie would have had no experience of mixing in any sort of society. In England the classes were sharply divided. This was something he loved about America, the freedom to be yourself, whoever you were and know you were appreciated for it. Not being of noble birth didn't prevent you sitting at the best tables.

"You're supposed to dance and enjoy yourself. Don't tell me you can't dance. I remember those Christmases when we danced here in this room. You remember don't you, Mrs Bundy?"

Dorcas chuckled, her heavy bosoms heaving. "Aye. And we had a right old knees up at the Crown and Anchor for New Year. You remember, Hettie. It was a grand night all round."

Corry didn't think a 'right old knees up' was exactly great preparation for dancing the night away at a Gala Supper Ball, but he said nothing.

"If it's something to wear you're worried about I have the name of an excellent dressmaker who'll make you something suitable. The ball's not for another week, so there's plenty of time."

"Plenty of time? For fittings and the like? Honestly Corry Flanagan sometimes I think you've taken leave of your senses. Me at a Grand Ball. It's ridiculous."

Corry bit his lip to stop from laughing. Despite her protestations he saw Hettie gradually warming to the idea. "It'd be a chance to find out what connects Lord Crenshaw to Miles Summerville," he said. He held out the card he'd been given for an excellent dressmaker. Hettie took it.

"I've taken a suite at The Grand Midland Hotel," Corry said. "It's where I've been staying."

Hettie's mouth dropped open.

"You need a good address here if you're to convince people that you have the wherewithal to do business. How else are we to find out about Annie if we don't mix with the people she mixed with?"

Hettie closed her mouth.

"You'll need to come and stay at the hotel with me," Corry said. "We need to be seen together if we are to pull this off."

Hettie stared at him.

"Don't worry, we'll have separate rooms and I'll employ a maid to help you dress. Mrs Bundy can come too if you're worried." Corry suddenly realised how anxious he was for Hettie's approval. If she wouldn't come with him...

"There's no need to bother Ma," Hettie said eventually. "A maid will suffice. But what about Billy?"

Corry swallowed. In his excitement at making the arrangements he'd forgotten about his nephew.

"Don't worry about Billy," Dorcas said. "With Sarah helping out I can manage him, and Sarah's mother, Mrs Mackie up at the pastor's house, has offered to have him anytime. She's three of her own to look after so one more makes no odds."

For the first time he could remember Corry could have hugged Dorcas. Perhaps she wasn't as bad as he remembered.

That evening Hettie received a note from Chloe. She showed it to Corry. "She says she'd like to meet us on Monday at the tearooms in Cavendish Square at two o'clock. She says she has some news."

Corry took the note. The handwriting was neat and the paper expensive.

"She must have an appointment with her dressmaker on Monday. She lives near there and Chloe often goes to the tearooms after her fittings." Hettie said.

Corry nodded. "Two o'clock on Monday it is then," he said. "I look forward to meeting her."

Chapter Twenty Five

Sunday morning Corry, Hettie, Dorcas and Billy braved the cold March wind and went to church. The church, next to the pastor's school, held so many memories for Corry. Everything about the large red brick building felt familiar: the tall arched windows, the slate roof with a small spire where a bell peeled out the call to service and the blue painted door still showing splits in several places.

Inside a hush fell over them, despite the number of people taking their places in the pews. A man Corry didn't recognise handed them each a hymn book and showed them to their seats near the front. Dorcas nodded to him as she led them into the pew.

Corry saw faces he remembered from the past in the congregation: shopkeepers, costers, factory workers, weavers and labourers; men who spent the week working, Friday nights drinking and came along on Sunday to atone for their sins. The women wore cloth coats and their Sunday best hats. All sat in reverence waiting for the pastor to remind them of their shortcomings, grant them forgiveness and restore their souls.

Several women nodded to Dorcas and Hettie, then stared at Billy. Corry saw the questions in their eyes and no doubt running through their minds as the looks of disapproval overcame their faces. Some raised eyebrows at his presence, trying to fit this well dressed young man into the equation that was Dorcas, Hettie and a baby. He grinned at the thought of the wrong conclusions they would be jumping to like a bull at a gate.

He gazed at the high stained-glass window above the altar dominated by a wooden cross, the carved wood of the choir stalls, where Annie sang every Sunday and the pulpit where Pastor Brown could survey his flock as he reminded them of their duty to God and their fellow man.

As the choir boys and girls filed in in their white cotton surplices he thought of Annie. She'd loved singing in the choir. He suspected it was her only reason for attending the lessons that bored her witless. She was quick to absorb the teachings and had little patience with the slower children. Once she'd finished her work she'd hand the teacher her slate and run off back to the streets where she could make a few pennies selling whatever she could blag from the sellers in the market. His stomach clenched. He should have been here to look out for her and protect her; even if it meant protecting her from herself. The guilt hung heavy on his heart.

Pastor Brown began his sermon by introducing Corry as a lost sheep – the prodigal son returned.

He attributed Corry's success to his hard work and in no small part to the influence of the church and what he referred to as the righteousness of his upbringing – thus making Dorcas puff out her chest and nod her head repeatedly.

He obliquely referred to his own influence and how proud he was of a young man from humble beginning who could, and indeed should, be an example to us all.

Corry blushed and fidgeted, but couldn't deny the pastor his reflected glory. The irony in the fact that his flight to America had been to avoid the consequences of an action he now knew to be less injurious, but at the time had been serious, didn't escape him.

After the service tea was served in the church hall. Pastor Brown approached them and asked how Billy, who was happily ensconced in Hettie's arms, was getting on. "Has he been christened?" he asked.

Hettie blushed. "I... I don't know," she said thrown by the question. "Annie never said."

The pastor sniffed. "Well does he have a Birth Certificate, or Certificate of Baptism? Anything like that?"

Hettie glared at him. Irritation lit her eyes, but Corry guessed it was annoyance at herself for not having thought of it before, rather than anger at the pastor for mentioning it.

"If he does," Corry said, riding to Hettie's rescue, "it would be in French."

"Ah," the pastor said. "Sorry I can't help you. If it were Latin however…"

"I'll have someone look through her papers," Corry said. "Although we don't even know if he was registered." He smiled at Billy and stroked his cheek. "He was very young when Annie brought him home."

After the service Dorcas and Hettie took Billy home leaving Corry to visit his mother's grave. He shuddered as he walked through the churchyard. There was an eerie feel about the silence after the hubbub of the church hall. He stared at the headstones of the graves he passed. Some were elaborately grand, others more humble. All bore inscriptions marking the passing of mothers, fathers, brothers and other loved ones sadly missed. Mary Flanagan's grave lay beyond them, close to the hedge at the far end of the churchyard.

The mound of earth, overgrown with grass and weeds, was surrounded by stones which he guessed Annie had laid shortly after their mother's funeral. He removed a bunch of decaying flowers and wondered how long they had lain there. Several months most likely. Since Annie's disappearance perhaps? It would be just like Annie to bring flowers to Ma's grave. Did she bring Billy too?

A picture flashed in his mind of little Annie, in her favourite dress with her white cotton pinafore over it, bending to arrange the stones so solemnly, yet not understanding the full impact of her situation. A wooden cross, with Mary Flanagan's name and the date of her passing painted on it, marked the head of the grave. An ache of grief caught in his throat.

He tidied the grave, replacing stones that had moved or fallen, then stood before it his mind teeming with memories. What could he say to this woman who bore him and Annie, and asked nothing more in life than that she be left in peace? He recalled moving from place to place as their fortunes increased or dwindled. Usually dwindled. Was that what had caused Annie to want so much more out of her life?

Visions of Annie ran through his mind; Annie when she was young, always outspoken and often in trouble, he smiled at that. Then Annie and the cress – she brought the world of cress sellers to life with her tales of the people she met on the street. Her passion for performing. Whether she was singing in the choir, giving a concert at home in front of an imaginary audience or performing on the stage, Annie gave it all she had.

Tears blurred his vision. "I'm sorry, Ma," he said. "You left her in my care. I should have looked after her better." He blinked away the tears stinging his eyes. "I would turn the clock back if I could," he said, "but I can't." He paused. "I'll find her, Ma. Whatever's happened to Annie, I'll find out and bring her back, you see if I don't."

He took a couple of deep breaths and a calmness fell over him. A soft breeze rustled the leaves of the trees and he imagined hearing his mother's voice. What would she say? 'It's not your fault,' she would say. 'Annie always was a wild child and there's no changing her. You were the sensible one, the reliable one. Don't blame yourself.' Yes, that's what his mother would say. She'd know what it was like to be an outsider trying to get in. That's how it felt, but the difference was, with money and a position behind him it would be easier now. The doubts and fears he'd felt before coming here evaporated. He had his mother's blessing, that's all he needed.

The next day after lunch, Corry and Hettie set out to walk to the tearooms in Cavendish Square. Early showers had wetted the roads leaving small puddles. Corry held Hettie's arm when she lifted her skirt to step over them. The dark clouds filling the sky in the morning had cleared and small patches of blue were visible between the high buildings. He noticed construction going on everywhere.

"Things have certainly changed while I've been away," he said.

"In more ways than one," Hettie said. She smiled at him. "It's mostly for the good, but not always."

He nodded and they walked on in silence until they came to the tearooms which appeared bright and cheerful despite the dullness of the cloudy day.

Hettie waved when she saw Chloe seated at a table near the window. She'd already ordered a pot of tea with three cups. A cake stand filled with finger sandwiches and fancy cakes stood on the white clothed table. Chloe rose to greet Hettie. "I was afraid you wouldn't come and I'd have to eat all these cakes myself," she said.

Hettie laughed. "No fear of that now," she said.

Then she introduced Corry and they all sat. Corry was the first to speak. "Have you any news of Annie?" he said, anxiety making him impatient. "Only your note said..."

Chloe looked puzzled.

"Angelique," Hettie said.

"Oh, yes, of course." Chloe glanced around before continuing. "You're not the only ones looking for Angelique," she said.

Corry's ears pricked up. "Not the only ones?"

Chloe picked up the teapot and poured them each a cup of tea. "No, there was a gentleman. He must have been a new client, an older man. I believe he met Sylvia at some Gala or other and asked about the girls."

She replaced the teapot and looked at Corry. "He said he was looking for someone to host a dinner he was planning. Of course Sylvia invited him to the house. He asked if any of the girls had ever been to Paris. Well, none of the others had, but I said I'd heard a lot about it from a girl who used to share my room."

"You mean Annie?"

"Yes. Anyway he invited me out to dinner at Simpsons in the Strand. Lovely dinner it was, really posh. Then he kept asking me all these questions. How many girls worked for Sylvia? Where did they come from? How long did they stay? What happened to them when they left? Did we ever keep in touch? He must have realised I was getting a bit suspicious, so he told me he was looking for one particular girl. He showed me a programme from the Folies-Bergère and said her name was Angelique and she used to dance there."

Hettie perked up, her interest aroused. "Did he say why he was looking for her?"

Chloe pouted. "No. He just kept asking questions about her. Did I know what happened to her, or where he could find her? Of course I said I didn't know, she'd just upped and left."

"Did he give you his name or a note of how to contact him should you hear from her?" Corry said.

Chloe shook her head. "Oh, I'm sorry. I should have asked shouldn't I? It was just so... well unexpected really. He was an older man, old enough to be her father, and I'd only just met him." She took a sip of tea. "Sylvia tells us to be careful until we get to know our clients. You hear so much about white slaves and that... Oh you don't think Angelique's been...?"

Corry stared at Chloe. "No of course not," he said. "White slavers don't go round to places like Sylvia's to find girls. They pick them off the streets. Annie would have more sense than to put herself in that position." Still, even as he said it Corry wondered. Was that what had happened to Annie? Hettie had mentioned the possibility earlier but Corry had dismissed it. What if Hettie was right?

"He asked if she knew anyone in London where she might go." She turned to Hettie. "I didn't want to tell him about you — not without asking your permission first, so I told him about her going to the church in Bromley by Bow which I thought was odd as we were living in Belgravia."

Chloe finished her tea and glanced at Corry. "I've not been much help have I? But at least now you know you're not the only ones looking for Angelique."

Corry's mind whirled. He'd heard about all sorts of things going on around the docks from opium and ivory smuggling to the abduction of young boys and women for all sorts of reasons... but white slavery... surely Annie wouldn't be involved in anything like that?

Hettie thanked Chloe and mentioned that Corry thought SM, the shipping merchant mentioned in Annie's journal, might be Miles Summerville, owner of the Summerville Shipping Line.

Chloe shrugged her elegant shoulders. "I can't help you there," she said. "I only ever saw him once. I never heard his name, and anyway it's doubtful he used his real one if he was up to no good."

"Well, Corry's got us invited to a Gala Supper Ball at Somerset House. He says Lord Crenshaw will be there and we may be able to find a connection between him and this Miles Summerville."

Chloe gasped. "The Gala Supper Ball for Joseph Bazelgette? I'm due to attend that very ball. In fact my fitting this morning was for a dress for that particular occasion." Her eyes lit up with excitement. "Miss de Vine has ordered new gowns for all the girls attending," she said. She blushed. "I'll be escorting a young American gentleman. He's newly arrived and in need of a partner for the evening."

Hettie almost jumped up in her delight. "Oh, how lovely," she said. "At least I'll know someone there so won't feel so alone."

Corry wondered whether the American gentleman might be someone of his acquaintance, but quickly dismissed the thought. "You won't be alone, Hettie," he said. "You'll be with me."

Hettie shook her head, suppressing a grin. "No, I'm going with a Mr James Fitzpatrick. I believe he's quite the man about town."

Much to Corry's amusement, after Hettie had explained to Chloe about his slight deception, although not the reason for it, the girls spent a pleasant hour discussing dresses, hats, gloves and other accoutrements necessary for an evening's dancing. Chloe recommended Miss de Vine's dressmaker. "She's very helpful and not at all stuck up," Chloe said. "She makes dresses for all Sylvia's girls. Runs them up in no time so you'll have no trouble."

Hettie wasn't sure she wanted something 'run up in no time'. She wanted something stylish and fashionable but simple and not over-fussy. Something that would knock Corry's eyes out would be good, or at least make him notice her. She sighed at the hopelessness of that particular dream. Chloe had assured her Madame Francine's establishment would be 'just the ticket'.

Chapter Twenty Six

The next morning Hettie visited the dressmaker Chloe had recommended. She checked the address on the paper Chloe had given her. The premises looked unprepossessing at say the least. A narrow doorway in the centre of a dingy grey edifice proclaimed it to be 'Madame Francine's Salon'. Hettie swallowed her doubts and rang the bell. A few minutes later a young girl in a parlour maid's outfit opened the door.

"Yes?" she said.

"I'd like to see Madame Francine if I may," Hettie said. "I am in urgent need of a ball-gown and understand she may be able to provide one."

"You'd better come in then," the girl said stepping aside. She showed Hettie into a room at the front of the building, overlooking the street. Sketches and designs of every conceivable type of outfit covered the walls. A table in the centre of the room was piled high with fabric samples, trimmings and boxes of braids, ribbons and beads. "If you'd care to wait I'll see if Madame is free," the girl said and left before Hettie could respond.

Hettie glanced around. Books of patterns filled the shelves either side of a huge, ornate, beautifully carved Adams fireplace. Heavy damask curtains covered the windows, making the room appear darker than it need have been. Hettie guessed it to be some sort of storeroom.

She didn't have to wait long. Madame Francine, a well upholstered lady with reddish hair piled in a bun on top of her head, glided into the room like a four-masted schooner under full sail. She looked Hettie up and down, taking in every detail of Hettie's thin cloth coat and felt hat. Her face twisted in dismay.

"The girl said you were in need of a ball gown," she said. "I don't deal in second-hand, my dear. All my gowns are bespoke."

"I'm glad to hear it," Hettie said matching Madame Francine's disdainful tone. "I would hate to think I would be attending the Gala Supper Ball celebrating Sir Joseph Bazalgette's knighthood, in a second-hand gown."

Madame Francine's expression changed in an instant. "Sir Joseph's Knighthood ball? Why didn't you say? I'm sure we can produce something eminently suitable. Please come through to my studio and we can begin."

Hettie followed her out of the room.

"Marie, to the studio please," Madame Francine called.

In contrast to the storeroom Madame Francine's studio was light, airy and bright. High windows, left bare of drapes, let in pale sunlight reflected by mirrors along the length of one wall. The room was empty save for one table on which sat a vase of spring flowers. A wheeled trolley containing pins, tape measures, tailor's chalk, scissors, rulers and other dressmaking paraphernalia stood alongside it.

Madame Francine took Hettie's coat and handed it to Marie. She indicated to Hettie to remove her blouse and skirt. Standing in her underwear, her image reflected in the mirrors adorning the walls, Hettie wondered what on earth she'd let herself in for.

"Now, let us begin," Madame Francine said, picking up a tape measure. She chatted to Hettie as she measured, asking what she had in mind, what colours she was thinking about, how would she be wearing her hair, what shoes, what underwear, what jewellery. All the time she would call out the measurements to Marie who noted them in a small notebook.

Hettie soon found herself warming to the woman who wasn't as formidable as she had at first appeared. Hettie told her about Chloe's recommendation. "I understand you make gowns for all Miss de Vine's girls," she said.

"Oh, yes. She's one of my best customers."

After all Hettie's measurements were taken, Madame Francine sent Marie for a book of patterns and some swatches of the finest silk for Hettie to look at.

While she was gone Hettie produced her picture of Annie. "I wonder if you may have made outfits for my friend Angelique?" she said.

Madame Francine looked at the picture. "Oh yes," she said. "Such a lovely girl. Very quiet, studious even. Not at all like the other girls." She flapped her hands and gazed skywards. "Those girls," she said. "So demanding."

She took Annie's picture and regarded it fondly. "She was different. So kind." She handed the picture back. "She saw my little grandson in the workroom one day when she came for a fitting. Every time after that she brought him sweets or a little toy." She gazed at Hettie. "She told me she had a little one of her own, but wasn't able to be with him. So sad." She sighed. "She said she missed him terribly."

Hettie's heart lurched. Annie had confided in this woman. Perhaps she could tell her more. "When did you last see her?" Hettie asked. "Only we lost touch and I would dearly like to see her again. Has she been in recently?"

Madame Francine thought for a moment, her brow creased. "No," she said. "Now that you mention it, it has been several months since I saw her. Let me think." She frowned. "It was before Christmas. I remember now. She had an appointment but didn't come in with the other girls for their Christmas and New Year outfits." Her brow puckered. "I thought it strange at the time." She shrugged. "These girls, they come and go. Still, I did think Angelique was different."

Marie returned carrying several pattern books and a basket filled with swatches of material, trimmings, ribbons and beads.

"Now, let us see," Madam Francine said standing back from Hettie and eyeing her up and down like a prize bull in the market. Hettie picked up a swatch of materials and selected a pale lilac.

"No, no, no," Madame Francine said, shaking her head. She gasped, her hands went to her chin. "I have it," she said. "With your colouring – the

Forest Green silk." She turned to Marie. "Fetch the Forest Green silk," she said. Marie hurried off.

Madame looked happier now as she picked up a pattern to show Hettie. Marie returned with a heavy bolt of the brightest, glossiest, deep green Hettie had ever seen. The colour of the forest, she thought. Well, that should appeal to Corry.

"Ah yes. This is it," Madame exclaimed, putting the bolt of silk on the table and unravelling a length. She held it under Hettie's chin.

Hettie caught her breath. Her eyes seemed to jump out a deep luminous green, reflecting the colour of the cloth. Her skin looked creamy in contrast to the deep chestnut of her hair.

"You see?" Madame said. "None of the other girls I dress could carry off such a vibrant colour, but you, you have the eyes, the hair, the skin, the perfect body..."

She draped the silk across Hettie's stomach. "Here we drape in folds across and catch up at the back to fall in pleated ripples from the bustle."

She showed Hettie how the fabric would fall. "The bodice will be fitted," she said. "Tight at the waist to flare over the hips. Such hips." She smiled. "Rarely do I have the pleasure of dressing such a body." She lifted the silk across Hettie's bust. "The neckline will be low. Off the shoulder – edged with white lace – very daring."

Hettie blanched. "I'm not sure I want to be daring," she said.

"Oh, but you must," Madame exclaimed. "Such a marvellous décolleté must be displayed. And your shoulders – such wonderful shoulders. It would be a sin to cover them up."

"I don't know," Hettie said. This was the first time anyone had admired her for the ampleness of her body. Annie was petite and vivacious, Chloe young and slim and Hettie guessed all Miss de Vine's other girls would be of similar build.

After the material, Madame Francine chose the trimmings, beads, underpinnings and accessories needed to make Hettie the belle of the ball. "Leave it to me," she said. "When I have finished every man in the room will want to dance with you and every woman will turn the colour of this gown with envy."

"The cost?" Hettie said, fearing that Madame was getting carried away.

Madame waved her hands. "Do not worry about the cost. When people see you in the gown they will flock to my door. That will be reward enough." She shrugged. "Miss de Vine pays for all her girls. Your friend Angelique did not come for her last fitting, so I have some material to spare. It is a very small thing."

"I am most grateful," Hettie said, relieved that she wouldn't be presenting Corry with a huge bill.

"The gratitude is mine," Madame Francine said. "I think of Angelique and her kindness to me and my grandson. If wearing my dress helps you to find her then I am satisfied."

When she left the Salon, everything Madame Francine had said about Annie was lodged in Hettie's brain. Annie had left Miss de Vine's with only the clothes she stood up in. She hadn't ordered anything new. That wasn't like the Annie Hettie knew of old, she was mad about new clothes and fashion. Then there was Billy. She'd confided in Madame Francine about him, making it clear how much she missed him and wanted to be with him. That didn't sound to Hettie like a mother who'd voluntarily abandon her baby. She was sure that when she told Corry, he'd have to agree with her.

Chapter Twenty Seven

The day of the ball arrived. The maid Corry had hired arranged Hettie's hair and helped her dress. She wore Madame Francine's exquisite creation in Forest Green silk trimmed with white lace. The fitted bodice, embroidered with sequins and pearls flared over Hettie's hips, just as Madame Francine had said. The skirt draped in folds cross Hettie's stomach and swept into the bustle to fall in a train behind her. Underneath she wore a whalebone corset tightly laced and several layers of petticoat.

"Good heavens," she said to the maid. "How on earth do these ladies breathe let alone dance?"

Once she was comfortable walking around in the dress she put on Annie's emerald pendant necklace, the one she had brought from Paris and kept for Billy. The maid pinned a padded slide trimmed with sequins and feathers into the chestnut curl of Hettie's hair, piled on top of her head in the latest fashion. Hettie added long diamond drop earrings and an emerald bracelet from Annie's collection, left in the wardrobe in Belgravia. A pair of long white evening gloves completed the outfit.

Corry waited for her in the lounge of the suite he had hired. When she walked into the room he stared. She twirled around.

"What do you think?" she said. "Will I do?"

He swallowed several times before he spoke. "You look incredible," he said. The admiration in his eyes brought a warm glow to Hettie's face.

Corry was dressed in a black tail coat over a white waistcoat and shirt. His high necked winged collar encircled by a white bow tie. His, glossy, black hair, freshly styled, curled onto his collar.

Golden flecks glinted in his soft brown eyes. His highly polished shoes shone. Hettie noticed the built up heel of his left shoe evened out his limp. Her heart hammered. He looked every inch the gentleman. She couldn't quite believe she was going to a ball with this gorgeous man, who made her heart leap the way no other man could.

A smile spread across his lips. "You look magnificent," he said. He bowed. "Your carriage awaits."

Hettie donned her cloak and with Corry went out and down in the ascending chamber, which Hettie still found miraculous. Outside they took a hansom to Somerset House.

A footman took Corry's hat and Hettie's cloak. The Master of Ceremonies announced them and they walked into the ballroom. A glittering mass of colour and light met their eyes. A rush of air filled Hettie's lungs. Men in evening suits and the most exquisitely dressed women spun around the floor to the music of a full orchestra. Lights in high chandeliers reflected in long mirrors along the walls. The overall impression was one of bright daylight, music and laughter. She was stunned by the glamour and elegance around her.

Corry offered his arm and said, "Shall we?" A playful twinkle lit his eyes as he pulled her into his arms and spun her out onto the dance floor.

Immediately Hettie was swept into the glittering throng of dancers circling the floor. Her feet hardly touched the ground, such was the joy she felt spinning around in Corry's arms. The music filled her head and she was completely lost in it. Nothing in her life had prepared her for such a thrill. If there was one thing she'd never, ever imagined it would be this; dancing around in Corry's arms with the whole world watching. It was something she'd never forget.

After the first dance they stopped, both breathless. Corry picked two glasses of champagne from a passing waiter's tray and handed one to Hettie. "That was fun," he said his eyes twinkling with amusement. "We really must do it again sometime."

Hettie struggled to control the chaos raging in her heart. She laughed, suddenly remembering why they were there. "We're not here to have fun," she said. "For all the effort I've taken to get into this dress I'm hoping we will have achieved a lot more than having fun."

"You're right as always, Hettie," Corry said. "But I can't deny the pleasure of the last few moments." His eyes sparkled.

Hettie glanced around. It really was magical. She was beginning to see the attraction of the sort of life Annie craved. Having a wealthy admirer brought ease and comfort beyond the reach of people like Hettie. Was that what had happened to Annie? Had the life of luxury and wealth turned her head?

Several people Corry had been doing business with during the week stopped to exchange a few words. Corry introduced them to Hettie. It soon became obvious to Hettie that he was immensely proud to have her on his arm. Her heart climbed another couple of notches.

They danced again. Hettie noticed all eyes upon them as they whirled around the floor. Light glittered on jewellery and dresses shimmered as the dancers spun around. She was grateful for Corry's broad shoulders and strong arms holding her. This was the closest they'd been since the day he ran way and Hettie wasn't about to let the memory slip from her mind, or the man slip from her grasp. When the music stopped her heart was still dancing.

Corry again picked up two glasses of champagne handing one to Hettie. She laughed. "If I carry on like this I'll be tipsy before the end of the evening," she said, but she did wonder if it was just the champagne that had gone to head filling it with wild imaginings.

"Look, there's Chloe," Corry said. "With her American. Should we join them?"

Hettie glanced over and saw Chloe dressed in a fabulous cerise gown complete with bows, pleats and flounces. The bodice was dotted with garnets and pearls. A discreet headdress of feathers rested in her hair. The man with her wore a wide lapelled tan jacket unbuttoned to reveal a blue and gold waistcoat over a high-necked white shirt with a black bootlace tie. He looked as though he'd be more at home riding the range than in an elegant London ballroom.

"Typical American," Corry whispered in Hettie's ear.

Chloe waved as they approached. She greeted Hettie with a kiss on each cheek. "This is Buck Masterson, my escort for the evening," she said. "Buck, I'd like you to meet..."

"James Fitzpatrick," Corry said before Chloe could speak his name. "Pleased to make your acquaintance." He held out his hand.

Chloe looked slightly bemused, but Hettie said, "I believe you and James may have much in common. He is recently returned from America."

"Is that a fact?" Buck said, pumping Corry's hand as though expecting to draw water from it. "I'm in beef. You?"

"Timber."

"Hmm. Timber's a good thing to be in. Always a market for timber," Buck said.

Corry smiled. "There's always a demand for beef too," he said. "You should do well."

Buck glanced around. "To tell you the truth I came here tonight hoping to meet some importers. I understand some of the men here virtually run the docks."

"It seems we do share some mutual interests," Corry said.

"Well, let me see who I can introduce you to," Chloe said looking around.

"Isn't that Miss de Vine?" Hettie said, seeing a group of well dressed and obviously wealthy gentlemen surrounding a vision in pale blue silk. "She looks amazing."

"Doesn't she?" Chloe said. "She outshines us all."

"Are there many of her girls here tonight?" Corry asked.

A wide grin stretched across Chloe face. "You'd be surprised," she said. "I think I saw Lord Crenshaw going into the gaming room. You may find the man you are looking for there also."

Buck rubbed his hands together. "Gaming eh? Well, I'm up for it. What do you say, James?"

"If the ladies have no objection."

Chloe bent over and whispered in Hettie's ear. "I believe the man with him may be SM."

"None at all," Hettie said. "After all we are here to enjoy ourselves and I'd love to see if James is as good a hand at cards as he says."

Green baize topped-tables dominated the gaming room. Four card players sat at each table while tail-coated men and silk-gowned women milled around or gathered near the roulette table at one end of the room. Oak panels lined the walls with sections picked out in white to add light. Corry gave Hettie some chips to try her hand at roulette while he went with Buck to pit their wits against the card players. Two people were leaving the table where Lord Crenshaw sat and Corry and Buck slid into the vacant chairs.

Corry studied the two men they were playing against. Lord Crenshaw was the elder. Grey haired, with a pathetic moustache and weary, watery blue eyes, he looked defeated before he began, as though he had the weight of the world on his shoulders. He dithered over his cards, his gaze filled with uncertainty, flitting between his hand and the man sitting opposite him.

Miles Summerville was the exact opposite. Young, with smoothed back dark hair, his whole demeanour exuded confident arrogance. A rich man who'd come by his wealth through nefarious means, Corry decided, but he did acknowledge he would be a cunning adversary and not easily fooled or outwitted.

Buck introduced them. "Buck Masterson," he said. "Rancher and producer of the finest beef you'll ever find. And this is my friend James Fitzpatrick, who's in timber." He glanced at the two men. "So who do we have here? I like to know who I'm playing against."

Lord Crenshaw leaned slightly forward. "Lord Crenshaw, from the Treasury," he said, obviously expecting them to be suitably impressed. Buck wasn't.

"Miles Summerville, shipping," Miles said. "Now, should we get on with the game?"

From the piles of chips on the table it was clear that Lord Crenshaw was losing heavily and Miles was winning.

After only two hands Corry could see why. Lord Crenshaw greeted good cards with a grin, poor ones with a frown. He laid reckless bets, seeming to enjoy the cut and thrust of the game more than the outcome. He was exuberant when he won and disgusted when he lost.

Miles on the other hand played his cards close to his chest. He folded quickly when Buck bet high and only pushed when Lord Crenshaw was upping the ante. After two hands Corry felt he had the measure of both men.

Buck and Corry played cautiously, but not so carefully as to lessen the excitement and challenge of the game. Soon the pile of chips in front of Corry mounted while Lord Crenshaw and Miles's shrunk. Buck's play was consistent and he remained even.

Between hands the men chatted idly. Buck introduced the difficulty of finding a partner in shipping to import his beef. Corry said he too was looking for someone who knew their way around the docks. Miles handed them each his business card. Corry put his in his waistcoat pocket.

He wanted to find out more about Lord Crenshaw and Miles's involvement with Annie and the house where she worked, so, to that end he said, "Where would you gentlemen recommend two single gentlemen go if they are looking for lively entertainment in this fair city? We do of course mean somewhere discreet where a gentleman's needs may be met."

Buck looked sideways at him. Corry silenced him with a glance.

"I dare say there are ladies here who would meet your needs more than adequately," Miles said.

Lord Crenshaw shook his head as though the subject was not one that had had ever worried his mind.

A new pack of cards was produced and the game started again in earnest. Corry became quite engrossed in the intricacies of the game and had forgotten about Hettie and Chloe until a waiter passed him a note. Surprised at the interruption he opened it and read: *Corry, Tibbs is here.*

He took a breath and said, "Gentlemen, I fear I have been called away on a matter of some urgency." He beckoned a waiter to collect his chips and cash them in. As he rose to leave Buck glanced around and said, "I regret, gentlemen, that I must leave also. I have neglected my lady friend for far too long and I promised her a dance before supper."

They both made their apologies and left the table. Corry heard Lord Crenshaw mutter something about them not being gentlemen.

"Phew, that was close," Buck said as they rejoined the ladies.

"What do you mean?" Hettie asked.

Buck grinned. "I've been around long enough to know a card sharp when I see one," he said, "and your boy here is one of the best I've seen."

Hettie looked horrified.

Corry laughed. "Don't worry, Hettie," he said. "I was only able to get the better of them because they were trying to cheat me. It's just that I'm better at it. Still, I was glad to get your note."

Chloe turned to Buck. "I've been dying to dance," she said pulling him towards the floor.

"And so you shall," Buck said, nodding goodbye to Corry and Hettie.

Corry watched them go then turned to Hettie. She really did look amazing. Why hadn't he noticed how beautiful she was before?

"Where's this Tibbs?" he said, suddenly serious. If he was involved in Annie's disappearance he wanted to find him and make him talk. Thinking about what may have happened to her turned his stomach to stone and hardened his resolve.

Chapter Twenty Eight

Hettie led Corry to the part of the hall near the door. "He's over there," she said, pointing out a man dressed in a black evening suit. The same height as Corry he was more slender. His blonde hair was neatly styled, his thin moustache well trimmed. He had an intelligent face. Interest shone in his inquisitive blue eyes. Despite being appropriately dress he looked out of place and mildly uncomfortable. He was talking to one of the waiters.

Corry waited until the waiter moved away, then he strolled up to Tibbs. "Good evening," he said. "It's Tobias Ebbs isn't it?"

Tibbs glanced quickly around. He looked put out by Corry's interruption. He stared at him. "Do I know you?" he said. "I'm afraid I don't recall ever having met you."

"No, but you've met me before," Hettie said, stepping forward into the light from the chandelier.

Tibbs blinked and stared. It took several moments before realisation dawned. His face spread into a smile. "It's Hettie, isn't it? Hettie Bundy?" He glanced up and down surveying her as though making an assessment. "Although I hardly recognised you. I do hope you are fully recovered from your ordeal."

"Yes, completely," she said. "Thanks to your timely intervention I suffered nothing more than a few bruises."

"I'm glad. I did mean to call again to see how you were but I see I needn't have worried. What a coincidence seeing you here." He glanced at Corry. "And who is your friend?"

"James Fitzpatrick, at your service," Corry said.

"Almost as coincidental as you being in Limehouse when I was attacked," Hettie said. "I have been wondering if your appearance, lucky for me though it was, was as accidental as it appeared."

He bridled. "What do you mean?"

"I mean, I can understand why Freda was there that night, but I don't suppose Limehouse is a regular spot for you to go walking. I can't help but wonder what business brought you there that night."

"I'd certainly like to know," Corry said.

"I don't know what you mean."

"I think you know exactly what I mean," Hettie said.

Corry recalled something Mugger had told him when he was talking to the mudlarks the previous day. Mugger had said he'd seen a 'rum cove' hanging around the docks. Corry wondered if the 'rum cove' could be Tibbs. "You've been seen around the docks too," Corry said.

"I don't know what business it is of yours," Tibbs said, his tone decidedly frosty. He glared at Hettie. "I might ask what a young lady like yourself was doing walking those streets at that time of night. It's a dangerous neighbourhood, as you found to your cost, and I dare say not one you regularly visit." His glance shifted from Hettie to Corry. "And your interest in Limehouse and the docks is?" he said, eyes wide.

Hettie glanced at Corry. They were getting nowhere. She decided honesty would be the best policy in the circumstances.

"Our sister has disappeared and we think she's been taken," she said. She couldn't stop her eyes filling with tears at the thought. "I'd been asking questions around the docks before I was attacked. The attack was a warning and your intervention came too readily to be by chance. I am right aren't I? You know more about the goings on at the docks than you're telling. You appear to be a decent man. If you know anything, anything at all, I beg you to tell us. We believe her life to be at risk."

Tibbs gasped. "Oh my dear," he said. "Is that what you were doing? Looking for your sister?"

Hettie bit her lip to stop the tears that threatened to flow.

"I had no idea," Tibbs said. His face creased with concern.

"So, what's your interest in the docks?" Corry said. "You haven't said."

"Nothing like taking young ladies off the street I can assure you," he said. "My goodness. Do you think that's what those men were after when they attacked you?"

Hettie shook her head. "No. The man who attacked me was quite specific. He said I asked too many questions and…" She had a sudden recollection, "…he mentioned what curiosity did to the cat." She swallowed the lump rising in her throat. Hot blood flooded her face.

Tibbs took a breath. "But that's what I said too. So you thought... Oh my lord... You thought I was one of them?"

"Not an unreasonable assumption in the circumstance," Corry said, jumping to Hettie's defence.

Tibbs looked aghast. "I was merely trying to warn Hettie to keep away from there. The streets of Limehouse are no place for a young lady at night. Perhaps I should explain myself," he said. He steered them to a side room, ushered them in and closed the door.

Red plush upholstered chairs lined the room. Pale blue walls with panels of white picked out in gold gave an impression of airy lightness despite the smallness of the room which was lit by a single chandelier. A retiring room of some sort, Hettie thought, but she didn't know what to think of Tibbs. He'd been surprised by her presence at the ball and obviously irritated by her questions, but she hadn't felt in any way threatened. Had she got him wrong? She soon found out she had.

"I'm a Revenue Officer working for Customs and Excise," he said. "I was watching the gang that attacked you." He smiled at Hettie. "I'd been following them for days. We know someone's bringing in large amounts of opium from the Far East which is unloaded somewhere out of sight of the Customs men." He turned to Corry. "With over a thousand ships in the docks and more along the Thames waiting to come in, it's an impossible task. They're a disreputable bunch and violent, but I don't think they're involved in anything like you're suggesting. I've seen no evidence of it anyway."

"Annie worked for a high class establishment providing services to some of the people here tonight," Corry said. "Lord Crenshaw and Miles Summerville were among her clients and we believe they are connected in some way."

"That's a possibility," Tibbs said, stroking his chin. "Since the Pharmacy Bill the importation of opium has been severely restricted. It's adversely affected a lot of shipping merchants, Miles Summerville among them." He paced up and down, hand over his mouth and deep in thought. Eventually he said, "I believe Lord Crenshaw is trying to get the law changed. He definitely opposed it."

"And was well paid to do so, I'll warrant. I understand his gambling debts far outweigh his income."

Tibbs nodded. "Yes, so I understand. He is under investigation, but that's not my department. It's the smugglers I'm after."

"Do you think they may have taken Annie?" Hettie asked. "If she knew about it... who they were and what they were up to?"

Tibbs shook his head. "I know many men, in their efforts to impress young ladies, will brag about their cleverness and how they are able to outwit and hoodwink the authorities. Secrets are often whispered and inhibitions lost, but even so, if she knew of their foulest deeds there would be no motivation to risk losing her livelihood by exposing them. Far better to keep quiet and enjoy the fruits of their ill-gotten gains."

Hettie recalled Annie saying that if you knew someone's weakness you could get them to do whatever you wanted. "If she tried to blackmail them?" Hettie persisted.

Tibbs took a breath. "Unlikely," he said. "In any event she wouldn't be believed and in no position to cast aspersions. It would be foolish beyond measure."

"But if they took her to keep her quiet..."

Tibbs's face softened as he looked at Hettie. "I'm sorry," he said. "She wouldn't be important enough to take such a risk." He touched her arm as if to comfort her. "Are you sure she hasn't simply moved on? Many girls in her position prefer to work for themselves, or she may have found an easier, more comfortable living elsewhere, where she has only to please one man, not many."

A furnace of fury burned inside Hettie. "Well, even if that is the case I still want to find her. Then we can all share her good fortune, can't we?" She tilted her chin and glared at Tibbs.

"This is getting us nowhere," Corry said. He turned to Tibbs. "I don't know how much you have found out about what goes on across the Thames but my guess is not much. The folk who know the river keep themselves to themselves and won't talk to the likes of you."

Tibbs let out a sigh. "I'm afraid you're right. I've one or two informants but they're unreliable. They tell me what I want to hear. I'll ask about a young woman being taken, if that's what you think, but I don't hold out much hope."

"But the people who attacked me..." Hettie said. "You were following them. They must be the same people who took Annie. I'm convinced of it."

Tibbs considered this for several moments. "If it's the smugglers who've taken your sister I may know some lads who can find out, although, as I said, I can't see any rhyme or reason why they should."

They talked some more about the likelihood of Annie being taken by the smugglers, but Tibbs still wasn't convinced.

"It wouldn't surprise me if Miles Summerville is involved in the opium trade," Corry said. "I understand from my business acquaintances that his ships come in from the Far East. It would be no trouble to anchor along by Rotherhithe Pier while they wait for entrance to the docks. From what I've seen he has quite a hold on Crenshaw too."

"I believe he was the man Biddy told me about," Hettie said.

"Biddy?" Tibbs raised his eyebrows.

Hettie smiled. "Biddy works for Lord Crenshaw. She told me about a row she'd overheard. Lord Crenshaw was quite put out. I'm sure it was Miles Summerville she was describing when she told me about it." She looked at Corry. "Expensive clothes and shabby shoes, she said, which describes him perfectly."

Corry grinned. So, he wasn't the only one who'd noticed Miles Summerville's footwear.

Corry promised to find out what he could about the ships mooring along the south side of the river and report back to Tibbs. Tibbs said he would ask his informants if they knew anything about a young lady being taken. They agreed to meet up again in a few days time.

Tibbs took Hettie's hand as he bade her goodbye. "I can assure you that if there's anything I can do to help find your sister I will," he said. He raised Hettie's hand to his lips. "If only to wipe the frown from your pretty face and replace it with a smile."

Hettie blushed. Corry hurried her out of the room and back onto the dance floor.

Dawn was breaking over the city when Hettie and Corry took a hansom back to the hotel. After the scene with Tibbs, Corry was determined to be the one to bring the smile back to Hettie's face. He was ridiculously pleased with the glow of pleasure he saw in her eyes as he spun her around the floor in his arms. They'd stayed for supper and joined Chloe and Buck. How different Hettie appears, Corry thought, released from the work and worries of her everyday life. The sound of her laughter when Chloe or Buck made some witty remark filled his heart with joy. If only life could always be like this, he thought. In any event he'd resolved to make the most of the night. The magnificent setting and glorious music would lift the spirits of the dowdiest soul. It was a once in a lifetime opportunity and he vowed to make the most of it. Suddenly, making it up to Hettie for all she'd been through whilst looking out for Annie became the most important thing in the world.

Corry insisted on ordering breakfast to be served in their rooms.

"That really isn't necessary," Hettie said. "A cup of coffee and a hot pie from the market on the way home will suffice." Hettie had packed all her things ready for the journey home before Corry awoke.

She'd smiled fondly at the dress she'd worn, wrapped it in tissue paper and put it back in the box it arrived in. She'd never get the chance to wear it again, but she'd keep it for a while anyway to relive the evening she had danced in Corry's arms as a never to be forgotten memory.

"So back to our old, ordinary lives," she said to him over breakfast. "I can't say I'm sorry."

"Didn't you enjoy it?" he said. "The music, the glamour, the ease and comfort that comes with wealth and status? I must say I did."

"Annie would have loved it," she said. "She would have been in her element, charming everyone in the room and having all the men pestering her for a dance."

"And you didn't?" He raised his eyebrows. "I noticed you charm enough people. I had to whisk you away onto the dance floor to stop you deserting me."

Hettie thought she'd never do that. Not in a million years. She beamed. "Yes, I did. But I wouldn't want to live like this all the time." She glanced around at the richly decorated room, the oil paintings on the walls, the ornate furniture and the highly polished floor. No effort had been spared to make the rooms as comfortable as possible.

"I wouldn't fancy having to dress up and be endlessly on show. It would be quite exhausting." She laughed. "And that dress – it was beautiful and amazing, but it was also the most uncomfortable thing to wear."

He chuckled.

"I expect you're used to it," she said. "All the glamour I mean – you being a member of Boston High Society."

Corry reddened and sighed. "I may have exaggerated that part a bit," he said. He looked shamefaced as he took Hettie's hand. "I'll admit now I wanted to impress everyone with my success. The truth is..." His blush deepened. "I am a partner in a timber mill, a very junior one. And it's a very small mill. I'm comfortably off but I'm little more than a salesman and what I've spent here will make a big dent in my fortune."

"So Annie isn't the only one who makes up stories," she said.

Corry's face crumpled. "I'm sorry," he said. "It was stupid. Starting over in America was hard and when I came home I wanted so much to be the all conquering hero. I didn't know about Annie. I just wanted to impress you and make everyone think I'd made it big in America." He gave a shy grin. "I realise now that money and status don't impress you. I got it wrong. I never meant to lie to you, Hettie. You of all people deserve the truth."

Hettie gripped his hand. "If what you're telling me is true we'd better pack up and get out of here as soon as possible. We don't want to be running up bills we can't pay."

Corry laughed. "It's not that bad, Hettie. I do have a little money, but you're right. It won't last long at this rate." He suddenly became serious. "I never lied to you about anything else, Hettie and I promise I won't ever lie to you again."

Hettie's heart swelled. This was the Corry she remembered; sometimes unsure and uncertain but always honest. "It's good to have you back, Corry," she said. "I enjoyed every moment of the ball, everything. But I'm not sorry to be going home. All I want is to find Annie so we can be a family again."

Once they had packed their things and settled the bill, Corry sent a runner to Hackney End find Jack to take them home.

Chapter Twenty Nine

Over the next few days Corry went out alone to talk to people from his past who knew all about the devious deeds and underhand dealings going on along the banks of the Thames.

"You certainly look the part," Hettie said when she saw him dressed in a faded collarless shirt and an old pair of moleskin trousers tied round his waist with rope.

"I got them from the market," he said. "The people I hope to see won't talk to anyone dressed in a suit."

"I wish I could come too," Hettie said.

Corry shook his head. "I'll be going places no young lady should see," he said. "They'll never talk to a girl neither. No, you best stay here and look after Billy. It may be dangerous anyway, if I ruffle the wrong feathers."

"In that case I definitely want to come," Hettie said but Corry was adamant.

"I'll do better on my own," he said. "But if I'm not back by supper you can call out the rozzers." He grinned but Hettie didn't think it at all funny.

She decided to go to the chop shop in Covent Garden again to speak to Veronique to find out more about the church at Le Peletier but Veronique wouldn't be drawn.

"It's not my secret to tell," was all she would say, so Hettie resolved to go back to the church at Bromley by Bow on Sunday and speak to Reverend Smythe.

Corry added a flat cap, a thick coat and shabby shoes to the outfit he'd bought in the market and walked to the docks to see what he could find out about the ships along the Thames waiting to come in. There were only two places the ships could dock, the West or East India Docks, the latter being the smaller. It was unlikely they'd choose to go further up river to St Katherine's Dock.

Ships came from all over the world; he was looking for one that had travelled from the Southern Indian Ocean, a square-rigged clipper in all probability. Clippers, acknowledged as the fastest vessels under sail, were ideally suited to low-volume, high-profit goods, such as tea, opium, spices, people and mail where the earlier the cargo could be delivered the more the trader would get for it. The returns could be spectacular.

The walled docks were closed to all except known Dockers and the entry gates were watched to ensure there was no pilfering from the cargoes being unloaded. Corry's only hope of discovering what he was looking for lay in the local pubs and bars around the less well guarded basins, piers, jetties, wharves and shipyards along the stretch of the river past Greenwich.

He caught a ferry from Wapping Steps to Greenwich Pier and found a pub called The Jolly Taverner. A wall of warmth hit him as he entered. The crowded room smelled of smoke, sweat and the sickly sweetness of stale cider. Men's laughter and the clink of glass and pewter engulfed him. He pushed his way through the crowd to the bar and stood listening to the men's banter and gossip. Most were complaining about the weather, their governors or their wives and mothers-in-law. Corry smiled.

He bought a pint of ale and asked the barman if he knew of any work going, unloading or labouring around there. He put him on to another man who couldn't be specific but he'd heard of ships being unloaded by Crossness. That was a long way from the docks and there was no crossing there unless by boat.

Corry thanked him and made his way east to the mudflats where he used to wade into the mud for what he could find when he was mudlarking along the south side of river. The tide was high, so most of the boys would be trying to sell their pickings in the chandlers' shops or round the markets. If they'd made anything they'd gather round the coffee stall near Phoenix Wharf where they could get a hot drink and a pie for a penny. He made his way there, bought a drink and two pies and found a place to sit. He didn't have long to wait.

"You needing that pie, Mister?" Mugger said. "Or are you gonna share?"

Corry smiled and handed him both the tea and one of the pies. "Thought I might find you here," he said.

"Yeah. Great detective ain't you? I'spect it's more information you wants ain't it? You ain't bought me a pie for nowt."

"So you're a great detective too," Corry said, biting into his pie.

Mugger grinned. "What is it you wants to know this time? I ain't no canary, so don't 'spect me to be grassing anyone up."

"I wouldn't dream of expecting any such thing," Corry said. "But when I was mudlarking I didn't hold any brief for the men who made their money exploiting the weaknesses of others."

"Who'd you mean?" Mugger asked staring at Corry, his pie poised between his hand and his mouth.

"Opium smugglers," Corry said. "The men who profit from selling that odious poison to people too befuddled by it to think straight."

"Oh," Mugger said, biting into his pie with fresh relish. "That all? I don't hold no brief for them neither."

"Good, then we are on the same side." Corry brushed the pie crumbs from his coat. "Now tell me about the dens in Limehouse. How much do you know about them, and the people who supply them?"

Mugger thought for a few minutes. "Two shillings," he said.

Corry grimaced. "One shilling and another pie for later," he said.

Mugger shrugged. "I knows there's someone goes over from Rotherhithe every day," he said. "Only takes small amounts but supplies several places along Causeway, Pennyfield, Bluefield, them places where there's Chinese sailors. Them's the best places. They must stash it somewhere this side of the river." He held out his hand.

Corry gave him a shilling and a penny for the pie.

They sat in silence while they ate their pies. Then Corry said, as casually as he could manage, "Do you ever hear anything about girls being taken off the streets?"

Mugger frowned. "Girls? Nah. I know of some young boys gone missing from the mudlarks, but they may be sick or dead. Never heard nothing about girls though."

Corry had heard rumours about the trade in young boys and the under-the-counter market for photos of young boys and girls too for that matter. Was that what had happened to Annie? She'd never do anything like that voluntarily. They wouldn't pay enough, not like hobnobbing with the gentry. That was much more lucrative. She'd never be involved in anything as squalid as dirty pictures for sale to dirty old men.

"If you hear anything, anything at all, you let me know. You know where to find me."

Mugger grinned. "Another shilling?" he said.

"Half a crown if the word is good and we find the girl I'm looking for."

"Sweetheart is it?" Mugger said.

"No, nothing like that." Although the thought did cross Corry's mind that if Hettie went missing he'd move heaven and earth to find her too.

"The bloke you're after with the gear usually goes over early evening," Mugger said. "You need to move quick if you wants to catch 'im."

Corry chuckled but got up. "See you again sometime, Mugger," he said.

"Not if I sees you first," Mugger said, smiling broadly as he pocketed the money Corry had given him.

Near the pier Corry managed to catch a ferry going to Wapping. All the way back he thought about Annie. Why hadn't he wanted to admit to Mugger that she was his sister? Was he so ashamed of her? He shook his head to dislodge the thought but couldn't. Sickness coiled in his stomach. He loved Annie, of course he did. Headstrong, passionate, fiery, feisty Annie. He smiled. Those were the qualities that had brought them both through the bad times. Annie had always been there for him, now it was his turn to be there for Annie. Still, he couldn't help wishing she was more like Hettie. Pious, strong, reliable Hettie, filled with gentle sweetness and effortless charm. He smiled at that thought too.

It was a good two mile walk to the street where Hettie said she had been attacked. Corry thought it as good a place to start as any. He walked a short way then turned down a side street where the lanes became narrower and the buildings shabbier. The smell of urine and rotting vegetables filled the air. Along the road men lounged in doorways, smoking foul smelling pipes; women sat on doorsteps, gossiping. A dog barked in the distance and the piteous cries of a child came from a nearby lodging house.

He took a couple more turns until he found the place. Here the street was empty save for a stray dog nosing at the rubbish piled along the gutters. The earlier rain has given up its efforts to clean the cobbles and moved on. Windows, grimy with dirt and shabby doors, their paint peeling, faced on to the street. His stomach churned at the thought of Hettie being in such a place. Even here in the early evening light the place looked forbidding. Whatever possessed Hettie to come at night?

He strolled down the street, glancing back and forth, as though just taking in his surroundings. No light penetrated between the awkward roofs. He saw a deep doorway flanked by soot-grimed buildings. Here the door was freshly painted and the step swept. He sniffed the air. The unmistakable smell of opium smoke filled his nostrils. The vision of what lay behind the door sprang into his head: men and women lost in the fog of smoke from the drugs that twisted their brains until they couldn't distinguish real life from fantasy. He shuddered. Once again the thought of Hettie being attacked filled his mind. Anger, sharp as a knife struck him. A quiet rage bubbled inside him. At the end of the street he paused, lounged against the wall and lit a cigarette. Standing in the shadows he watched and waited.

Two men ambled along the street, one stopping to light a pipe another to kick the dog, but none gave the opium den a passing glance.

After about an hour a young man, about nineteen from the look of him, hurried past carrying a package wrapped in brown paper. The ships brought in raw opium which would have to be shredded and properly prepared before it could be turned into the substances that were smoked. Corry pressed himself back against the wall. The lad knocked on the door looking furtively around as he did so. When the door opened he went in. Corry waited. A few minutes later he came out, his hand thrust deep into his pockets.

Corry dodged into a doorway as he ran past. He couldn't help thinking he'd seen him somewhere before, then it came back to him. He was called Rabbit, mainly due to the size of his ears. He was one of Gander's boys. Older now, filled out and taller, but there was no doubt in Corry's mind that he was one of the gang of boys who regularly thieved for Gander.

Corry let him get a little distance ahead of him then followed him to the river where he caught a ferry. Corry watched him as the ferryman rowed to midstream to catch the outgoing tide to carry him further down river towards Greenwich. He was more convinced than ever that the smugglers Tibbs was looking for were unloading ships across the river and that Gander and his gang were involved.

The next morning he dressed in a suit and topcoat with a crown derby hat, just like any city gent going about his business. He walked to London Bridge where he caught a steamer for a round trip to Gravesend. Luckily the weather was fine. The early mist had cleared and a light breeze blew across the water. By the time he got to the pier the steamer was crowded and ready to sail. Once on board he stood by the rail, the wind ruffling his hair.

Before long they were travelling midstream past Greenwich and Corry watched the ships moored along the south bank. He took careful note of their names and liveries writing them in a notebook. A bubble of excitement stirred inside him when he saw two ships moored along by Greenhithe pier each flying flags displaying the emblem of the Summerville Shipping Line. By the time the steamer returned from Gravesend the ships had gone.

Chapter Thirty

That afternoon Hettie insisted on going with Corry to the meeting with Tibbs. "If he's heard anything about girls being taken I want to hear it," she said. So Corry relented.

They met Tibbs in The Duke of Wellington, a hostelry in Silvertown near the India Rubber factory. Tibbs chose the venue as it was unlikely to be populated by men from the docks or the Revenue offices who might recognise him. The nauseous smell from the nearby gas works kept most people away.

When they arrived Corry ordered them each a drink, ale for him and a glass of porter for Hettie, and a couple of ham sandwiches. Hettie was glad she'd worn her good suit and best hat. The room looked gloomy and drab, the oak panelled walls stained with smoke and age. The seats were padded but the fabric worn. It was not a place she would choose to be if it weren't for her hopes of Tibbs having news of Annie.

Tibbs walked in a few minutes later. Hettie noticed again how well dressed he was. He took off his hat and a lock of blonde hair fell across his forehead. When he saw them his eyes lit up. He bought himself a drink and joined Hettie on the bench seat, placing his glass on the table in front of him. His hands were pale with long slender fingers. Not at all like Corry's, Hettie thought.

"Is there any news?" she asked as soon as he sat down. "Have you heard anything?"

He shook his head. "I am afraid I have heard nothing. I was hoping you would be able to bring me better news. The gang I've been watching seems to have gone underground, as have my snouts. I'm really lost for any new leads."

Corry sat up straighter in his chair, leaned toward Tibbs and told him about the lad he'd seen taking a package into the house in Limehouse. "I recognised him as being one of Gander's gang."

Hettie shuddered at the memory of Gander threatening Annie when they were selling cress. Plus, she hadn't forgotten it was Gander who'd got Corry into thieving. "That makes sense," she said. "It was one of the men from the street gangs that attacked me, I'm sure of it."

Tibbs nodded. "I've heard the name," he said. "I think he works for Miles Summerville, rather than the shipping company. Some sort of personal assistant. We've been watching his comings and goings for some time now but never managed to catch him at anything. I've heard he's a bad lot all round."

"You can say that again," Hettie said and swallowed a gulp of porter to fortify herself. The idea of Gander having any regular job, let alone being someone's personal assistant shocked her to the core.

"Summerville's ships were moored east of Greenwich," Corry said, showing Tibbs the notes he'd made on the steamer. "By the time I returned from Gravesend they had moved on. Probably into the docks."

Tibbs rubbed his chin. "It'd be too late to raid them anyway, once they've anchored," he said. "Any illicit cargo would have been unloaded either midstream or as soon as they tied up." He glanced at Corry. "We've tried raiding several ships but always come up empty. They somehow get to know we are coming. You'd be amazed how clean and honest the captains are when we raid their ships."

"Summerville's ships must come in fairly regularly," Corry said. "If we knew when they were next due..."

Tibbs smiled. "I can look into their arrivals. We should be able to work out when the next ones are due in."

"So you'll organise a raid?"

Tibbs nodded, but glanced around before whispering. "This time I'll use the River Police. Their boats are faster and they have more men than I can gather. Also, if there is a leak in the Revenue offices..."

"Do you suspect anyone?" Corry asked.

"Well," Tibbs said. "The Revenue Office liaises closely with the Treasury..."

He didn't need to say any more. He sipped his drink. "I'm sorry I can't find out anything about your sister. If she's been taken by someone from the docks no one I've spoken to knows anything about it." He placed his glass back on the table. "I've seen where you live. She's hardly been taken for a ransom, unless they think one of her suitors would pay up to get her back and that's very unlikely. Someone in her position would be easily replaced."

Hettie frowned. It was true. She would have very little value to the men who used her services. "Miss de Vine thinks she's left for a better life," she said. "If she'd received a ransom demand she'd have gone straight to the police."

"The police?" Tibbs said.

"Several of her clients are high ranking officers. No, it's not for money. I'm still convinced her disappearance has something to do with the drugs and the ships coming in and out of the docks."

"I've put the word out among the street gangs and mudlarks," Corry said. "If she's been taken by someone on the river I'll soon get to hear about it. But that's a matter for the police, not Customs and Excise."

Tibbs's face darkened. "If you find anything and need help, let me know. I can marshal a few officers of the law who won't hold back if it's young boys or girls being abused. All they need is a wink."

Hettie smiled. "Thank you," she said. "That's reassuring to know."

Tibbs smiled.

On Sunday Hettie took Corry to the church at Bromley by Bow. After the service they waited at the church doorway for Reverend Smythe. They watched him gather up the hymn books and place them in a pile on a table behind the pews. Corry caught him just as he was about to leave. "I believe you knew my sister in Paris," he said.

Reverend Smythe looked at him, then at Hettie. A hint of recognition shadowed his eyes. Hettie took a photo of Annie out of her reticule and showed it to him. "I was here before, remember?" she said.

Reverend Smythe took the photo and twisted his lips as though trying to think. Trying to work out how little he could say to satisfy them, Hettie thought.

"I'm sure Hettie told you how desperate we are to find her," Corry said. "Anything you can tell us would be helpful."

"We're not the only ones looking for her are we?" Hettie said, her impatience growing. "I believe a gentleman came to see you for the same purpose. Did you tell him anything more than you were able to tell me?" She stared at him.

"Veronique said to ask you about the church at Le Peletier."

At the mention of the church Reverend Smythe glanced around. The congregation had dispersed and only Corry and Hettie remained standing in the church doorway.

"Come inside," he said and ushered them to a pew at the rear of the church near the font. "It was a long time ago," he said. "I was a young theology student studying in Paris." He glanced at the photo and sighed. "Angelique was very beautiful. She had many admirers." He smiled at Hettie. "I didn't know about the baby," he said.

"So?"

"So, when you arrived with him I wasn't sure. You could have been anybody. I only knew Angelique vaguely. I was a friend of a young subaltern calling himself Charles Langtry who was billeted in Paris before joining his regiment."

"Billy's father?"

"I assume so. I didn't know any more than that then. Angelique didn't tell me about the baby. I thought she was merely looking up old friends from Paris." Sadness filled his eyes as he spoke. "Many of the young blades visiting Paris for the first time change their name to protect their families from any scandals arising from their wild behaviour, and believe me their behaviour was excessively wild." He took a breath. "I have since learned that he was in fact Charles Landridge and that he was killed in action in Egypt."

"So you didn't even tell Angelique?"

"I didn't know it at the time."

"And the church at Le Peletier?"

Reverend Smythe sank onto a nearby pew. "It was a stupid prank. We'd been drinking when Charles suggested it. He thought it would be fun if he and Angelique got married. It wasn't a real wedding. I wasn't even ordained then. I think he wanted Angelique to know that his intentions were honourable, but of course his family would never have allowed such a union. A son of the gentry marrying a dancer from the Folies-Bergère! It was a ludicrous idea." He shrugged. "I couldn't tell Angelique that when she came looking for Charles Langtry could I? I mean – it would have hurt her deeply."

"So you allowed her to go on looking for someone who didn't exist? Surely that would have wounded her more deeply?" Hettie bridled. The anger she thought she'd managed to keep at bay rose up in her chest.

Reverend Smythe grimaced. "I'm not proud of what I did. I thought it best at the time. They say when ignorance is bliss, it's folly to be wise," he said, as though that excused his actions.

"Well, for a man of the cloth you have a very poor idea of honesty," Corry said.

Reverend Smythe stood up. His face glowed. "I told Angelique that I had no idea where Charles might be, which was the truth then. I'll tell you the same as I told the gentleman looking for her. I have no idea where she is."

Hettie only just managed to repress her fury. "And the gentleman looking for her? Have you any idea who he might be?"

Embarrassment coloured Reverend Smythe's face. He took a breath as though trying to control himself. "He gave me a card. I have it in the office," he said.

Hettie and Corry stopped at a small teashop on the way home. Hettie gazed at the card Reverend Smythe had given them. "Why would a solicitor be looking for Annie?" she said.

"Not more trouble I hope," Corry said lifting his cup to sip his tea.

Hettie frowned. "I'll keep this just in case," she said. "But we don't want to go stirring up trouble for Annie. He obviously doesn't know any more as regards her whereabouts than we do. Perhaps it's best we keep it that way."

Chapter Thirty One

A few days later a runner brought a note to Corry from Tibbs to the effect that he'd be in The Prospect of Whitby in Wapping that afternoon. Corry met him there.

"Summerville's got a ship coming in on the morning tide," Tibbs said. "I'll be on the river with twenty men at dawn. You're welcome to join us if you've a mind to. After all, without your information we wouldn't be going anywhere."

"It'll be my pleasure," Corry said, beaming.

"There a reward too, if we find anything."

"Even better," Corry said. He took a gulp of his beer.

The next morning Corry crept out at dawn. The air was cold, street sellers, costers and market traders the only people out. He passed a man setting up a coffee stall. A newspaper cart rattled by, stopping to throw papers to the news-stand on the corner. Tibbs was waiting with a boat at Wapping Old Stairs. Several other boats, each manned by four men, were gathered nearby, ready to set out. Gradually they shifted into the river, moving silently in the still morning air, the dipping of their oars the only sound.

"We'll board as they round Gallions Reach," Tibbs said. "The water's deep and the current strong enough to take us quickly into midstream. We'll wait by Hobart's Wharf until we see their lights. Then we'll go."

Waiting was the worst part for Corry. What if he'd got it wrong? What if they found nothing? What if he'd got these men early from their beds on a wild goose chase – just because of some irrational notion about a man who'd paid well enough for services his sister was quite willing to provide? A gnawing ache filled his belly. The minutes ticked away with only the lapping of the water against the boat's hull to count its passing. An eerie silence fell over the boats, until one of the men in the foremost boat called, "Ship ahoy! I see her!"

Sure enough a tall-masted clipper emerged from the mist.

Without warning the light from twenty police lanterns broke through the gloom. Oarsmen pulled into the stream, the lights from their boats dancing on the dark water. Within minutes they were alongside the ship.

Tibbs lifted his loud hailer to his lips. "Customs and Excise!" he called. "Prepare to be boarded!"

Faces materialized over the ship's railings, appearing white in the reflected light of the lanterns. Ropes were thrown from the boats, ladders were hoisted and climbed, shouts filled the air. Within minutes Inspector Barnes and the men of the Thames River Police, acting on instructions from Tibbs, were aboard the ship.

Tibbs was first up from their boat, Corry followed. The ship's sails were furled as the Captain, with Tibbs standing at his shoulder, steered the ship into the jetty.

The sun rose slowly in a pewter sky, lights reflected on inky water and the swell of passing boats crashed against the hull. The sound of creaking masts, scurrying boots, men cursing and swearing filled Corry's ears. He could hardly breathe. Police officers swarmed over the ship, lifting the canvases, moving the boxes and examining everything on deck. Ten men went below to search the holds. The ship's crew stood around glaring but were powerless to intervene. There were several false alarms, mysterious boxes explained away, excuses made for things in the wrong place and a general air of hostility all round.

After several hours of searching, to Corry's great relief, a cry came up from below decks. A large amount of raw opium had been found along with tea and ivory tusks that would be smuggled in to avoid the duty. "It was hidden under a false floor," the police sergeant said. "An old mariner's trick. Thought they could fool us." He grinned. "More fool them though." At last Tibbs had the evidence he needed to launch a full investigation into the Summerville Shipping Line.

"Once we seize the illegal cargo and threaten the crew with incarceration it's amazing how quickly they turn Queen's Evidence. We'll have no trouble finding the men behind it. Thanks to you," he said.

Filled with greater satisfaction than he'd ever imagined, Corry couldn't wait to get home and tell Hettie all about it. It was mid-day before the police were able to round up the men and the illegal cargo for transportation back to Customs House. Corry was preparing to leave when he spotted Mugger hanging about in the shadow by the tow path.

"What are you doing here, Mugger?" he said. "Come to watch the fun?"

Mugger looked horrified. "Nah, not me. I ain't a copper's nark, but I seen a girl on a boat. You said you was looking for a girl on a boat."

"A girl on a boat? Nothing unusual about that. I've seen lots of girls on boats," Corry said his eyes narrowing.

"Tied up below decks?" Mugger asked.

Corry's heart beat faster. "Where?"

"Up by London Bridge."

"How come you saw below decks?"

Mugger looked sheepish. "Wasn't me," he said. "Tommy, one of the larks. He told me he saw it. A white girl tied to a bed."

"And this Tommy? Reliable is he?"

"Straight as a church pew."

Corry's stomach churned with excitement. To catch Summerville and find Annie in the same day was almost too much to hope for. "All right. Sounds like a matter for the police. If you're having me on..."

"I ain't. Honest."

"Well come on then." Corry grabbed Mugger and pulled him towards the boats where police officers were preparing to return to Wapping. "You show us which boat and the police can take a look."

Mugger pulled his arm away. "I ain't going in no police boat. What d'you take me for?"

Tibbs appeared by Corry's side. "Is there a problem? Can I help?"

"No problem," Corry said. "This honest citizen has reported seeing a girl tied up on a boat by London Bridge. If it's Annie..."

Tibbs didn't hesitate. "We're going back to Wapping anyway. London Bridge isn't much further. Come on."

On the journey up to Wapping, with Mugger squirming in the presence of so many men in uniform, Tibbs told Inspector Barnes about Corry's missing sister. "If it's her it's kidnapping and abduction," he said. "The least we can do is take a look."

"Two raids in one day, Mr Ebbs. You're spoiling us," the inspector said.

As they neared London Bridge Mugger pointed to a large, single-masted sloop which had obviously seen better days. A cabin covered most of the deck. It was large for a river boat, but not so big as not to be able to move up and down the river as the need arose. It looked like the sort of boat that would once have been used by a wealthy merchant for leisure or a not so wealthy one for fishing.

At first sight it looked deserted, but as the police boats approached a man peered over the railings. He was close enough for Corry to recognise him as Rabbit.

"Gander's somewhere at the back of this," he said to Tibbs. "If he's taken Annie..."

The police boats made for the steps by the bridge where the men scrambled ashore. As they did so the lad on the sloop jumped to shore and ran. A couple of officers from the boats ran after him, but he was swift on his feet and had a head start.

Corry walked the length of the boat staring in at the portholes. All were covered by curtains. The first men on the boat put down a gangplank. Tibbs and Corry boarded.

Below decks all the doors were locked. All Corry could think about was Annie, possibly being drugged and tied up to be used for Gander's pleasure. Despair swept over him. A cauldron of rage bubbled up uncontrollably inside him. He ran up to the top cabin and grabbed an axe from a bracket on the wall. He almost slipped as he rushed back below.

He smashed the first door open. Shock froze him to the spot. The stench alone made him want to vomit. He tried to turn his head away but the image before his eyes held him riveted. A fury of rage swirled inside him. Upward of ten young boys, all in various states of undress, lay in stupors that could only be the result of opium. He stood motionless, too sickened to move.

Tibbs, standing beside him, rushed in and grabbed the nearest boy, calling to the other men in alarm as he did so. Corry came to. He breathed heavily, trying to quell the nausea rising inside him. Blood pounded through his veins. His fists clenched.

He went to the next door and, using all his strength, broke it down. Inside he found photographic equipment, manacles, whips and other instruments of torture. Several rows of chairs were set out in front of a platform with curtains where young boys could be forced to perform for the entertainment of deviant men who enjoyed such perversions and could afford to pay for them. Corry swallowed back the bile surging up his throat. His blood boiled. This was worse than seeing Annie on stage for the first time performing at that so called musical hall. At least she'd volunteered for it.

Thin lipped with fury he smashed down the next door. Here he found the young girl Tommy must have seen through the half-pulled curtains at the porthole. She was young, beautiful and probably not more than fifteen. But she wasn't Annie.

He swore, cutting the rope tying her to the bed. She was light as a feather and just as fragile as he carried her up to the deck. The boys, all malnourished and some badly beaten, were being attended to by the officers on deck. "I've sent for an ambulance to take them to the nearest hospital," Inspector Barnes said.

"Is this your sister?" Tibbs asked when Corry lowered the young girl gently onto the deck.

Corry shook his head. "No, but I wouldn't be surprised if Gander has something to do with taking her. It would be just like him."

"If he has, be sure we will find him and then her," the inspector said. "I only hope we are in time."

Corry blinked. In time? Then it dawned on him. With the arrests at the ship and the lad escaping from the boat, Gander would want to move on. He'd go somewhere he wasn't known and he wouldn't want to leave anyone or anything that could incriminate him behind.

"But you'll find the boat's owner?" Tibbs said to the inspector. "At least you can prosecute although I doubt you can find punishment enough for his foul, depraved trade."

The inspector shrugged. "If the boat's registered we can find who owns it, but they'll deny all knowledge. They always do."

It was obvious to Corry that this wasn't the first example of the abduction and abuse of young boys that Inspector Barnes had seen. "It makes me sick to my stomach," the inspector said. "Hanging's too good for 'em"

Corry's heart pounded. "The man on the boat was the same one I saw in Limehouse," he said. "If they're still delivering there..."

The inspector grinned. "Limehouse is on my beat too," he said.

Chapter Thirty Two

That afternoon, while Corry was out with Tibbs, Hettie met with Chloe. Over tea Chloe told her all about the balls and functions she'd attended. She smiled and her eyes glinted with pleasure when she showed Hettie the pearl and ruby Tiffany brooch Buck had given her.

"It's pity you don't have a friend like Buck," she said, grinning mischievously. "Although the way Corry, or was it James Fitzpatrick, was looking at you at the ball, I do believe you have."

Hettie coloured. "He's Angelique's brother," she said. "We just want to find her."

Chloe's eyes sparkled. "Maybe that's all you want, but from the look in his eyes that night, I think he's after a good deal more."

"Nonsense," Hettie said. "Have some more tea." She lifted the pot to pour. A wave of pleasure washed over her. If only that were true, she thought.

Sipping her tea Chloe said, "Did you ever find out who that gentleman was who was looking for Angelique?" She pouted. "I'm sorry I didn't find out more about him. It's quite infuriating."

Hettie remembered the card she'd put in Annie's box after the visit to the church in Bromley by Bow. In the excitement of the last few days she'd forgotten about it. "As a matter of fact I did," she said. "He's a solicitor. As I recall he did have an address in London. I may pay him a visit."

"Good for you," Chloe said. "You must tell me all about it when we next meet up." She picked up a cake. "It's a bit of mystery isn't it? I love a good mystery." With that she bit into the cake and a squirt of cream landed on her chin.

When Hettie got home she went to look for the card Reverend Smythe had given her. She'd put it in Annie's box with her other things. Kneeling on the floor she opened the box. She smiled as she rummaged through the now familiar objects: the clothes Annie had bought in Paris and left behind, the hair ornaments and bits of jewellery, programmes, photographs and papers. She sighed. Would any of them be able to help her find out what had happened to her?

She picked up the bundle of letters addressed to Angelique Bouvier in the Boulevard Montmartre. This was an area Veronique had told her where students, artists and showgirls lived, as well as those engaged in less salubrious professions. Most of the lodgings were cheap and the landladies didn't ask too many questions.

According to Veronique it was the liveliest area in Paris.

Hettie fingered the letters. She undid the pink ribbon tying them together and picked out the one in the first envelope. Her heart beat faster as she did so, but if the letters threw any light on who Billy's father might be, and therefore where Annie may have gone to search for him, the invasion of Annie's privacy would be justified. She took a breath before reading the letter.

She scanned the writing. A good hand, obviously educated. The writing flowed clearly and was readable. The sentiments brought a blush to Hettie's face. She stuffed the letter back into the envelope. The words were meant for Annie alone to read, that much was obvious. She felt a flush of guilt for even thinking of reading them. She sat back on her heels and closed her eyes, steeling herself to carry on.

They were obviously written by her lover, the man calling himself Charles Langtry. Hettie now knew his real name was Landridge but had no idea about his background or where his family may be found. She picked out another letter, scanning only for a name or an address. There were neither. The letter, addressed to 'My Darling Angel', was merely signed with the initial 'C' and lots of crosses. Hettie sighed in exasperation and put it back.

Her heart ached for Annie. Not only did she not know how her lover had deceived her, she also knew nothing of his death. Annie's dreams of a life with Billy's father would be ground, like falling sparrows, into the dust.

She picked up the card from Reverend Smythe. Perhaps this was a lead after all. The man was a solicitor. Who was he acting for? Could it be anything to do with Annie's dead lover? Hettie hoped with all her heart that this was true. It would mean that Annie was right, he did care for her. He wasn't just leading her on as so many men did. It was a game to them. Was Annie a fool to take them seriously? Or was it Hettie who'd got it all wrong? Perhaps it was time to find out.

She tucked the card and a photo of Annie and her beau into her pocket and vowed to investigate further. If nothing else she'd feel she was doing something positive, instead of sitting back waiting for something to happen. "Oh, Annie," she said. "Why did you have to make things so difficult? What has happened to you? Where are you?"

She didn't expect a reply but her heart crunched all the same.

Later that evening Tibbs called on Hettie and Corry to update them with progress. This time Dorcas welcomed him with the offer of tea before he'd hardly crossed the threshold.

"That would be lovely," he said, smiling and handing her his hat.

In the front room Billy was standing at Corry's knee while Corry fiddled with a boat he had carved for him with two levers shaped like figures to work the oars. Corry and Billy were both engrossed but Hettie jumped up at the sight of Tibbs.

Corry put the boat on the floor for Billy and stood up.

"Good evening, Hettie, Corry," Tibbs said. He looked at the child now playing with the boat on the floor and smiled, but said nothing. "I'm sorry to call so late but I've come straight from the office," he said. "I thought you'd want to hear the latest news."

"Indeed we do," Hettie said beaming him a broad smile.

"Well?" Corry said.

"We've charged the ship's captain and questioned the crew. We've got them bang to rights. He'll lose his Master's licence but other than a fine..." He frowned. "Miles Summerville is under arrest. The ship's crew are singing like canaries and papers found in his office confirm his hand in the transportation and importation of illegal opium and evasion of custom's duty." He gave a satisfied grin. "There's to be a full enquiry into his shipping company. Lord Crenshaw has resigned from the Treasury pending investigation of his business arrangements."

Dorcas came in with the tea. She placed the tray on the table, poured the tea and handed it round. She handed Tibbs one of her freshly baked scones. "I like to see a man with an appetite," she said. Hettie had the strongest notion that she was trying to make up to him for her brusqueness the last time he had called.

He smiled his thanks and turned back to Corry. "The bad news is, although we've caught the men bringing the opium in we haven't got the distributors. There was no sign of the unloaders when we docked."

"So there's no connection to Gander?" Corry looked aghast.

Tibbs shook his head. "No one knows anything about that end of the operation," Tibbs said. "Or if they do they're keeping quiet about it. Even the lad we picked up in Limehouse is saying nothing. It's possible they're more afraid of Gander than they are of us."

"Well, you won't cut their throats will you?" Hettie said, more sharply than she intended. Memories of the man's hands around her throat when she was attacked filled her head. A shiver ran down her spine. She put her teacup on the table. Her hands were shaking.

"I'm sorry," Tibbs said.

"So! He gets away with it again," Corry said, bitterness souring his voice. "What about the boys from the boat, or the girl? Can't they tell you anything?"

Tibbs shook his head. "They're so traumatised they can barely speak. Not surprising after what they've been through." He sipped his tea before putting the cup on its saucer. "Physically they can be made better, but mentally..." he shrugged. "Who knows? They'll all be found good homes, but for some the scars will never heal."

Chapter Thirty Three

The next morning Hettie set out to visit the solicitor's office at the address in Leadenhall Street. The sun sparkled on the windows of the shops she passed. She stopped to check her reflection in one of them and wished she hadn't. She looked like a dowdy old maid.

When she arrived at the address on the card, the building looked forbidding. She glanced up and down the street. A brass plaque on the wall identified one of the occupants as Mr Ackerman. This was it, this was the place. She squared her shoulders, took a deep breath and knocked on the door. Nothing happened. After a few moments she knocked again. Then the door opened and a man stepped out. He smiled and held the door open for her. She went in. Ahead of her, along a short corridor she saw a door with the words 'Mr Josiah Ackerman, Attorney at Law' on a wooden nameplate. She knocked.

A clerk opened the door and ushered her into a small office which looked like some sort of reception. "Is Mr Ackerman in?" she asked with as much confidence as she could muster.

"Do you have an appointment?"

Hettie's heart dropped. Of course she didn't, she should have thought of that. "It's about a young lady he was looking for," she said. "I may be able to help."

"Mr Ackerman is very busy. I can make an appointment for you if you wish." He picked up a large black diary. "Next week perhaps. Say... er... Wednesday?"

Hettie shook her head. "No. No that won't do at all." She glanced around in the vain hope she might see the gentleman Chloe had described. She didn't. She took a breath and pulled herself up to her full height. "I would have thought a missing girl might claim a higher priority than sometime next week," she said. "I can see I'm wasting my time here. If Mr Ackerman wishes to know more about the girl named Angelique, he may contact me. Of course I'm very busy too, so I hope he has a lot of patience."

"Er..." the clerk glanced around, obviously torn between asking Hettie to wait and sending her away with a flea in her ear. Conflicting emotions flashed across his face. Luckily fear of the consequences of letting her go without telling Mr Ackerman won. "Er... if you'd care to wait I'll see if Mr Ackerman can see you," he said.

"I should think so," Hettie said and plonked herself down on one of the chairs, prepared to wait.

She didn't have to wait long. Within seconds of the clerk informing Mr Ackerman of her presence he reappeared, closely followed by the gentleman himself.

"I hear you have information about a certain Angelique Bouvier," Mr Ackerman said. "Please come in." He glanced at the clerk. "Perhaps you could organise some refreshment," he said. He turned to Hettie. "This way, my dear."

Hettie smiled and followed him into another office. She gave the clerk a sideways glance, tempted to poke her tongue out at him, but settling instead for a disdainful stare.

Mr Ackerman was just as Chloe had described him. Old enough to be Annie's father rather than a possible client, although, Hettie thought, one never knows. Mr Ackerman however, appeared to be every inch the gentlemen, although again, Hettie thought, looks can be deceptive.

He offered her a seat in front of his desk and sat in his own well-padded chair behind it. The office was sparsely furnished. Files of papers were piled on top of a long bookcase filled with official looking, leather-bound books. A kerosene lamp stood on the corner of the desk. A large blotter lay in the centre. A silver inkstand holding a variety of pens stood in front of the blotter. Several framed certificates graced the walls. The window overlooked the road muffling the clatter of hooves and the clank and rumble of wheels from the passing traffic.

"Now, my dear," Mr Ackerman said. "As you are aware I am looking for Miss Angelique Bouvier. When my clerk announced a young lady had called with knowledge of her whereabouts I had hoped it would be the lady in question. However, I see that my hopes are to be dashed."

Hettie grimaced. Was the unlikelihood of her being a dancer from the Folies-Bergère so obvious? "No. I'm not Angelique," she said. "My name is Hettie Bundy. I'm a friend of hers."

"Ah!" Mr Ackerman said. "And you have an address where I may find her?"

Hettie didn't respond.

He gazed at her, as though assessing her motives. "If it's a matter of a reward," he said spreading his hands, "I'm sure something appropriate may be arranged."

Hettie's brow furrowed. This was not at all what she was expecting. "Perhaps if you tell me the reason you're looking for her," she said, "I may be able to help."

Mr Ackerman leaned back and contemplated Hettie. She blushed under his scrutiny but didn't move. She was beginning to see the folly of her visit. If he was after making trouble for Annie she didn't want to help him, and if that was the case he was hardly likely to tell her so.

"That would be strictly confidential," he said.

Hettie stood. It was clear he had no more idea of Annie's whereabouts than she did and she wondered why she'd thought coming here would be such a good idea. "It seems we cannot help each other after all," she said and prepared to leave.

Mr Ackerman jumped up. "If you know where I can find Angelique Bouvier I implore you to tell me. It will be to her advantage I can assure you."

Hettie sat down again. Perhaps she should trust this gentleman, after all he was an officer of the law. Then again, perhaps that was a good reason not to trust him. She took a deep breath.

"I came here hoping you could help me find her," she said. "I heard you were looking for her and hoped you may have been more successful than I. The truth is that she has disappeared. I haven't set eyes upon her since before Christmas and I am seriously worried about her wellbeing. Something has happened to her. I am sure of it."

At that moment the clerk reappeared with a tray of tea which he placed on the desk. Mr Ackerman waved him away. "Hmm," he said, "Perhaps it would be best if you told me the whole story. How much you know about her and what you think may have happened to her." He picked up the teapot and leaned forward to pour Hettie a cup of tea.

"I think she's been taken. That's what I think."

Mr Ackerman stared at Hettie. "Taken? By whom?"

Hettie shrugged. "I don't know," she said. "All I know is that we were like sisters. We grew up together. Then she went and got a job in the music hall and I hardly knew her after that." Snakes of anxiety curled in her stomach. Mr Ackerman appeared genuine enough; he looked properly concerned as he poured the tea. She wasn't sure she was doing the right thing, but if she didn't tell somebody she would burst. The fears she'd tried so hard to control were now rising like flames inside her. She had visions of Annie being abducted and of the treatment she may be subjected to. Corry telling her about the girl they'd found in the boat with the young boys didn't help.

"She was fine until she went to Paris," she said. Tears stung her eyes, she blinked them away. She was being completely irrational and goodness knows what Mr Ackerman must think of her, but she had to get it out. The anger she felt towards Annie, suppressed for so long, burned in her stomach.

"I can see this must be terribly distressing for you," Mr Ackerman said. "Tell me about Paris."

Hettie's eyes blazed. "She went to dance at the Folies-Bergère, but you know that. You asked about a dancer from there. You must know all about what happened to her in Paris."

Mr Ackerman shook his head. "I know very little," he said. "I would very much like to know more."

"She got herself pregnant, that's what happened in Paris," Hettie said. "And from what I heard the man involved led her on and then left her. She came home with a baby, very little else and left me to look after him." She bit her lip. "And her name isn't Angelique Bouvier either. It's Annie Flanagan. Plain Annie Flanagan from Wapping." She paused. Mr Ackerman looked shocked. He wrote something on the notepad in front of him.

"I don't suppose you're so keen to find her now are you?" Hettie said.

Mr Ackerman swallowed. He stared at Hettie. "I can assure you I am keener than ever to find her if what you tell me is true." He paused. "The baby," he said. "Was it a boy or a girl?"

Hettie frowned, calm now after her outburst. Mr Ackerman seemed to be taking everything in. "What's it to you?" she asked. Then relented. "A boy, if you must know. He's called Billy and he's nearly sixteen months old."

Mr Ackerman made a note. Hettie didn't know whether to stay there or leave. Her hopes of Mr Ackerman being any help were quickly fading.

Mr Ackerman picked a photo from his file. "Is this the Angelique Bouvier you knew as Annie Flanagan?" he said. The picture was the same as the one in Annie's box. Hettie had brought it with her so she took it out of her bag and placed her copy on the table next to his. "That's her," she said. "I believe the man in the picture to be the father of her child." She half-smiled at Mr Ackerman. "This photo was one of the pictures she brought back from Paris. We are talking about the same person."

Mr Ackerman nodded. He made another note.

Hettie went on. "The last I heard of Annie, who you call Angelique, she was working for a woman in Belgravia. I'm sure I don't need to tell you in what capacity. I understand you made enquiries there yourself."

Mr Ackerman looked discomforted but merely coughed and inclined his head in agreement.

"I understand you also visited St Leonard's, in Bromley by Bow. Reverend Smythe gave me your card, which is what brought me here."

"Yes," Mr Ackerman said.

"And did Reverend Smythe tell you about the fake wedding between Angelique and her beau?" Hettie huffed. "He went to a lot of trouble to deceive her. She came home to England to find him." She clenched her jaw. "Reverend Smythe said the man she knew as Charles Langtry had been killed in Egypt. I don't know how true that is, it may be another deception, but Annie wouldn't know that and I fear it may be her continuing attempts to find him that have been the cause of her disappearance. I myself was attacked for asking too many questions when trying to find her."

Mr Ackerman sat back and put his hand to his mouth. He shook his head.

"If you were attacked I can assure you it was nothing to do with your friend's search for her lover."

Hettie raised her eyebrows. "You can *assure* me of that can you? How come? You seem to know a lot more than you're letting on. If you're a party to her disappearance or to my being attacked..."

"My dear Miss Bundy." Mr Ackerman folded his arms and leaned back in his chair. "I cannot reveal how I know her disappearance and the attack on your good self were nothing to do with her search for him. Suffice to say you have my word. I'm afraid you will have to be satisfied with that."

She shrugged. "If you say so." It was clear she'd get no more out of him. He was obviously acting for a client. Who his client might be was a mystery too deep for Hettie to worry about. She had enough to do worrying about Billy and Annie and Corry and the rest. "It appears we are each as wise as the other and neither of us any nearer to finding her," she said. "I shall continue looking and asking questions and I hope you will do the same. Perhaps between us we can come up with something."

He smiled and appeared to relax. "If I hear any news or my extensive enquiries turn up anything of value you will be the first to know," he said. "How may I contact you?"

Hettie gave him her address. "I do hope we find her soon," she said. "Every day that passes I grow more afraid for her."

"I'll do everything I can," Mr Ackerman said.

And in her heart Hettie believed he really would.

Chapter Thirty Four

Corry spent the morning after the raid looking for Mugger. The tide was low so he expected to find him prospecting along the banks of the Thames. He tried the Wapping flats and the area around London Bridge. When he found him Mugger was up to his knees in mud along the banks by Vauxhall Bridge. With the promise of a shilling he was easily persuaded to accompany Corry to the narrow street in Limehouse where Corry had seen Rabbit deliver a package to the opium den.

"If he's daft enough to come today I want to follow him back to Gander's," Corry said. "If we find where Gander's hiding we may need the rozzers."

Mugger's eyes widened but he didn't say anything. Corry guessed the promise of a shilling overrode his ethics about fraternising with the police.

Although the midday sun cast its light over the city, the area round Limehouse Basin was dark with shadow. The buildings either side of the cobbled streets overhung the road, their roofs almost touching. The air felt dank despite the warmth of the April day.

They entered the alley from the direction of the river, the way Rabbit would come if he had a delivery to make. Corry walked past the opium den and settled in a doorway on the opposite side further along the road, a doorway deep enough for him to hide in the shadows. He leant against the boarded up door. Mugger sat on the stone step, munching on the pie Corry had bought for him. Neither of them spoke.

The hours passed slowly. Corry smoked cigarettes at intervals, in between whittling a piece of wood into the semblance of a horse for Billy. He recalled the hours he'd sat on doorsteps in New York, whittling his models. He'd wait here as long as it took. If Rabbit was coming there was no way he was going to miss him.

Mugger changed position several times and walked to the end of the road to look around. Now and then someone ambled past, on their way to the wharves or the boats. No one gave Corry a second glance. A woman with a bundle of washing on her hip bustled along the road. Church bells struck faintly in the distance marking the hours as they passed.

Dusk was falling when Corry heard footsteps coming towards them. His body tensed. He threw the rest of the cigarette he was smoking to the ground and stubbed out its glow.

Mugger stood up.

"I thought I might find you here," Tibbs said, sliding into the doorway beside Corry. "Too good an opportunity to miss, eh?"

Corry relaxed. "Great minds think alike," he said.

Tibbs took out a case and offered Corry another cigarette. In the flickering light of the match Corry saw the determination on Tibbs's face.

Another hour passed. Lights appeared in one or two windows of the forbidding building. Lodging houses for sailors, Corry thought although he couldn't imagine why anyone would want to lodge in such a godforsaken place.

A Chinese sailor stumbled along and went in through a door near the end of the road. Several more lights appeared at windows along the length of the building, but the roadway was still as quiet as the grave.

Then, in the half-light from the windows Corry saw him. Wearing a heavy overcoat with his cap pulled low over his face, Rabbit walked towards them carrying a brown paper parcel.

He came from the direction of the river just as Corry had predicted. Corry watched as he glanced up and down the road before knocking softly on the door of the opium den.

Tibbs started forward, but Corry grabbed his arm. "We want the organ-grinder, not the monkey," he whispered in Tibbs's ear.

Tibbs grimaced but nodded. After about fifteen minutes the door opened and Rabbit came out, empty handed. He glanced up and down the road again before setting off back the way he had come.

Corry waited a few minutes before stepping out to follow him. Seconds later Tibbs left. He followed a few feet behind Corry with Mugger alongside him. Corry swore softly when Rabbit jumped into a boat and rowed away. He'd expected him to get a ferry from the steps, not to have brought a boat of his own. He dashed to the steps and managed to catch a ferry. Tibbs and Mugger were close on his heel. The ferryman was a more experienced rower than Rabbit and more familiar with the river. They soon caught sight of Rabbit about twenty yards ahead of them.

Rabbit pulled in and tied up at Rotherhithe. Corry, Tibbs and Mugger were close behind. Corry and Mugger scrambled up the steps as soon as the ferry docked while Tibbs paid the ferryman. For several anxious moments Corry thought they'd lost him, then Mugger grabbed his sleeve and pointed to an alleyway where Corry saw Rabbit disappearing into the gloom.

Tibbs took one side of the street, Corry the other. Silently they edged their way along, pressing themselves into the wall whenever Rabbit paused or turned around. The warren of passageways and alleys was shrouded in an all-pervading darkness. They'd left the flickering glow of gaslight far behind.

About fifty yards in, the alleyway narrowed until there was barely room for one body to pass along it. Corry's heart almost stopped when Rabbit disappeared into a building on the right. The road was a dead-end. We've got him, he thought. If Gander's here I'll have him too.

He turned to Tibbs and grinned. He made a circle with his fingers and pointed to show they were in the right place. Tibbs grabbed Corry's arm to hold him back.

"There may be a whole gang of them in there," he whispered. "Let me send Mugger for reinforcements. We may be outnumbered."

Corry shook his head. "No, we need to go in now. Don't give him time to get away."

"It's madness to take on a gang on our own." Tibbs turned to Mugger and pulled a notebook and pencil out of his pocket. "Can you get this note to Inspector Barnes in Wapping and bring him here?" he said. "The Thames Tunnel'll take you straight to the station. It'll be quicker than going by boat."

Mugger grinned. "Half a crown," he said.

Tibbs sighed. "Half a crown," he said. "When you bring him." Mugger grabbed the note and ran.

Meanwhile, Corry walked up and down the alley, assessing the possibility of breaking into the house. The windows were boarded but the front door looked flimsy enough. He had no tools and wished he'd thought to bring something. The only weapon he had was the penknife he'd been using to whittle the wood. He glanced around. If he could find a large stone or even a wooden pole he'd have something. At the entrance to the alley he'd noticed a metal bin outside one of the houses. He went back and picked it up.

"Hey, wait on," Tibbs said. "What do you think you're going to do with that?"

"Break into the house," Corry said. "If this is Gander's hideaway this is where he'll be treating the raw opium to sell over the river. This may be where he's holding Annie."

"If he's taken her," Tibbs said. "We have no proof of that do we? We should at least wait for Inspector Barnes and his men."

"You can wait if you want," Corry said. "I'm going in." With that he lifted the bin and smashed it against the door. The door splintered and Corry pushed his way into the house.

Inside was in darkness and at first Corry saw only the blackness around him. He breathed heavily, smashing the door down had taken more effort than he'd thought. He heard movement ahead of him and a lamp flickered. Rabbit appeared carrying the lamp.

Corry rushed at him, pushing the bin he still held into Rabbit's stomach, catching him off guard and knocking him to the floor.

The lantern smashed, the oil spilled and flames spread along the wooden floorboards.

Corry went to kick Rabbit in the head, but Rabbit grabbed his leg and pulled him over. He fell on the flames, snuffing them out. Heat scorched his side, burning a hole in his shirt.

Rabbit was the first to his feet, but not for long. As Rabbit turned to kick Corry, Tibbs felled him with a blow to the back of his head with a split plank from the shattered door.

A door opened at the end of the hall and a voice called out, "What the hell? What's all the racket?" He soon found out. Corry was on his feet and at the door in seconds. He punched the man in the stomach, following that with an uppercut to the jaw. The man fell back, hitting his head on the wall and sliding to a sitting position on the floor.

Tibbs stepped from behind Corry and they both went into the room. A kerosene lamp on a table shone a dull light on large metal pans used to shred raw opium and boil it into the hard waxy substance sold for smoking. The acrid smell filled the air. Corry took out his whittling knife and picked up the lamp. "Let's have a good look round," he said.

Tibbs followed him into the hallway. Corry opened one door after another, swinging the lamp into the rooms but saw nothing. Then, out of nowhere came a mighty roar and Gander was on him. Before Corry had time to act Gander jumped on his back and hooked his arm in a choke hold across Corry's throat.

Corry grabbed his arm and tried to twist him off. Foul breath brushed his face. Corry recognised the scar on Gander's cheek and the meanness in his eyes as he twisted to face him. He swung the lamp wildly, struggling to free himself from Gander's grasp. Back and forth they struggled until Corry managed to swing the lamp high enough to smash it against Gander's head, loosening his grip.

They were plunged into darkness. Before Corry could regain his balance Gander roared again, knocked him out with a punch to the jaw, lifted him bodily into the air and threw him against the wall.

Another man grabbed Tibbs and punched him. Tibbs swung the wooden plank at his opponent sending him reeling. He stood ready to continue the fight but the man stumbled to his feet and ran, following Gander, out of what remained of the broken-down door.

Half-an-hour later, when Corry came round, his back ached and his head pounded. He felt as though he'd been trampled by a thousand horses. Tibbs was kneeling by his side. "He got away," he said.

Corry groaned. He glanced around. The hallway was full of men with lamps looking into every room in the house.

Mugger appeared next to him.

"There's a girl..." he said. "Laid out in a back room. Drugged from the look of it."

Corry scrambled to his feet. A searing pain shot through his brain. He staggered. Mugger pointed to a door that led to a basement. Corry borrowed a lamp from one of the policemen and, with Tibbs's help went down into the basement.

Sickness welled up inside him when he saw Annie. His passionate, feisty, vivacious sister lay drugged, emaciated and ill on a rough bed where she'd obviously been kept for Gander to do whatever he pleased.

It was all he could do not to vomit. Tibbs stepped forward, knelt beside the bed and lifted Annie's head gently from the pillow. "Is this your sister?" he said, the look in his eyes more eloquent than words. Corry nodded.

Together they wrapped Annie in the grubby sheet that covered her. Her chemise and petticoat were torn and stained. Tibbs's jaw clenched as he lifted her and carried her upstairs.

"Is this the girl you were looking for?" Inspector Barnes asked.

Corry nodded. "Yes. She's my sister." A wave of deep emotion washed over him. His wild, spirited, beautiful sister lay like a corpse in Tibbs's arms.

"There's an ambulance on its way," one of the young constables said.

The inspector nodded. "We thought there might be casualties," he said.

Inspector Barnes and his men rounded up all the evidence they needed. The opium processing equipment was carried out to a waiting police wagon. "We should at least be able to prosecute the landlord of the house for allowing the distribution of drugs," he said. "And I'm sure we'll have no difficulty in finding the men who've escaped."

Corry wished he felt as confident.

When the ambulance arrived Tibbs carried Annie out. He'd stayed by her side since finding her.

"You both look like you could do with a bit of medical attention an' all," the inspector said. Tibbs and Corry grinned but they both went in the ambulance with Annie.

Corry held Annie's hand while Tibbs bathed her face and stroked her hair.

"She'll be all right when the drugs wear off," he said, probably more to convince himself than Corry. "She'll just need a bit of looking after."

"Yes," Corry said. He had a feeling she'd be in safe hands with Tibbs. "I wish we'd caught Gander though. I could kill him for what he's done."

Tibbs looked at Corry and nodded in silent agreement.

Chapter Thirty Five

As soon as Hettie heard from Mugger that Annie had been found and taken to hospital she lost no time in getting there herself. Not sure what to expect, she left Billy with Dorcas. Mugger said

Corry and Tibbs had rescued her from a house in Rotherhithe. Hettie could only guess what sort of place that was and what went on there.

Breathless, she rushed up to the reception. She shivered. The last time she'd been here was when Corry had had the accident that left him crippled. She took a breath and asked to see Miss Annie Flanagan.

The girl on reception asked her to wait while she found a doctor.

Hettie paced the floor, wringing her bag in her hands. Visions of the last time she'd seen Annie, so full of life, laughing and dancing around with Billy, played in her mind.

She'd been there about ten minutes when she saw Corry limping towards her along the corridor. His hair was awry, his clothes torn and spattered with blood. One eye was so swollen and bruised it was half-closed. His hands were bandaged and a bloody graze filled his cheek. Hettie raced towards him.His attempt at a smile when he saw her made her heart crunch. "Mugger said you'd been in a fight, but I never imagined..."

Corry put his arm around her shoulders. His good eye shone with tears. "They got away," he said. "The bastards got away."

Hettie helped him to a seat. The knot in her stomach tightened. "At least you're alive," she said, "and Annie. How is Annie?"

"She's alive too, but barely. It was Gander. The evil bastard drugged her. Lord knows how long she's been like that, or what else he's done to her." He turned to look at Hettie. "I'll swing for him, Hettie. As God is my witness I'll have him." The anger that consumed him was plain to see.

The receptionist returned. "You can see Annie Flanagan now," she said. "Follow me." Hettie asked Corry to wait for her and followed the girl to the charity ward where Annie lay. Hettie was surprised to see Tibbs leaning over her. He looked up when he saw Hettie. "I think she's coming round," he said.

Hettie rushed to the bedside. She swallowed when she saw Annie. Her face, pale as marble, felt as cold. Her eyes were closed, her cheeks sunken. Hettie brushed a lock of auburn hair from her cheek. "Oh Annie," she said. "I'm so glad to see you. I thought we'd lost you."

Annie's chest rose as she took a breath. Her eyes opened slowly. Eyes that had no spark of life in them. "Annie, it's me, Hettie. You've been poorly but you're back now. We're going to take care of you, aren't we, Tibbs?" She glared at Tibbs who was still holding Annie's hand and gazing into her face.

He came to with a start. "Yes, yes we are," he said. He smiled. The smile lit up his face. A smile for Annie, Hettie thought and was glad.

"You just get yourself fit and well and you'll be home in no time," Hettie said, relief at seeing Annie calming the horror she'd felt seeing Corry in such a state. She glanced at Tibbs and noticed his face too was bruised, his coat torn and muddied and the collar of his shirt hung loose around his neck. Annie stared at Tibbs.

Of course, Hettie thought. Annie had never met Tibbs. "This gentleman saved your life, Annie, with Corry's help." Then she realised Annie wouldn't even know Corry was home from America. Annie stared at her as though she didn't even know who Hettie was.

Hettie stroked Annie's hair. "Don't worry," she said. "You've a lot of catching up to do, but in time, and with proper rest and care you'll be right as rain." Even as she said it Hettie wondered if she was being overly optimistic. She'd heard about people losing their minds and never recovering from taking drugs. They'd do everything they could at the hospital and at home, but ultimately it would be up to whether Annie was strong enough. A shiver ran down her spine.

The next morning Hettie and Corry visited Annie in hospital, taking in small bites of food and messages from Dorcas and Pastor Brown. Most of the time Annie lay transfixed, staring at the ceiling with unseeing eyes.

"It'll take a few days," the doctor said. "Recovery takes time, but the human body is wonderfully resilient."

The following day Hettie went on her own while Corry went out to look for Gander. Annie still lay pale and fragile as a fallen leaf pushed this way and that by a sudden breeze. Occasionally she'd glance at Hettie and smile, but she never spoke, lost in a dream world of her own.

Hettie noticed fresh flowers and a card by the side of Annie's bed. She picked up the card. *'Get well soon, Tibbs'*, she read.

The next day there were chocolates with a card from Tibbs. Hettie smiled as she put the card back. Each day she saw a slight improvement in Annie as the effects of the opium wore off. She thought Annie's confusion and disorientation a blessing and thanked the Lord that she was unable to recall what had happened to her, but gradually her memory returned.

"I was drugged," she said one day. "That's why everything is so confused. I thought I was dreaming, imaging things, terrible things. Some of it seemed so real."

Hettie soothed her. "You don't need to think about that now," she said. "It's all in the past. All you have to do is get better."

But she did have to think about it when Inspector Barnes called that afternoon. Hettie was with Annie and Annie asked her to stay while she told the inspector all she could remember.

"I wasn't drugged all the time," she said. Her face darkened, like a thundercloud passing over the sun. Hatred glowed like burning coal in her eyes. "I'll never forget what they did to me. If I live to be a hundred years old I'll never forget." She said it with such vehemence that Hettie worried for her.

Inspector Barnes pulled up a chair, set it next to her bed and sat on it. He took out his notebook and pencil. "Now," he said. "Start at the beginning and tell me everything."

Annie took a breath. Hettie squeezed her hand. "It was Gander," she said. "Gander Thomas, who used to run the street gangs when we were growing up." She looked at Hettie. "You remember?"

"I do," Hettie said.

"He must have seen me with Miles Summerville, one of my, erm... Miss de Vine's...

erm… well a man I was escorting to the opera, or so I was told." She glanced at the inspector who was making notes. "I often visited the opera and other functions with men of wealth and standing. Miles Summerville was one such man, or so I thought." She paused and a great sigh escaped her lips. "I'm not naïve when it comes to men, Inspector," she said. "But it appears I was quite wrong about him."

"Wrong? In what way, Miss?" Inspector Barnes said, his brow furrowed.

"When I got into the carriage he had sent for me, Gander was there with him. I recognised him at once. 'So, what do you think, Gander? Will she do?' he said. Gander said, 'I think she'll do very nicely.' 'There must be some mistake,' I said. 'I'm here to escort you to the opera. They both laughed at that. Then Miles told Gander he could do what he liked with me – I was bought and paid for." She sniffed. Hettie handed her a handkerchief. Annie blew her nose, wiped her tears and held her head high. "Well, Gander must have seen me before and recognised me. Miles thought it a great game to offer me to Gander as some sort of… some sort of… what would you call it?" She stared at Inspector Barnes. "A prize? A bonus? I don't know what." She sniffed again. "'So, it's Miss Annie Flanagan from Wapping is it?' Miles said. 'And I was expecting Angelique Bouvier from Paris.' He laughed. I tried to get out of the carriage but he and Gander stopped me." She paused for breath. "Gander said I owed him for getting Corry to leave the gang. He said Miles had promised he could have me. He said I'd rue the day I ever crossed him. Oh, Hettie it was awful. I tried to fight him off but he was stronger than me, and Miles held me down."

Anguish and shame filled her eyes. "I thought it was some sort of sick game. I pleaded with them to let me go but the louder I pleaded the louder they laughed." She drew herself up as best she could and looked at Hettie. "I expect everyone thinks I got what I deserve, but I didn't deserve what he did to me, Hettie. I really didn't."

"No, no of course you didn't," Hettie said. "No one deserves that. Gander should hang for what he did to you. If Corry ever finds him..."

"Corry?" Annie took a deep breath. "How can I face him again after what I've done? He's probably disowned me. He hated it when I joined the music hall, how much worse must he think of what I've done since?"

Hettie stood and put her arms around Annie. "Corry doesn't blame you, Annie. It's Gander he's after." She put on her best smile for Annie. "Corry understands a lot better than you think."

"Do you think he'll ever forgive me?"

"I think he already has," Hettie said.

The inspector coughed. "So, Miles Sommerville was party to the abduction was he? Well, that's another thing to add to his charge sheet. Don't worry, Miss. He'll be going away for a long time, if they don't hang him."

"And Gander? What about Gander?"

"Erm. Unfortunately he got away. But don't you worry. We'll find him and when we do..." The inspector shuffled uncomfortably. "It's very unpleasant I know, but I have to ask, what happened after that?"

"The next thing I knew I woke up tied to a bed in a cold, dark, smelly room with no windows," Annie said. Her brow puckered. She shook her head. It was as though she'd remembered something too terrible to talk about and was shutting down. "It's all a bit of a haze. I can't tell you how much of it was real and how much hallucination. I remember waking up screaming and being beaten to keep quiet. I remember several men coming in and out of the room. Then there was Gander... he... he..." She broke down sobbing, her head in her hands.

"That's enough," Hettie said jumping up to put her arms around Annie again. "I think she's had enough."

The inspector nodded. "Well, thank you for your frankness," he said, closing his notebook. "I think we have enough to go on. Certainly enough to bring a case for kidnap and abduction. You've been very brave." He patted Annie's shoulder.

Annie sniffed and removed her hands from her face. "Thank you, Inspector," she said.

Once Inspector Barnes had gone Annie asked Hettie about Billy. "Where's Billy?" she said, eyeing Hettie suspiciously. "You haven't mentioned him since I've been here. Is he all right?" She stared at Hettie "You do still have him don't you? Please tell me you've been taking care of him."

"He's fine, growing up and full of life, which is more than I can say about you. We need to get you better before you see him."

Annie sighed. "I don't even know how long I was in that dreadful place." She glanced at Hettie. "You must have thought I'd deserted him. I bet Dorcas thought that when I stopped paying. Go on admit it, she thought the worst of me." Her face drooped with sadness, misery filled her eyes. "I couldn't blame her. Oh, Hettie. I've been such a fool."

Hettie squeezed Annie's hand. "Ma didn't always approve of what you did but even she knew you didn't deserve what happened to you. She's looking after Billy as though he were her own. He's really charmed her. She wouldn't hurt him for the world." Hettie pushed the memory of Dorcas wanting to take him to the workhouse to the back of her mind.

"Now," Hettie said. "We need to get you tidied up. Corry and Tibbs will be in to see you this evening and you'll want to look your best." She took a mirror and comb out of her bag and handed it to Annie. Annie grinned as she took it. A spark of life came into her eyes. That's it, Hettie thought. I knew appealing to your vanity would get you better quicker than a lightning flash.

Chapter Thirty Six

Annie was well enough to be allowed home at the end of the week. "There's nothing more we can do for her," the doctor said. "She needs rest and feeding up to put the bloom back in her cheeks, but apart from that..." He smiled.

Corry arranged to go with Jack to collect her from the hospital. He took some fresh clothes and a gaily coloured shawl for her. Dorcas made up a bed for Annie in Hettie's room so Hettie could keep an eye on her and laid on a welcome home party with fish paste sandwiches, cakes and scones. Hettie dressed Billy in his best blue and white outfit and brushed his golden hair until it shone. "Mummy's coming home," she told him. He giggled. She wondered whether he'd remember Annie; it had been so long since he'd seen her.

When Annie arrived home Corry helped her from the carriage. Still wobbly on her legs she clung to him. As soon as she saw Billy she rushed to him and tried to pick him up, but her arms couldn't hold him. She bent down to hug him close, tears running freely over her cheeks. Billy looked bemused and wriggled from her grasp. Hettie picked him up and he chuckled. Hettie's heart squeezed.

Corry led Annie to a seat while Sarah handed out cups of tea. "We're glad to have you home," Sarah said. "Everyone's been so worried."

Annie smiled. "Some more worried than others no doubt," she said looking at Dorcas.

Hettie bridled. "That's not fair," she said. "If it hadn't been for Ma, Billy would be..."

Pastor Brown stepped in before she could finish. "I'm sure we've all worried," he said, "and are all equally pleased to see you returned to the fold."

Dorcas handed Annie a cup of tea and said, "If I've been a bit harsh in the past it's been with your best interests at heart. You were never the easiest child, but you've grown into a responsible adult. I'll give you credit for that."

Annie nodded her thanks. "I guess that's the nearest I'll get to an apology," she whispered to Hettie when Dorcas's back was turned.

"Well, I'm glad you're safe and well," Corry said. "We've got a lot of catching up to do."

Watching him, Hettie realised the bond between brother and sister had never been broken, despite the early animosity and long separations.

"I want to hear all about America," Annie said. "It seems I did you a favour making you so mad you started a fight, then ran away."

Corry laughed. "It didn't feel like a favour at the time," he said.

A little later Tibbs arrived with Inspector Barnes. "Well, I must say you're looking a lot brighter," the inspector said, smiling at Annie.

"And as beautiful as ever," Tibbs added handing her the flowers he had brought.

"Thank you, kind sir," Annie said taking the flowers and handing them to Hettie. "I understand I have a lot to thank you for. I can assure you I won't forget your kindness."

Tibbs took a seat next to Annie. "I can only imagine the horrors you went through," he said. "I'm sorry we didn't find you sooner."

"Is there any news about the kidnappers, Inspector?" Corry asked.

Inspector Barnes shook his head.

"They should all hang for what they did," Tibbs said.

"We have to catch them first," Corry reminded him.

The inspector sighed. "We have Miles Summerville, his crew and a couple of Gander's boys in custody," he said. "It's my eternal regret that Gander got away. But the arm of the law is long. We will catch him one day."

"Well, it can't be soon enough for me," Annie said.

Towards the end of the afternoon Billy was getting fractious, anxious for his tea, and Dorcas said Annie needed to rest. Sarah, Tibbs, Inspector Barnes and Pastor Brown all said their goodbyes and wished Annie a swift recovery. Corry said he'd go with them to the river.

"I owe Mugger half a crown and a good deal more," he said. "I think it's time I treated him and the boys to a slap-up meal, or at least a few pies." No one could argue with that.

Dorcas went to the kitchen to feed Billy and put him to bed.

"Corry's told me how good you've been looking after Billy and always speaking up for me," Annie said once she and Hettie were alone. "I won't forget it, Hettie. Whatever happens I'll always be grateful to you."

Hettie blushed. So Corry had spoken well of her. Somehow that thought gave her the greatest pleasure. "Billy's never been any trouble and Ma helped. I knew you'd never desert him."

"So, how did you find out about Miles Summerville and Lord Crenshaw, Hettie?" Annie asked. "And Mr Tibbs? How did you meet him and what's he really like?" Interest sparkled in her eyes. "His was the first face I saw when I woke up in the hospital, you know. You must tell me all about him."

"Let me make us both some hot chocolate," she said. "Then I'll tell you everything."

But, in view of Annie's poor state Hettie didn't tell her everything. She couldn't bring herself to tell Annie about the visit to St Leonard's and finding out that Billy's father had deceived her or that he'd been killed. She'd save that for a later day.

Corry and Tibbs walked by the river each deep in thought. They watched the boats going up and down the Thames, into and out of the docks.

"When the Royal Albert Dock opens the Pool of London will be the biggest and busiest port in the world," Tibbs said. "If Gander's got a ship we'll never find him."

"I'll find him" Corry said. "If it takes every breath in my body I'll find him."

"If there's any more I can do you only have to ask," Tibbs said. Then he removed his hat, turning it in his hands. "You have a beautiful sister," he said. "Would you object to my calling on her?" He blushed. "To see how she is of course."

A wide grin spread across Corry's face. "No objection whatsoever," he said.

Corry continued on to the mudflats where he found the boys digging for their finds. He gave them each a shilling. "There's a sovereign for the lad who can tell me where Gander Thomas is. That's if I find him."

He left the boys wide-eyed, pocketing their new found wealth and grinning.

Next he went to the church. He wanted to visit his mother's grave and tell her that Annie was safe and being looked after by Hettie. The more he thought about Hettie the more confused he became. She'd been like a sister to him but he wasn't indifferent to her charms. He recognised the goodness in her heart and wondered how he could have been so lucky to have found her again. But his feelings went deeper than that. He was perturbed by how often her face appeared in his thoughts and how every vision of her sent his mind spinning. He recalled how happy she made him, how different she was from Annie, how blessed he felt in her company and how his problems disappeared in the warmth of her smile. He had feelings he shouldn't have for a sister. But then, she wasn't his blood sister was she?

On his way to the church he bought some flowers from one of the street girls on her way home from the market. Inside the church he gave thanks for Annie's deliverance and prayed for guidance. Then he walked to the back of the churchyard where he put the flowers on Mary Flanagan's grave.

He glanced around. The churchyard was empty. Dusk was falling. "She's home, Ma," he whispered. "And I'm going to stay and look out for her. You don't need to worry about Annie anymore. She's going to be fine." Even as he said it he wondered whether Ma had ever worried about Annie, but he was her big brother and he knew where his duty lay.

About a month later, Annie was well on the way to making a full recovery. Dorcas's lodger had moved out and Annie had been restored to the room she'd occupied on her return from France. Hettie's heart ached when Billy moved in with Annie, but she knew it to be for the best.

Corry went out to meet Tibbs in The Duke of Wellington in Silvertown. "You have some news for me?" he asked as soon as Tibbs walked in the door.

Tibbs nodded. He got himself a drink and sat with Corry. "It's not good news," he said. "I've spoken to a few people around the docks. Gander was last seen jumping a ship to America. He's gone, Corry. Out of reach, but at least he'll leave Annie alone now. He can't hurt us from there."

Corry's brow creased. He bit his lips together. Part of him was glad for Annie, at least she could put him out of her mind now, but he still harboured the desire to find him and bring his reign of terror to a permanent end. He sipped his ale slowly. Hadn't he done the same all those years ago, when he thought he'd be pursued by the police?

Corry had contacts in America, a business over there and enough clout to make sure Gander paid for his sins. The thought made him feel better. He remembered what Inspector Barnes had said about the long arm of the law.

"Does Inspector Barnes know?" Corry asked.

"Yes, I've spoken to him. He's sending details of the Warrant for Gander's arrest on the next ship out."

Corry smiled. "All is not lost then," he said. The inspector was right, there'd be no place for Gander to hide.

"Let's drink to rough seas and long journeys," Corry said.

"Rough seas and long journeys," Tibbs repeated.

After leaving Tibbs, Corry walked back along the banks of the Thames. It was the first time thoughts of returning to America had entered his mind. What he'd told Hettie was true; he did have business interests there, a home and friends. He'd been setting up sales of timber from the mill to agents in London, but since he'd been back...

The familiar streets felt like home to him now. Then there was Annie and Billy to look after, although, judging by his frequent visits, Tibbs may be planning to take over that responsibility. He smiled at the prospect. Then there was Hettie...

He sat for a while watching the river, trying to sort out the thoughts running through his mind. He sighed. He'd do what he always did when faced with a dilemma; he'd go and see Pastor Brown.

Chapter Thirty Seven

By the beginning of May, Annie was well enough to go out with Hettie and Billy. The sun warmed the streets and they needed only to wear their knitted shawls. Billy was happy to toddle along beside them while they walked over the park or along by the river. Hettie decided it was time to talk to Annie about her and Billy's future.

They went to the tearooms in the park where Annie had first announced her intention to leave Billy with Hettie and live with Miss de Vine. Could it really have been only a year ago? So much had happened since.

Annie gazed around. "Do you remember the last time we came here?" she asked.

"Yes," Hettie said. "Vividly. But that's the past. I want to talk about the future." She sighed and her shoulders sagged. "There's something I haven't told you."

Annie eyed her suspiciously. She didn't respond immediately. She picked up the teapot and poured the tea. "I can't think what it could be," Annie said. "I hope it's not bad news."

Hettie swallowed. "I'm afraid it is," she said. "I didn't tell you before because I didn't think you strong enough, but there's something you need to know."

"That sounds ominous. Go on."

Hettie took a breath. "Corry and I went to see Reverend Smythe at St Leonard's," she said. "He told us about Charles Langtry, or..." she paused, watching Annie closely. "Charles Landridge to give him his real name."

Annie stared at her.

"He told us about the fake wedding. You did know it was fake didn't you? Or did he deceive you in that too?"

Annie paled. She took a breath, her mouth twisted into a pout. "Charles and I were lovers," she said. "The wedding was our way of showing our intention to marry. He was leaving to join his regiment. It was to show me he meant to come back and marry me for real. When I find him he will confirm everything I've said." She pulled her shawl closer around her. "Now let's not hear any more nonsense about deceit."

"You knew his real name?" Hettie paused. "So why not contact his family on your return to England? Why go to the trouble of working in a place like Sylvia de Vine's? If he was as honest as you say he'd have given you his real name and address in England."

Annie flushed scarlet. "You know nothing about it. Nothing about what it was like in Paris then." She bit her lip. "How difficult it was for us." She tilted her chin. "I'll not sit and listen to any more of this cruel rubbish, Hettie Bundy." Tears shone in her eyes. "Of course he loved me. He wanted to marry me. I don't know why you have to be so mean spirited. I can only assume you are jealous. You always did have a mean, jealous streak."

With that she tried to stand. Hettie leaned over and grabbed her arm. "I'm sorry, Annie," she said. "I was only trying to make a point. You didn't know as much about him as he let you believe." She raised her eyebrows. "Anyway, it matters little now. Reverend Smythe told us he'd been killed in Egypt. I don't know how true that is, or if it's another deceit, but..."

Annie sank back into the chair. The blood drained from her face. Hettie thought she was about to faint. "Killed?" She stared at Hettie.

"That's what Reverend Smythe said. Some sort of skirmish by insurgents." Hettie's heart raced. The last thing she'd wanted to do was upset Annie with the abruptness of the revelation, but it was time she knew.

Annie blinked. She looked deflated, like a rag doll with the stuffing knocked out of her. Her face twisted as she tried to absorb the news. Eventually she took a handkerchief from her bag and wiped tears from her face.

She took a breath to compose herself. She fingered the locket she had taken to wearing around her neck since her return, delighted to have it restored to her. "I wrote to him, you know, at the regiment. He said to send letters there. I told him I was with child. He never replied. I thought... well, I thought..."

Hettie could guess what she thought. The same as any single, expectant mother would think in the absence of communication from the father of her child.

"There was someone looking for you. Someone apart from me and Corry." She fished in her bag and brought out Mr Ackerman's card. "He's a solicitor. He said if I found you to contact him. He said you would learn something to your advantage." She handed the card to Annie. "It might be something to do with Charles Landridge. He's the one told Reverend Smythe about him being... you know..."

Annie looked at the card. She shrugged. "He couldn't give me any worse news than you have," she said. She put the card in her bag. "What you've told me has turned my whole world upside down. I don't know what I'm to do now." She looked at Billy, sitting happily on the floor playing with his wooden train. "One thing I do know. I'll not be leaving Billy again. Not for anyone."

Corry knocked on the pastor's door. Standing outside the study brought a flood of memories. He never walked into the pastor's study without being spun back in time. He felt like a young boy again, called in for a telling off or a reward for a special effort. Sometimes the pastor would give him a drink and a biscuit, if he'd been really good. He smiled at the memory.

Pastor Brown sat at his large mahogany desk. He stood as Corry entered. He indicated the chair in front of his desk and said, "It's good to hear Annie is well again. It brought me great joy to see her in church on Sunday with Billy. I hope all is well with the family."

"Yes, thank you, Pastor," Corry said. "It's about Gander I've come to see you."

"Gander? Gander Thomas? The last I heard he was on a ship to America." He looked serious. "And you are contemplating going back to find him? Is that it?"

Corry shuffled his feet. "I don't know what to do, Pastor. I have business in America but I'm not unaware of my duties here. The reason for my absence from London is past, but I have responsibilities in America too."

"And where is your heart, Corry? Is it here in London or over there?"

Corry considered but deep down he knew where his heart lay.

"I'm glad you came to see me, Corry," the pastor said. "There are matters we need to discuss." He looked uncomfortable but pressed on. "How much do you remember of your mother's life, or more accurately, how much do you know of her circumstances?"

"My mother?" Corry said, puzzled. "I know we fell on hard times and our life was easier before we came here. Other than that... But what has this got to do with anything? My mother lived the life she chose and died too young. God rest her soul."

Pastor Brown nodded. "Mary Flanagan was a beauty in her day." He paused for reflection. He coughed and carried on. "She came over from Ireland when she was fifteen to work in the house of a wealthy gentleman with two sons. The elder son was brash, handsome, enormously arrogant and blessed with a sense of entitlement second to none. When she was eighteen, to his family's absolute disgust, he forced himself on her and she became pregnant." He glanced at Corry. "You were the child she carried."

Corry stared in disbelief. His stomach churned. It took several minutes before he found his voice. "You knew my father?"

"I regret that I knew him well. He was my brother." Pastor Brown opened a drawer in his desk and took out a folder of papers. Corry continued to stare at him. "Your brother? So you're my..."

Pastor Brown nodded. "To my shame and deep regret, Corry, I've never acknowledged it. But I've always been proud of you. As proud as if you were my own son."

Corry shook his head. Nausea swirled inside him, turning to anger. A deep rage washed over him. He started to stand but before he could speak Pastor Brown held up his hand. "Don't judge me yet, Corry, nor my family, before you know the whole story. Then you must do whatever you think right."

Corry sat again, his hands balled into fists in his lap. Clearly it wasn't this old man's fault. His brother was to blame.

"Mary Flanagan was paid to keep her mouth shut and turned out of the house when my father learned of her condition. It wasn't unusual for single, pregnant women to be treated thus. I'm not proud of what my family did. If it's any consolation my brother Linus, the eldest son and the favourite, was bought a commission in the army. I myself, being the younger son, was sent to a seminary to study theology." He took a breath. "I kept in touch with your mother and sent money when I could, but I was a poor theology student. I couldn't afford much."

He glanced at Corry. "I'm sorry to say we let her down. Like any young girl in that position she did what she had to do to make a living. She was lively, gregarious and wild. She got in with a fast crowd, young blades out for nothing but a good time. When she became pregnant with Annie they abandoned her. Gradually her fortunes dwindled and she found it more difficult to make a living." He shook his head. "You mustn't judge her too harshly, Corry. She was only doing what a lot of girls in her situation would do." He frowned.

It was several minutes before the pastor could continue. "My father had a breakdown when Linus was killed in the Crimea. He was the favourite son. My mother died of a broken heart. Father moved to the country to live in remorseful solitude."

He looked up at Corry, his eyebrows raised. "Why am I telling you all this now? You may well ask."

"Well?" Corry said. His relationship with the pastor was still sinking in. True he'd always favoured him over the other boys and shown pride at Corry's achievements, but he'd thought it pride in a talented student, nothing more.

The pastor sighed. "My father died a few months ago. I've been going through his papers. He leaves a house in Kent with enough land rented out to bring in a comfortable living. As far as I am aware you are his only living blood relative. This property could be yours if you want it."

Corry looked aghast. "Mine?" He couldn't take it all in. "What about you? You are his nearest blood relative. The property surely belongs to you?"

The pastor grimaced. "I renounced all worldly goods when I joined the church. If you don't want it the property will be sold and the proceeds given to the state."

He sat back in his chair and gazed at Corry. "After the way my family treated your mother she's due some recompense." His face was shadowed with grief. "It's something I've struggled to live with all these years. I helped her out when I could, paid the rent and kept an eye on you and Annie, but it was never enough. I had hoped that by giving you this it might make up for some of the deep wrong we did her."

Anger seethed inside Corry, not for himself but for his mother who'd been forced by the pastor's family into a life she never deserved. The pastor's offer was generous, but to Corry's mind it was too little too late.

The pastor breathed a deep sigh, as though he had the troubles of the world on his shoulders. He closed the folder in front of him. "Think about it and let me know," he said.

Corry left the pastor's house in a daze. Far from easing his dilemma the pastor had made it several times worse. What on earth was he going to do now?

Chapter Thirty Eight

After visiting the park, Hettie helped Annie go through Billy's things. "He's growing so fast," Annie said. "He'll be needing new shoes soon and a coat. I don't know how I'll manage with nothing coming in."

"I was wondering the same thing," Hettie said. "Corry's been generosity itself paying all the bills, but if he goes back to America..." Her heart plunged into her boots. Having found him again, losing him would bring more heartache than she could bear. She pushed the thought out of her mind. "I could try going back to the bakery," she said. "The money's not good but it's better than nothing."

"I need to get a job too," Annie said. "But who'll look after Billy?" She glanced at Hettie. "I'll not be going back to the music hall. I don't want that life anymore. Once the glamour and glitz has worn off and you see the sordid reality..." She grimaced. "Perhaps I could get a job teaching dance and music." She brightened up at the thought. "I'll ask Veronique if she knows of any openings."

They packed Billy's things away. Annie took Mr Ackerman's card out of her purse. She stared at it deep in thought. "What do you think, Hettie? Should I go and see him? If he can tell me something to my advantage it might be worth hearing."

Hettie recalled her visit to Mr Ackerman's office. He'd made her feel welcome and seemed genuine. She remembered his interest in Annie's baby. "I'll come with you if you like," she said. "We can take Billy."

The next morning Hettie, Annie and Billy set out to Mr Ackerman's office in the city. "Will he see us without an appointment?" Annie asked.

Hettie recalled her last visit. "He'll see us," she said.

The clerk remembered Hettie. As soon as she walked into the office he jumped up. He glanced past her to Annie standing behind her, holding Billy in her arms.

"We've come to see Mr Ackerman," Hettie said. "If he's in."

"I'll see," the clerk said and scurried off.

On his return the clerk showed them into the office. Mr Ackerman pulled out two chairs and smiled at Billy. He ordered tea for the ladies, "and milk for the little one, if that's permitted?"

Annie smiled and nodded. The clerk raced away. Hettie noticed how Mr Ackerman's gaze lingered on the child. He appeared to be taking in every feature of his chubby, smiling face. He glanced up at Annie. "Do I have the pleasure of meeting Miss Angelique Bouvier at last?" he said.

Any nervousness Annie may have had at coming to the solicitor's office evaporated in an instant. She smiled her most gracious smile. "You do," she said, holding out her gloved hand. She glowed with pleasure.

Mr Ackerman touched her hand and returned to his seat behind the desk, a bemused look on his face. "The same Angelique Bouvier who danced at the Folies-Bergère?"

"The same," Annie said.

Mr Ackerman nodded. "You will excuse my caution," he said, "but I must be sure you are the person I have been looking for."

"Of course," Annie said. "You may ask me anything you like about my life in Paris. I have no secrets from my friend here." She nodded at Hettie.

"Good." Mr Ackerman passed Annie a sheet of paper and pen. He flicked open the lid of the silver inkwell on his desk. "Please write your address in Paris and the name of your landlady."

Annie glanced at Hettie, shrugged and wrote as requested. Mr Ackerman took the paper. He opened the folder on his desk and took out a letter, laying it next to Annie's note. Hettie saw the handwriting was the same.

Annie gasped. She reached over and picked up the letter. "This is the last letter I wrote to Charles," she said. Her brow puckered. "How did you get it? What am I doing here? Why were you looking for me?"

Mr Ackerman stretched across the desk and took the letter back. He rested his elbows on the table and steepled his fingers. "I have the unfortunate duty to inform you of the death of Mr Charles Landridge, known to you as Charles Langtry."

Annie huffed. "You're a bit late. I already have that particular bit of bad news. Reverend Smythe at St Leonard's church informed my friend here of his demise. If that's all you had to tell me..." Annie went to rise, but Hettie stopped her.

"I'm sure Mr Ackerman has more to say," she said. "Isn't that right, Mr Ackerman?"

The solicitor nodded. "I have been hired by Mr Landridge's father, Mr Horace Landridge, to find the sender of this letter and ascertain the truth of it."

"The truth of it?" Annie's face flushed. "Of course it's true." She gasped. "Oh, I see. That's the letter telling Charles that I was carrying his child." She glanced at Billy, happily playing at her feet. "Well, you can see the truth of it yourself."

Mr Ackerman leaned back, deep in thought. He nodded slowly as though coming to a decision. Hettie imagined the thoughts running through his mind. Anyone could turn up with a child hoping to cash in on some family's misfortune and pass the child off as a descendant in the hope of gaining some financial advantage. He may believe Annie to be who she said she was, but Billy could be anyone's child.

"We're wasting our time here," she said to Annie. She turned to Mr Ackerman. "You said you were looking for Angelique Bouvier. I have found her for you. Now, if that's all..."

She rose from her seat. "Come on Annie. Let's go home."

"No. Please wait." Mr Ackerman stood up. "I'm sorry but when I tell you Mr Landridge's reasons you will realise that I must be sure."

Annie sighed. She lifted the locket from Charles she wore around her neck and opened it. "Charles gave me this as a token of his love. He wanted to marry me and I him."

"I know." Mr Ackerman said. "Charles wrote to his father. He told him about a girl he'd met dancing at the Folies-Bergère and how he wanted to marry her. Well, marriage was out of the question of course, a man in his position. His father would never permit it... but..." Mr Ackerman grimaced. "Your letter was among Charles's effects returned to his father by the regiment. When Mr Landridge senior realised a child was involved he knew he had a duty to provide for it – even given it was conceived the wrong side of the blanket, so to speak."

Annie's eyes flared. "Wrong side of the blanket! You're calling my son a... Charles and I were in love. Had he lived he would have married me with or without his father's permission." Sparks of anger shone in her eyes. "I regret having troubled you, Mr Ackerman, but I think our business here is finished." She went to rise.

"No wait. I'm sorry I put that very badly. You must understand. Sir Horace's family are of good reputation and some standing in society. The idea that Charles may have sired an offspring outside of marriage, well, it troubled him greatly. He engaged me to find out for sure and, if it were the case, to make some sort of settlement upon the child."

Annie sat. She took a breath. "I can assure you, Mr Ackerman, that Billy here is Charles's son. He is all I have left to remind me of the man I loved. I wanted to marry Charles, not his family or his money. Billy is my son and I will never part with him, not for all the money in the world if that is what you have in mind, and certainly not to usage an old man's conscience."

Hettie grabbed Annie's arm. "So tell us Mr Ackerman, what form would this settlement take?"

"Merely a monthly sum to pay for his keep and a trust fund set up to pay for his education."

"I don't want their charity or their guilt money," Annie said, her jaw clenched.

"Annie, think of Billy. And his father. What would Charles have wanted for his son? Not for him to be brought up in a back street in London with no education to speak of and no opportunities in life. Every child should know of his father," Hettie said.

Annie put her hand over Hettie's. "You are right as always, Hettie." She turned to Mr Ackerman. "Draw up the necessary papers and you will not find me ungrateful. It's Billy's future I am concerned about."

By the time they left Mr Ackerman's office Hettie and Annie were reassured. Billy's future would be secure. "I told you Charles loved me," Annie said, a satisfied grin on her face. She fingered the locket around her neck. "I'll never forget you Charles," she said.

Corry walked along the banks of the Thames stopping now and then to watch the boats making their way to the docks. He saw the children scavenging in the mud. Memories whirled though his mind, memories of hardship, pain and feelings of utter hopelessness.

Then he remembered the Christmases at Hettie's with Dorcas and Pastor Brown making him and Annie feel welcome and part of the family. What sort of home life did these lads have today? He recalled the pastor telling him about the night shelter and the homes being built by Doctor Barnardo in the East End and he was glad.

Then he thought about his life in America. It had been hard at first, so many immigrants landing in New York, like himself, with nothing. But he'd survived. He owed that to the pastor and, in a way to Dorcas. They'd given him an education, a home and the determination to succeed. He'd thought of them often in those early days. He'd always hoped to come home one day and show them what he'd become. Of course, then it had been a distant dream, the threat of arrest hanging over him. But it was always in his mind. Now his dream had become a reality and he wasn't sure how he felt about it.

He walked through Limehouse, gazing at the run-down buildings, the grime, the litter-filled streets. A young lad with a broom rushed ahead of him waiting to clear a crossing for him through the mud and horse droppings. He gave him sixpence, more than he'd probably earn in a week. The delight in his face brought a stab of guilt to Corry's heart. Could he settle here? He wasn't sure.

Then he thought of Annie and now Billy. He thought of Dorcas, who'd been like a mother to him and Pastor Brown and the father he'd never known. But most of all he thought of Hettie.

Chapter Thirty Nine

That evening Hettie served supper while Annie told Corry and Dorcas about Mr Ackerman and Billy grandfather's wish to provide for him. "He wants to see him now and then and take an interest in his future," she said.

"Are you happy with that, Annie?" Corry asked.

She smiled. "I'm happy that my feelings for Charles and his for me have produced a child his family are willing to acknowledge. I don't think I can ask for more than that."

Corry grinned. "What about Tibbs?" he asked. Tibbs had been a regular visitor and Corry, as Annie's brother, had wondered whether he should enquire about his intentions.

Annie blushed. "I'm sure I don't know what you're talking about."

Hettie laughed. "Go on, Annie," she said. "Be honest. Don't tell us you don't have hopes in that direction."

Dorcas huffed. "If he comes any more often I'll be making up a room for him," she said.

Annie laughed. She looked at Corry. "Would you mind?"

"Me? I'd be pleased as a dog with two tails. He's a good man. I know he'll treat you well. I couldn't be happier." He bent over and kissed Annie's cheek. "You have my blessing," he said.

"He hasn't asked me yet." Annie's eyes widened.

"He will," Corry said. "He will."

After Hettie had cleared the plates Corry asked her to go for a walk with him. "It's a fine evening," he said. "And there's something I want to show you."

Hettie's heart stumbled. Now Annie and Billy's futures were assured there was no reason for

Corry to stay. He'd be wanting to tell her about his plans to go back to America.

She donned her cape and bonnet, her heart heavy with sadness. She chided herself. She was being selfish wanting Corry to stay. He had business interests in America. Surely that was where his heart lay?

He offered his arm as they walked towards the river and along by the docks. The air was still warm from the early summer sun. Strolling along with Corry Hettie felt she'd come home at last. If only it could always be like this, she thought. Then the memory of America clouded her mind and the happiness fell away.

They came to the part of the river where Corry used to delve in the mud for anything he could sell. They paused by the pump where he'd tried to wash the mud from the gash on his foot. That was the day Hettie had tried to help him.

He put his arm around her. "Do you remember the day I cut my foot and you tried to stop me going back in?"

She smiled. "Of course I remember. You were stubborn as a mule and wouldn't be told. It could have been serious you know."

"I know. I think that was when I fell in love with you," he said.

Her jaw dropped in amazement.

"Or it could have been when you nursed me back to health after my accident. I thought you were an angel." He stroked her face. "I missed you, Hettie. All the time in America I carried the memory of you with me. It was you I thought of most. How stupid I'd been and how things might have been different if I'd stayed."

"It wasn't your fault," Hettie said. "You did what you thought was right." Her heart was still pounding at the words he'd said and she wondered if she'd heard right. She wasn't going to spoil it by asking him to repeat it. Being here with him was enough.

He led her to a nearby seat and went down on one knee. Her heart thumped even louder. He took off his hat, holding it close to his chest. A lock of coal-black hair fell across his face. He gazed at Hettie and the world tilted. The look in his eyes sent her pulse racing.

He took a small box from his pocket. When he opened it Hettie saw the most exquisite diamond ring twinkling in the fading light. "I love you, Hettie Bundy. I want to spend the rest of my life with you. I don't have much to offer but everything I have is yours. Will you do me the greatest honour and become my wife?"

Hettie's breath caught in her throat, her heart leapt uncontrollably, her legs turned to jelly. She felt as though the sun had come out after a long period of rain. It was the last thing she'd expected. Thoughts whirred through her brain. A huge swell of happiness bubbled up inside her. She leaned forward and kissed him, something she'd dreamt of doing ever since she could remember. "Yes," she said. "Yes, yes, yes."

Six months later

The last remains of early frost had melted away. The air was crisp and bright. The pale winter sun shone through the windows in Hettie's bedroom. Piles of discarded clothes were heaped on the bed.

"You look amazing," Annie said. "As radiant as I always imagined a bride should be. Why you're positively glowing."

Hettie laughed. "You look amazing too," she said. It was true. Madame Francine had produced breathtaking creations for next to nothing. Hettie's, in white satin with an overskirt of tulle and lace, pooled around her feet and trailed out behind her as she walked. Swirls of lace decorated the neckline and lace panels were inset into the sleeves. A watercress design, picked out in pearls decorated the bodice. Around her neck she wore Dorcas's pearl chocker with a simple gold cross pendant. White orchids were pinned into the chestnut curls of hair piled on top of her head.

Annie's dress, the one Hettie had worn to the Gala Ball, had been suitably altered by Madame Francine to fit her shorter, more slender figure. The shimmering silk matched her eyes. She wore the emerald necklace and earrings she'd brought from Paris.

Hettie glanced around the room, the room she and Annie had shared for so many years. "I'll miss it," she said. "This room holds so many memories."

"Yes," Annie said. "Memories of icy mornings, never enough to eat and freezing pavements when we were out selling cress." She smiled and glanced at the ring sparkling on her finger. Her smile widened. "Look at us now. You going to America and me marrying a Revenue Officer. Who'd have thought it?"

"Not me," Hettie said. "Never in a million years would I have foreseen our futures."

She looked in the mirror and touched the flowers in her hair. "We'll be back for your wedding." She turned to Annie. "You'll make a lovely bride." She sighed. Annie had changed since her ordeal. She was more withdrawn, quieter and less confident than she had been, but every now and then Hettie saw signs of the wild streak she'd once had. Recklessness, spontaneity and passion had always been part of Annie's nature. She supposed Tibbs saw it too. That's probably what attracted him, she thought. That, or her charming sensuality allied with her fragile grace and beauty. "He's a good man, Annie. Treat him well," she said.

"I will," Annie said. "I've learned my lesson. I'll still enjoy outings to the theatre and the glamorous world of parties, the opera and entertainment, but I've come to appreciate and cherish the comfort of security." She sat beside Hettie in front of the mirror.

"What about you, Hettie? I wonder what your future will hold."

Hettie took a breath and gazed at the reflection of them both in the mirror. So different and yet, so close. She'd always admired Annie and, if truth be known, often been overawed by her when they were young. Now they were going their separate ways and part of her felt saddened by it. "By the time we get back the school will be open. Corry and I will be kept busy." She glanced at Annie. "It was your mother's inheritance really," she said. "I know it came to Corry, but do you mind?"

Annie thought for a moment. "Ma never took to me. Corry was always her favourite. I think what he's done, giving the estate to Doctor Barnardo is an admirable thing. You and Corry will make wonderful teachers for those waifs and strays.

Taking them off the streets and giving them a home means more to me than I can say. I think you're both being very brave. What would I want with a country estate anyway? It sounds quite boring."

She stood up. "Now, Hettie Bundy. Are you ready for the big day?"

Jack's hackney was decorated with white ribbons and Covent Garden white roses. Dorcas went with Hettie, Annie and Billy who fidgeted and pulled at the collar of his new pale green outfit all the way to the church. Organ music swelled to the rafters as Hettie walked down the aisle on Jack's arm to marry the man she had loved since childhood.

Corry grinned as she took her place beside him. A glance passed between them and Hettie's heart melted like a snowflake when the sun comes out. Pastor Brown conducted the ceremony with fitting solemnity and, in front of a packed congregation, they made their vows.

The reception, held at a local hostelry, was attended by half of Wapping. Mugger and the boys from Hettie's class at school clustered round the food table.

"Are you going to live in America, Miss?" Weasel, one of the boys in Hettie's class asked, his mouth full of meat pie. "And if you are, can I visit?"

Hettie laughed. "No. We're only going on honeymoon and for Mr Flanagan to make arrangements for his business. I'll be back to see how you're getting on, so no slacking." She ruffled his hair. "Aw," he said, squirming. Then he dodged away to the table where they were serving desserts.

Tibbs made a speech praising Corry's courage, and not least because of his marriage to Hettie which should keep him on the straight and narrow. "The next wedding I'll be attending will be mine and Annie Flanagan's," he said, proudly. "And you are all invited."

Hettie circulated, bidding goodbye to her friends and neighbours. So many friends she'd made over the years. Each goodbye brought a special memory.

She overheard Chloe talking to Annie. Buck and Chloe were travelling with them to America. Buck would be helping Corry sort out his business affairs. Hettie and Corry would be splitting their time between visits to America and working in the school Doctor Barnardo was setting up at the property in Kent.

"We're going on a steamship from Southampton," Chloe said. She glanced around and whispered to Annie, "When we're married you must come and visit." Annie laughed. "Chloe, you're incorrigible," she said. But the warmth of their friendship was obvious.

Corry joined Hettie. "Well, Mrs Flanagan," he said. "Are you going to get changed? Jack's ready to take us to the station."

Hettie gazed into his eyes. Something she felt sure she'd never tire of doing. She brushed his cheek with her lips. "Two minutes," she said, although she knew she'd be much longer than that.

Dorcas went with Hettie up to the room Corry had booked for her to get changed into her travelling outfit. She helped Hettie undress and carefully folded her gown into the box Madame Francine had kindly given them.

Hettie dressed in her best blue suit. She'd wear a heavy cape too, in view of the coldness of the day.

"Are you all right, Ma?" Hettie asked. Dorcas had been unusually quiet all day.

"Course I'm all right," Dorcas said quite brusquely. She sighed. "It's not every day my daughter gets wed." She gazed at Hettie. "Your father would be proud," she said.

Hettie's heart skipped a beat. Dorcas hardly ever spoke of the man she had married. Hettie hugged her. "Thanks, Ma," she said.

"The pastor's asked me to move in with him," Dorcas said, as though it was the most natural thing in the world.

Hettie gasped. "Ma!" she said.

"As his housekeeper for now," Dorcas said. "Mrs Mackie is leaving to look after her ever expanding brood. Once Annie's married and Billy's off to school..." she shrugged. "Well, it'll suit."

A broad smile stretched across Hettie's face. She guessed 'it'll suit' was as excited as Ma was ever going to get. "I'm glad, Ma. I'm happy for you." She hugged Dorcas and planted a kiss on her forehead. "I hope you'll be as happy as me and Corry."

"Get away with you," Dorcas said, pushing her off. "Daft beggar."

Hettie laughed. This really was the happiest day of her life – so far she added at the thought of the adventures that lay ahead of her.

Epilogue

Shortly after arriving in America Hettie and Corry learned that Gander Thomas had been killed in a fight between two of the gangs that ruled the streets of New York.
Neither Hettie or Corry shed a tear, but both prayed for his soul.

Acknowledgements

Firstly my thanks go to my family for their patience and support, especially to my husband Mick for doing the shopping and cooking while I was busy writing. Also thanks to my daughters for reading the ms and to the brilliant Helen Baggott who made enough sense of it to proofread and copy edit.

I'd also like to record my gratitude to Henry Mayhew (1812-1887) who's interviews with *The London Labour and the London Poor* gave valuable insights into the real lives of Londoners during the nineteenth century and inspired the characters in this book.

A huge 'thank you' to my writing friends, ALLi members and supporters for their continued encouragement and, once again, to Jane Dixon-Smith for the wonderful cover.

Lastly I want to thank the readers of *The Water Gypsy* who prompted me to write this novel and made it such a pleasure.

If you have read and enjoyed this novel I would love to hear from you via my website:

www.kayseeleyauthor.com

or through my Facebook page

https://www.facebook.com/kayseeley.writer/?ref=aymt_homepage_panel

If you enjoyed this book you may also enjoy Kay's other books:

If you've enjoyed this book you may enjly Kay's other books which are also being put into Large Print.

A Girl Called Hope

A heart-wrenching saga of love, loss, courage and resilience from the author of *The Guardian Angel*.

In Victorian London's East End, life for Hope Daniels in the public house run by her parents is not as it seems. Pa drinks and gambles, brother John longs for a place of his own, sister Violet dreams of a life on stage and little Alfie is being bullied at school.

Silas Quirk, the charismatic owner of a local gentlemen's club and disreputable gambling den her father frequents, has his own plans for Hope.

When disaster strikes the family lose everything and the future they planned is snatched away from them. Secrets are revealed that make Hope question all she's ever believed in. Can Hope keep them together when fate is pulling them apart?

What will she sacrifice to save her family?

A captivating story of tragedy and triumph you won't want to put down.

This is the first book in the Hope Series

A Girl Called Violet

A gripping saga of courage and human relationships from the bestselling author of *The Guardian Angel*

When the feckless and often violent father of Violet Daniel's five-year-old twins turns up out of the blue, asking to see them she recalls the abuse she suffered at his hands. He never wanted them before, why would he want them now?

Terrified that he might snatch them from her she takes them to a place of safety. There she meets the handsome and charming Gabriel Stone who shows her a better way of life.

But is he all he appears to be?

When Violet decides to stop running and finds the courage to return to London, vowing to confront the children's father, she finds a far greater evil than she ever thought possible.

How far will Violet go to protect her children?

Set against the background of two very different worlds in Edwardian London's East End this is the second book in the Hope Series.

Perfect for fans of Catherine Cookson and Dilly Court.

The Guardian Angel

When Nell Draper leaves the workhouse to care for Robert, the five-year-old son and heir of Lord Eversham, a wealthy landowner, she has no idea of the heartache that lies ahead of her.

She soon discovers that Robert can't speak or communicate with her, his family or the staff that work for his father.

Robert's mother died in childbirth. Lord Eversham, a powerful man, remarries but the new Lady Eversham is not happy about Robert's existence. When she gives birth to a son Robert's fate is sealed.

Can Nell save him from a desolate future, secure his inheritance and ensure he takes his rightful place in society?

Betrayal, kidnap, murder, loyalty and love all play their part in this wonderful novel that shows how the Victorians lived – rich and poor. Inspired by her autistic and non-verbal grandson, Kay Seeley writes with passion and inspiration in her third novel set in the Victorian era.

A love story

The Water Gypsy

Struggling to survive on Britain's waterways Tilly Thompson, a girl from the canal, is caught stealing a pie from the terrace of The Imperial Hotel, Athelstone. Only the intervention of Captain Charles Thackery saves her from prison. Tilly soon finds out the reason for the rescue.

With the Captain Tilly sees life away from the poverty and hardship of the waterways, but

the Captain's favour stirs up jealously and hatred among the hotel staff, especially Freddie, the stable boy, who harbours desires of his own.

Freddie's pursuit leads Tilly into far greater danger than she could ever have imagined. Can she escape the prejudice, persecution and hypocrisy of Victorian Society, leave her past behind and find true happiness?

This is a story of love and loss, lust and passion, injustice and ultimate redemption.

The Victorian Novels

BOX SET

Romance, mystery and suspense come together in these heart-pulling tales of love, loyalty and sacrifice. Beautiful evocative writing and compelling characters bring Victorian London to pulsating life. These three historical novels and their feisty heroines will grab you by the heart-strings and won't let go until the last page.

Contains:

The Water Gypsy

The Watercress Girls

The Guardian Angel

You may also enjoy Kay's short story collections:

You may also enjoy Kay's short story collections:

The Cappuccino Collection
20 stories to warm the heart

All the stories in *The Cappuccino Collection*, except one, have been previously published in magazines, anthologies or on the internet. They are romantic, humorous and thought provoking stories that reflect real life, love in all its guises and the ties that bind. Enjoy them in small bites.

The Summer Stories

12 Romantic tales to make you smile

From first to last a joy to read. Romance blossoms like summer flowers in these delightfully different stories filled with humour, love, life and surprises. Perfect for holiday reading or sitting in the sun in the garden with a glass of wine.

A stunning collection.

The Christmas Stories

6 magical Christmas Stories

When it's snowing outside and frost sparkles on the window pane, there's nothing better than roasting chestnuts by the fire with a glass of mulled wine and a book of six magical stories to bring a smile to your face and joy to your heart. Here are the stories. You'll have to provide the chestnuts, fire and wine yourself.

Please feel free to contact Kay through her website www.kayseeleyauthor.com She'd love to hear from you.

Or follow Kay on her Facebook Page
https://www.facebook.com/kayseeley.writer/

Printed in Great Britain
by Amazon

44442298R10233